SHAM SHAMUS

SOFT-BOILED NOIR – WHERE SHADOWS LAUGH

CHARLOTTE STUART

To Pam, Robin, & Bruce for your ongoing encouragement.

"It's no use going back to yesterday, because I was a different person then."
—Lewis Carroll, *Alice in Wonderland*

"My yesterdays walk with me. They keep step, they are gray faces that peer over my shoulder."
—William Golding

CHAPTER 1
MASQUERADE

I have always had sensitive feet. My mother used to argue with the shoe salesmen at J.C. Penney's about my high arches and long toes, but their only response was to cram my protesting metatarsals into penny loafers and sneakers mass produced for kids with ordinary feet. Those shoes pinched and rubbed the joy out of my boyhood. I was nearly thirty before I discovered the Scribe, a handmade shoe by Bally. For a time, my feet were happy.

Massaging the aching arch of my left foot and cursing the corn that was threatening to erupt on my little toe, I glared at the shoes on the floor beside Eric Henderson's desk. Henderson was a man without taste or distinction. I should know; he was my creation. His shoes with their worn synthetic soles and imitation leather uppers were to the Scribe what Hershey is to Comptoir du Cacao of France. I hated Henderson's shoes. I hated Henderson.

At that moment I thought I heard a familiar squeak. If someone was turning the handle of the office door, I would know soon enough. I bent down and put on Henderson's shoes, waiting for the inevitable "thunk" as the caller tried to push the door open. It wouldn't open unless I unlocked it, and I wouldn't do that until I had a look at who wanted in.

"Thunk."

Pause.

"Knock, knock."

I got up and quietly retreated through the adjoining door to the empty neighboring space which I lease but don't use, except as an alternative way to enter and exit. It opened onto the corridor around the corner from the official entrance to Henderson's place of business. I had looked a long time before finding this exact setup.

As I peeked around the corner, I saw a man delivering a controlled rap just below the sign that said, "Eric Henderson, Private Investigations." His appearance was as moderate as his three-knuckle knock, gray and neat, inexpensive tweed jacket that almost, but not quite, matched his polyester slacks, hair trimmed but not stylish, sloping heels on his highly polished oxfords. In his left hand he had a faux leather vinyl briefcase with plastic initials under the brown plastic handle. It probably wasn't filled with hundred-dollar bills.

If he didn't look rich, he didn't look dangerous either. Playing Henderson, I drew myself up to my full height and came out of hiding, pretending to be just coming down the hall.

"May I help you?" Henderson asked.

The man turned around, startled. Then he pointed a narrow thumb at the door. "Do you know if this guy's around?"

"Yeah. He's around." Acting as Henderson, I took out his keys and moved forward, keeping an eye on the stranger's hands.

When I stopped in front of the door, the man asked, "Are *you* Henderson?"

"Last time I looked."

"There ought to be a sign on the door stating your hours."

"You're right. Maybe one of those cardboard clock things that says 'out to lunch' on the back side." I swung the door open and stepped aside for the man to enter first.

Even after two years I was still self-conscious about Henderson's office. With its battered desk, gray metal filing cabinet, patched Naugahyde couch, linoleum floor, and dirty Venetian blinds, it looked like the set for a Sam Spade movie. Admittedly, that's what I'd had in mind. There was even an ashtray with the name of a hotel in block print on the bottom. It was the kind of room that was supposed to conjure up the image of a tough, determined private eye, one barely making ends meet, but ready and willing to take on the roughest assignment. Used to more aesthetic surroundings, to me the place was just depressing.

I went around behind Henderson's desk, careful not to turn my back on his visitor who was trying to make himself comfortable in Henderson's Edwardian client chair. It was a high-backed monstrosity made when rear ends were smaller and people more formal. Henderson's persona hadn't picked the chair, I had. I didn't like his office and saw no reason why anyone else should either. With a sign of resignation, Henderson's visitor settled in, posture erect, knees clamped together, briefcase in his lap.

"So, you're Eric Henderson," he said heartily.

"Uh huh."

"Well, Mr. Henderson, we're in the same business."

"So...you want career counseling?" Henderson was a snide bastard.

"No, I want to hire you." The man took a card from his simulated leather wallet and handed it across the desk. I noted it was a computer-generated card. All Henderson saw was the name: Stephen Foster. Henderson's lips puckered in anticipation of a flip remark, but Foster interrupted before he could follow through.

"I'm with Langdon, Fennerman, and Wetzel Investigative and Security Consultants," he announced with pride, even though he apparently wasn't a name partner.

Henderson realigned his lips over his teeth and waited for him to continue.

"We've been asked to locate a husband who deserted his wife. I've traced him to this city. That's where you come in. It's your town, your turf. You know where to look."

My "turf"? "You pick my name out of the Racing news?" Clever, Henderson, clever.

"You *do* specialize in missing persons, don't you?"

"You've been reading the small print."

"What we need is someone who can devote his full time to this matter, er, right away."

"The landlord let it slip that I'm behind on my rent?"

"Please don't misunderstand. I'm here because Captain Castaldo spoke highly of you."

"Money can buy anything, even a good reputation." Easy, Henderson, you don't want to libel the good captain.

"You *are* interested in the job?" He was starting to sound doubtful.

"Do I look like the kind of guy that would turn down good money?"

Judging from the deepening creases in Foster's forehead, Henderson's banter was beginning to get to him. I decided to ease off. I didn't think much of an investigator who couldn't appreciate a good wisecrack now and then, but Henderson needed the money.

"I have the file right here." Foster flipped open his briefcase in his no-nonsense manner that was beginning to grate on my psyche. Inside were several files, all neatly marked, a row of pens on the left tucked in their little pockets. "Here it is." He extracted a manila folder and handed it over. His fingernails were chewed to the quick. What did someone like him have to worry about, I wondered, losing money in a football pool?

As Henderson, I made a show of slumping down and propping my feet on the edge of the open bottom drawer of his desk, laid back, self-confident, the man to go with the setting. Then I opened the folder and looked down at the glossy photograph of the man Foster wanted found. Henderson's self-confidence vanished as quickly as a wallet on a park bench. I had to struggle not to let it show, not to lose sight of who I was supposed to be.

My eyes involuntarily went to Foster's face, but he wasn't even looking in my direction. He was leering at the girlie calendar on the wall behind my desk. It was yellowed with age and the wrong month was on display. But it had come with the place, and I hadn't bothered to take it down.

My breathing had become noticeably audible and one foot had slipped off the edge of the drawer. Trying to cover, I straightened up, blew my nose into a crumpled Kleenex from my jacket pocket, and flipped through the remaining pages in the file without really seeing anything.

When I had myself under control, Henderson commented on the file. "Seems straightforward."

Foster turned toward Henderson with a condescending smile. "Straightforward, perhaps, but certainly not your run-of-the-mill missing person's case."

Was he testing me? "Runaway husband, a wife who wants him back–it happens all the time."

"You don't recognize the name?"

Henderson hesitated as I racked my mind to decide if that was a trick question. "Sounds vaguely familiar."

"Warren Stevick," Foster said, favoring Henderson with another patronizing look. "He made the headlines a few years back. Prominent tax and corporate attorney who wasn't too careful about his clientele. That is, he didn't care how they made their money as long as they had lots of it and he got his share. His job was to 'clothe their incomes in legitimacy.' Like putting a whore in a white wedding dress."

His eyes darted to the calendar, then back to Henderson. "That's how most of those fancy lawyers earn their keep, you know, helping the fat cats stay fat."

What a creep! With his personality he had to be for real.

"Then one day Stevick testifies against a couple of minor crime figures. Not clients of his, but probably connected to some of his clients. It was part of a crackdown on gambling. They were convicted on his testimony. The affair made quite a splash. The police were happy, the public was happy, but Stevick, well, he disappeared. The press couldn't decide whether he went into witness protection, took out on his own to avoid having to testify against bigger fish, or was eliminated by one or more dissatisfied customer."

"The mafia remedy for malpractice," Henderson quipped.

"Hmmm. Yes." Foster didn't smile.

"His wife thinks he left on his own?"

"Maybe witness protection, but he absconded with some of their money. Either way she wants him found."

"Oh."

"She knows he's still alive; he sends money to the kids. Warren Jr. and Tamara." Foster rolled his eyes and leered. A bead of spittle appeared at the corner of his mouth. "You should see her, little Tammy. Sixteen and just begging to be laid."

I kept Henderson's face expressionless, but it wasn't easy. After an awkward pause, Foster took the hint.

"Stevick has been sending his kids money and presents off and on since he disappeared. That's how I traced him."

"To this city . . ."

"Right. He was smart, but not smart enough. He's got mail drops in different cities to cover his real address. One in New York, one in Minneapolis . . ." He hesitated. "I guess you know how that sort of thing works."

I did.

"And he's figured out ways to cover his tracks when he orders gifts for the kids online. Still, he wasn't as clever as he thought he was."

Are any of us?

"I tried to buy the information, but that didn't, ah, pan out. You've got to have an 'in' to get anything out of these techie nerds." He shook his head in disgust; everyone ought to have their price. "And private postal box service employees have high turnover and short memories."

"But you got onto him anyway."

Foster grinned, displaying crooked but well cared for teeth. "Perseverance," he said. "Perseverance and a little luck. That's what it takes in this business, right?"

Why did the room suddenly seem cold? It must have been that damned linoleum. Floors need rugs. Preferably one-of-a-kind, hand-knotted rugs.

"Anyway, last month was Warren Jr.'s birthday. Right on schedule, Papa sent him a present. A backpack. Top of the line. Sent it through the usual channels, but forgot to remove the label. Only one company makes that particular backpack. And that one company sells it at their one and only retail store right here in this city." He paused for dramatic effect.

It had been a stupid move on Stevick's part, stupid and perhaps dangerous. If Foster knew enough to look up the brand and discover it had a sole retail distributor, the bad guys wouldn't be far behind.

"He could have been passing through," Henderson observed. "Or he could have ordered it online from another state."

Foster impatiently tapped the sides of his briefcase with his manicured fingertips. "He might have been passing through," he conceded, "but it wasn't an online sale. Those come with different paperwork. This pack was bought right here, in this city, and I think it's the mistake that's going to finally nail him. All we, that is, all *you* have to do is follow up on this lead."

He made it sound easy. But if there wasn't a snag somewhere, Foster wouldn't be sitting in Henderson's Edwardian client chair. He was right about one thing though: Henderson stood a better chance of success than he would.

Henderson rifled through the file again. Without looking up, he asked, "Kid like the backpack?"

"Huh?"

"The kid like the backpack? You said it was top of the line."

"He never saw it."

"Why? You have it?"

"Nah. The wife got rid of it as soon as I had a chance to look it over. She doesn't want the kids thinking about their old man anymore."

"Bitter, huh?"

"Bitter as hell." He leaned forward. "I can tell you one thing. I wouldn't want her after me. No way. She's a cold bitch. Once she catches up with him, she's going to squeeze him dry, then chew up what's left and spit out the pieces." He smiled, either at the thought of all that squeezing and chewing, or at his own ability to turn a cliché. "Not that I blame her, you understand. I mean, after all, the guy ran out on his own kids."

"What makes her think there is anything to 'squeeze' out of him?"

"Be serious. Do you honestly think he would leave without taking a stash with him? Besides, his wife says she always suspected he was putting a little something aside for a rainy day. Probably has two or three Swiss bank accounts."

"Is she guessing, or does she have some evidence?"

"Hey, this was a hotshot lawyer with big-time clients. *Connected* clients, if you get my meaning. His job was to hide their 'incomes.'

That doesn't come cheap. And someone like that had to know his future was shaky. There's no way he didn't plan an exit strategy for himself. Use your head."

"I'm just trying to get a clear picture of what happened. You say he planned the whole thing in advance and absconded with a bundle of money that rightfully belongs to the wife and kiddies. What I want to know is whether it's possible he left with empty pockets and his former clients breathing down his neck. If so, there may not be any more to squeeze out of him than the proverbial turnip." Henderson threw in the bit about the turnip because he thought the platitude would appeal to Foster.

"He testified before a grand jury, for Christ's sake. He had plenty of time to make plans." Foster snapped his briefcase shut with an air of finality. "He brought the whole thing on himself. You eventually become like the company you keep."

Had Foster learned to speak from greeting cards? Or was this some kind of innuendo intended to put Henderson on the defensive?

"What do you care for, anyway?" Foster added. "Stevick isn't your client. *Mrs.* Stevick is the one paying the fee. Once we find her husband, our job is over."

Yeah. If Foster was on the up and up, what the hell did I care? Henderson could certainly use the money.

"This will cost you," Henderson warned.

Foster raised his eyebrows and both hands simultaneously, as if they were connected by invisible threads. "Hey, I bring you a nice straightforward job—that's your own word, 'straightforward'—and you start acting like you're the only P.I. on the block. You get the going rate. Take it or leave it."

"That was *before* you mentioned his 'connections.' That puts the case on a different footing. I'm entitled to hazardous duty pay, up front." Henderson held out his hand, palm up. It was a crass gesture, the kind I imagined as 'tough."

They argued back and forth awhile. Henderson wanted to see how far he could push Foster. He didn't back off until he was certain Foster had reached his approved limit. In the end, Henderson settled for a little less than he'd wanted, but Foster ended up giving him a little more than he'd probably intended. Life was like that. At least Henderson's life always seemed to be.

After Foster had gone and I was once again locked in the office, I opened the Stevick file and went through it, page by page. Did Foster really have the jump on the mob? Or was he working for them? Maybe the Mrs. Stevick client bit was a ruse.

I took out the enlarged photo of Warren Stevick and propped it against an ashtray that had Harrah's printed around the rim. There he was, deserter, fink, and loser. A man on the run, his former clients snapping at his heels. And a bitter wife leading the pack, hell bent on revenge.

The setup made me nervous, real nervous. Automatically I reached into my jacket pocket. Damn. Only a pack of cigarettes. That's right, Henderson didn't eat gourmet hard candies when he got upset, he smoked. Cheap tobacco and cheap liquor. When he ordered a drink, he didn't ask to see the label.

I was becoming more adept at inhaling like someone who craved smoke-filled lungs, but I still hated the taste of cheap tobacco. It was a disgusting habit. A good cigar with a glass of aged Armagnac brandy—now *that* was different. If only Henderson could afford genuine Cuban cigars, the ones smuggled into the country for those willing to pay for the best. But he couldn't. Not even if they became legal would he be able to afford them. Just like he couldn't afford Scribe shoes. Henderson would always have blackened lungs and sore feet.

For the most part I tried not to think about what might have been, but sometimes when I looked around Henderson's sleazy office, I couldn't control my thoughts. Instead of a dingy room and three squares a day, I could have had a plush carpeted suite with a view of the city from glass walls cleaned weekly by somebody else. Then there was troll-caught king salmon flown in fresh from Alaska, black truffles from Périgord, French wines from private collections, the best of whatever I wanted from anywhere in the world.

I turned the photograph of Warren Stevick face down on the desk.

With the money Henderson made from the case, he could have a mechanic work on the rattle in his car. It had been getting worse of late, about time he got it fixed. Dammit. I should have been driving a new car, not a junker with rust spots, poor shocks, and rattles.

In spite of the wrinkles in the case, it was, in a sense, straightforward. He could lay his hands on Stevick any time he wanted. There was, however, one tiny snag, one teensy obstacle that took the farce out of being between a rock and a hard spot.

Unless Foster had already guessed and I was being set up, my continued existence depended on the tenuous deception of cosmetic surgery. The picture from the Stevick file was a photograph of me. I had just been hired to find myself.

CHAPTER 2
LUCKY HENDERSON

L angdon, Fennerman, and Wetzel had a web page with a Chicago address and telephone number that matched the information on the card Foster had given Henderson. But then, I'd expected it would. Business cards were a cheap prop. What I had to find out was whether the firm had a Stephen Foster on their staff, and, if they did, if *their* Stephen Foster was *my* Stephen Foster. Since there were no names or pictures of non-partner employees on the site, I dialed their number and waited for someone to answer.

"Landonfennermanandwet-zel," a pleasant, feminine voice intoned.

"May I speak with Stephen Foster."

"He's unavailable at the moment. May I have him return your call?"

The name was apparently legit, but I still didn't know if I had the right man. "He's unavailable" can mean anything from "he's in the john" to "he's out of town" to "he's picky about answering phone calls." I had to find out which.

"Can you tell me when I can best reach him?"

She put me on hold and Muzak was piped over the line. Classy. Given what my phone service with unlimited text and data cost me, I figured that I was paying the equivalent of a concert ticket for that

medley of near music. She didn't come back on the line until inter-
mission.

"He won't be in until tomorrow, I'm afraid."

That left out the john.

"I'm hoping I have the right Stephen Foster. Stephen G. Foster—
tall, athletic fellow, snappy dresser, witty."

"Well, er, I wouldn't *quite* describe him like that."

"Oh?"

"I think his middle initial is 'G,'" but he isn't very tall. Average
height, I would say."

If we *were* talking about the same man, she was the type of person I
hoped would someday write my epitaph. We made a few more guarded
comparisons. Then I thanked her and hung up. Even without being asked
whether their Stephen Foster wore oxfords with sloping heels, it was a safe
bet that the investigator at "Landonfennermanandwet-zel" was my guy.

The next thing I knew I was working on a list. Making lists is a
lawyer's habit, but for some reason, if Henderson didn't make a list, he
couldn't remember what he was supposed to do next. Stevick had used
little boxes in the left-hand margin to check off each item as it was
completed. Henderson omitted these. In addition, Henderson made
sloppy lists, sometimes even failing to cross off completed assignments. Stevick despised Henderson's untidy approach to list making,
but I was slowly becoming accustomed to them. Any list is better than
no list at all. It was a compromise I couldn't resist.

Henderson actually needed two lists for this case, one for checking
out Foster, the other for finding himself. Using a dull number two
pencil, I made a faint checkmark by the first item on the Foster list: I
needed a sense of accomplishment this morning. Then, impulsively, I
made a square around the checkmark, a thick, smudged line. Sharp-
ened pencils were for tidy people. Henderson wasn't a tidy person. He
was just someone irritated as hell by a dull pencil.

A glance at Henderson's calendar told me that at least two other
files needed immediate attention. They weren't big moneymakers,
none of his cases were, but he had accepted the jobs and therefore had
an obligation to complete them. Follow-through was part of the poor-

but-honest image. Besides, Henderson needed every dime they would bring in to pay the rent and keep himself in pencils.

The first thing Henderson always did when settling down to work was to call his telephone answering service for messages, just as Stevick used to check with his secretary at the start of each working day. Surely that didn't constitute a traceable habit. He could have used an automated answering service, but he liked having a real voice to talk to about messages, and he assumed his clients felt the same. He had chosen the service partly because they were local. But they were also efficient, and his message taker's name, Coral, reminded him of sunny days spent scuba diving in exotic locales before he became Henderson.

I dialed the number and Coral answered, her voice as delicate and pink as her name.

"Sorry, Mr. Henderson. No messages today."

There was something sensual about the way she said Henderson's name. Since he supposedly viewed all women as objects, he considered it his duty to *think* like an animal. He had a number of secret nicknames he imagined whispering to her in a moment of passion. What I often wondered was whether Coral—assuming her name really was "Coral"—had any secret names for him.

"Thanks, Coral." Sometimes Henderson kidded around with her a while, reaching back to Stevick's early college years for something to say, often provoking an incredulous, "Why, Mis-ter Henderson!" No time for that today though.

After organizing and reorganizing Henderson's assignments, making two fruitless calls and pacing back and forth for almost five minutes, I finally managed to convince Henderson that spending more time on the Stevick case was essential, to both of us. I couldn't rely on a single telephone call to verify Foster's identity. And if he wasn't who he claimed to be, our double life was over.

I gathered up Henderson's lists, took one last look around, and left through the front door. If anyone wanted to follow Henderson today, I intended to make it easy for them. Foster had passed the first test, but Henderson was a cautious man. No, that wasn't accurate. Henderson was a *thorough* man, thorough but reckless, a good detective. I kept forgetting.

Without looking over his shoulder once, Henderson went directly to his car. He took plenty of time to warm up the engine, listening with displeasure to the loud rattle. Then he pulled out of the parking space and proceeded slowly enough to allow anyone who wanted to follow him wanted plenty of opportunity to fall into line.

Several honks from impatient drivers failed to ruffle Henderson. Signaling well in advance of each turn, he continued at a snail's pace, keeping one eye on the road, the other on the rearview mirror.

A red Honda followed for two blocks before turning off. Other cars came and went, but none seemed to stay in sight for very long. Once Henderson stopped and ran into a drugstore. No one seemed to care. By the time he arrived at police headquarters, I was fairly certain he wasn't being followed.

Al Castaldo was behind his desk looking out of sorts, like a man suffering from low back pain should. He'd had the pains ever since he'd been promoted to captain. Probably from too much sitting around. Crease lines had formed along his nose from frowning at the stacks of forms that seemed to multiply faster than crime statistics. He was always thwacking the piles with a ballpoint pen, like a cop on the beat brandishing a nightstick. If it hadn't been for a wife and five kids, there was no doubt he would have asked for his old job back.

'Morning, Alph . . .'' Henderson let his voice trail off. It was an old joke, and not a very funny one.

Al tipped his nameplate on its side so Henderson couldn't read "Captain Alphonso Castaldo" and thrust a yellow piece of paper at him. "Read this," he said.

ORDER FILLED PREVIOUSLY was stamped sideways across the form. "You mean they actually have a rubber stamp that says 'order filled previously'?"

"They told me to fill out a requisition form, so I did, and this is what they sent me back. What the hell do they think I went to all that trouble for?"

"You could put a piece of masking tape over the 'phonso.' Or get another desk."

"My father, he had to have an Uncle Alphonso. Uncle Alphonso, lots of money, and no heir. Not until *after* I got stuck with his damn name. Then he remarries and has a kid."

Henderson had heard it all before, but he liked Al, so he listened patiently.

After Al ran out of complaints, he asked, "So, what do you want?"

"I could ask why you think I want something." Henderson grinned. "But I won't. I'll tell you what I want instead."

Al put the yellow copy of the requisition form on top of the pile in his IN box and got up to pour two cups of coffee. Henderson waited until the ritual was completed before asking about Foster.

"What is this?" Al said. "He asks about you, you ask about him— why don't you two save yourself time and skip the middleman?"

"What do you know about him?"

"You see his business card?"

"Yeah."

"Then you know everything I know." Al sat down, shifting in his chair as if trying to find a comfortable position. The requisition form had obviously upset him—and the muscles in his back.

"Did he come in here specifically to ask about me?"

"You think your name is on everyone's lips, like some movie star or something?"

"I once ran an ad in the *New Yorker:* 'Henderson, Private Dick for Hire.'"

"Very funny."

"So?"

"So? So . . . he asked for the name of a good investigator special-izing in missing persons."

"And *you* gave him *my* name."

"It was an off day."

"Did he seem to know who I was?"

"Maybe he doesn't read the *New Yorker.*"

Al was sitting up a little straighter. There had to be some reason for Henderson's interest in Foster.

"The job seems legit," Henderson said, "but the mob may be involved. I'm not sure I like that."

"Any particular mob, or are you using the generic term?"

"*A* mob. *The* mob. What difference does it make?"

Al reached out to straighten his nameplate. "You going to tell me who you're supposed to be looking for?"

"Ever hear of Warren Stevick?"

"Stevick. Stevick. Not the lawyer from Chicago who ratted on some criminal friends of his a few years back."

"That's the one." He had the right Stevick, but I couldn't say I cared much for his characterization of events.

"He's here?"

"That's what I'm supposed to find out."

"Is it a possibility?"

"Anything's possible. I'll let you know what I come up with."

"If I remember right, he disappeared, didn't he?"

"I'd have disappeared too if I'd been in his shoes," I said with feeling. Actually, it was his Scribes I missed the most.

As I left Al's office, I mentally checked off another item on the Foster list: It had been a stroke of luck that Foster had been referred to Henderson, not necessarily a coincidence Sherlock Holmes would have questioned. It was beginning to look as though I was worried over nothing, well, not exactly over nothing, but at least things probably weren't as bad as I'd feared. Stevick had made a stupid move, but Henderson could cover for him. He could go through the motions and reassure Foster that if Stevick had indeed been in the city, he was no longer around. That would even be the truth—there was no such person as Warren Stevick in this city, or anywhere else for that matter. Not Warren Stevick as he used to be at any rate. The old personality and tastes occasionally surfaced, although that was happening less and less of late. I wasn't entirely certain I was pleased about some of the changes, but I had little choice in the matter. If Henderson was to exist as a believable and whole person, I had to forget I was an actor playing a part. I had to *become* the character. And at times I feared that I had. Except for the pop-up yearning for luxuries.

I stopped for a quick lunch at one of the dives Henderson

frequents, then ran two quick errands on other files to ease my conscience and to placate Henderson's clients. Afterwards I went to the recreational equipment store where another one of my pseudo identities had purchased the backpack for Warren Jr. It was a logical starting point for Henderson, and it would allow me to assess just how much Foster actually knew.

The manager was an attractive middle-aged woman, attractive in an efficient, professional way, not at all like the bouncy young clerks Henderson had ogled on the way in. Had she ever been like them, I wondered, or had she emerged from puberty wearing a tailored suit with stodgy tortoiseshell glasses? Henderson resisted an urge to rip off her glasses and fluff out her hair. Instead, he asked about the backpack.

"Another man made similar inquiries just last Friday," she replied, her tone critical.

"Don't tell me we're duplicating assignments." Henderson shook his head in disgust. "Fellow about medium height, short brown hair, polished shoes, vinyl briefcase?"

I knew by the look in her eye that she had noticed Henderson's own scuffed shoes and generally tacky appearance, but all she said was, "Yes, that describes him."

"Could I trouble you to go over the information again? I'm afraid it may be impossible to catch up with Mr. Foster today, and it would speed things up considerably if you could share with me what you told him." Henderson was being nauseatingly polite. Not that she would know that wasn't his usual approach.

She hesitated a moment, then acquiesced. It only took a few minutes to locate the information. "I'm afraid I can't tell you much," she said. "We don't have a Warren Stevick on our preferred customers' list. Nor does the name appear in any of our other records. He apparently didn't request a catalog, give us a bad check . . ." she smiled apologetically ". . . or get caught shoplifting. I can, however, tell you that we got those particular backpacks in only two months ago. They're a new line developed for greater durability and carrying capacity. The style is very popular with our younger customers."

Damn Caron. Warren Jr. would have liked that backpack.

"But you're certain someone purchased it here?" I tried not to look around to see if I could spot the clerk who processed the pack sale originally. Henderson looked different than Norton, but it was best not to push it.

"I can assure you that no one else would be selling anything with our label."

"But you advertise nationally."

"In some select magazines."

She seemed to imply Henderson wouldn't be familiar with those particular publications.

'You *do* have online sales."

"Yes, but our records would show if it had been an online purchase. We track store and online purchases separately as part of our stocking and distribution plan. And, if it had been purchased online, we would have a record of his name and address from his credit information."

"One last thing, do you have security camera coverage from a month ago?" Ordinarily Henderson would have been anxious to look at any camera footage, but under the circumstances, he was hoping the answer was "no."

"I'm sorry. We only keep videos for thirty days. They're recorded over after that." She paused. "Your Mr. Foster asked the same thing." The tone of disapproval was back. "Sorry I can't be of more help." Definitely a dismissal statement.

I stood up. "I appreciate you taking the time to talk with me. Especially since you already went over all this with Mr. Foster." See, Ms. Manager, Henderson doesn't call all women broads and slap them on the butt for an exit gesture.

We shook hands. Her skin was cool and her grip firm. Stevick appreciated her professionalism, but Henderson labeled her cold and asexual. Although he was still speculating about whether she had a kinky streak under the pinstripes and buttoned up silk blouse.

As I left, she gave me a penetrating look as if trying to see the inner man, or so I fantasized. To her I was probably just a tacky, but polite, private investigator. Her cooperative attentiveness had undoubtedly been her customer service training kicking in.

Feeling out of sorts, I headed uptown to a small office supplies and services store that Henderson always used for his printing and copying needs as well as for getting the occasional report typed. They were efficient, and they had Angie. I had a rule against forming attachments, but panting and patting didn't constitute forming an attachment.

When Henderson said he only needed a few minutes of her time in one of the back rooms, the other employees snickered. Angie pretended she didn't get the joke, but winked at Henderson as she said to come along. Henderson wiggled his eyebrows at the others and gave a fair imitation of undisguised masculine lust. Then he turned and followed Angie's well-rounded figure down the hall, admiring the way her skirt followed the line of her buttocks down to the top of her thighs.

Although Angie was a flirt and seemed to enjoy Henderson's inane banter, she never seemed surprised or disappointed when he didn't follow through. After their usual exchange of double entendres, he told her what he wanted, and she quickly settled down to business.

One of the things I had done when bringing Henderson into the world was to take some drama and voice lessons, ostensibly to improve my speaking voice. What I had secretly tried to accomplish was to learn how to alter my voice sufficiently so it would not give me away if I ran into anyone from Stevick's past. Even though I considered the lessons a success, I didn't relish testing them now. There was too much at stake.

After just a few minutes of practice, Angie was ready. I dialed the still familiar number and the telephone started to ring. Angie nodded at Henderson to let him know someone had answered. "Mrs. Stevick?" Angie said.

Pause.

"I'm calling for Mr. Foster to see if you've received anything else in the mail from your husband that might be helpful in the investigation." The implicit message was that the area code for the call indicated Foster was still in the city and wanted the information before he headed back for Chicago. "Oh, you talked with him this morning? I'm sorry, I must have misunderstood. I didn't realize he was going to take care of this directly."

Pause.

"Fine. Sorry to have bothered you. Goodbye."

She put down the phone and twirled the chair around, her skirt stretched taut and hitched upward to reveal the shapely length of her long legs.

"Sounds like she definitely hired this Mr. Foster. And she thinks he's still here in the city. That's what you wanted to know, isn't it?"

"Exactly. Thanks, Angie. You're a doll." Did calling her a "doll" make him sound like someone who read too many Raymond Chandler mysteries?

Angie dropped her businesslike demeanor and crossed her legs to give Henderson a better view. Her smile reminded him of a line from *Farewell My Lovely*: "She gave me a smile I could feel in my hip pocket." He lingered just long enough to make a fool of himself.

As I left the building, I pulled out the list and made a nice, neat checkmark right in the middle of a perfect square. Foster was legit.

CHAPTER 3
UNLUCKY STEVICK

Warren Stevick had never been the master of his own ambitions. In high school he'd taken college prep classes because he was bright and his counselor said he should. He had worked hard, but he'd had no particular long-range goals. After college he went to law school because it was his dying mother's wish. Then he met Caron. *She* knew exactly what his future held.

Her father got him a job in one of Chicago's top law firms, the firm that handled the work for her father's construction company. After that came the opulent home, the garage full of showy cars, and two children in exclusive private schools, all applauded by a wife who stood behind him 100 per cent—as long as the money kept coming in.

Unfortunately, Stevick's salary as an associate wasn't enough to cover his family's constantly expanding needs. To acquire more money meant Stevick had to acquire clients of his own. When Rollo Langley walked in one day and asked for advice on how to get around a Chicago anti-gambling ordinance, Stevick was quick to oblige. Langley might be a crook, and the advice might be badly disguised counsel on how to violate the law, but he was Stevick's own client, a client who appreciated the advice and paid his bills.

First Langley, then Chen, and after him Shaw, Shields, and Trent. As the clients trickled in, Stevick's status with the firm grew. The partners actually knew very little about these clients. They didn't want to know.

They were pleased to have another big rainmaker among their numbers. When they made Stevick an offer of partnership it was more than generous. Caron and her father were pleased with Stevick's new status. And Stevick was pleased because everyone else was pleased.

Without consciously making the decision to become the local mob's "go-to" lawyer, Stevick slowly acquired more and more clients from the organized crime community, including a few who were fairly high up on the food chain. The money and the power that came with having his own client base in the firm made it easier to rationalize some of his misgivings about what he was doing. Besides, his clients' requests were seldom tangibly illegal, although there was a fine line between advising someone on how to avoid committing a crime and advising them on how to avoid getting caught. Beating the system; it was an all-American sport. As long as it made everyone happy, Stevick tried not to worry about whether the line dividing the legal from the illegal became blurred from time to time.

In the long run, Stevick was just too smart. He never asked unnecessary questions, but many of his clients had overlapping interests. A fact here, a bit of gossip there, and, as the years passed, Stevick found himself in a position to know more about the criminal elite than was good for anyone's health. Still, he didn't think any of his clients were worried about him using any of what he knew against them. The money was too good.

Then he made his big discovery.

The facts came to him one at a time. The identity of the secret owner of two major sports equipment manufacturing chains. The salaries being paid to certain athletes for advertising the products of those companies. The knowledge that two specific games had been fixed. And suddenly he knew the payoff system. He not only knew the *how*, but, even more dangerous, the *who*.

The man at the top wasn't a known mob figure; he was supposedly one of Stevick's straight clients, an upstanding community activist with political aspirations. Stevick was fairly certain that few, if any, of the man's mob associates knew the extent of his activities. And as long as Stevick didn't let on how much *he* knew, he thought he was probably safe. But if the man at the top ever decided Stevick was a potential obstacle between him and the United States Senate, Stevick had no doubt that he would become "expendable" in the worst sense of the word. He had every intention of making sure that never happened. He did as he was told and kept his mouth shut.

Then one day, FBI agent Calvin Edwards walked into Stevick's high-rise office and marched him out wearing handcuffs and a grim smile, right past open-mouthed secretaries, horrified senior partners, and bewildered clients. Stevick's professional life was over. His neck was on the line in more ways than one.

The only way he was able to avoid a jail sentence was to agree to testify for the government in exchange for immunity. Once it was clear that he would have to take the witness stand, he had carefully strategized the nature of his potential testimony for its minimal impact on the mob and maximum impression on Edwards. But that didn't solve his problem. No matter what he held back, he couldn't count on the mob's benevolence. After considerable negotiation with the government, Stevick and his family were offered admittance into the Witness Security Program. But his wife dug in her heels and said, "No way." She didn't want to leave her family and friends and start over in some "godforsaken hellhole" with no money and no prospect for a future of societal prominence and power. "No way."

Edwards shrugged his shoulders and said that Stevick could go into the program on his own, but he didn't push it. Stevick felt trapped. If he stayed, he risked retaliation for his testimony. If he left, he had to do so without his family. And he would no longer be a lawyer. They had made that clear. Nor was he entirely convinced that the program couldn't be penetrated by someone with enough money and influence. No, if he was going to disappear, he would do it on his own terms.

Stevick knew he needed more than a backpack and a one-way bus ticket to Des Moines to make his escape. He had to have both a bankroll and a new identity. He could come up with a little money, but most of his assets were tied up in properties and investments, and Caron quickly mustered forces to see that he wouldn't get even a penny without a fight. He didn't blame her. But he needed enough to get a jumpstart on a new life. She would have to make due with getting 99 percent of their combined assets.

What he couldn't manage on his own was a new identity. But he was sure Edwards could do that for him without using the formal government program. Edwards was savvy. And he understood Stevick's situation. They bargained right up to the last minute, Edwards badgering for more information about the people at the top. Stevick holding firm.

Stalemate.

Finally, Edwards agreed to help him. Maybe he felt sorry for Stevick. Maybe he felt the government owed Stevick at least that much. In any event, he came through with a birth certificate, social Security number, and driver's license, all in the name of Nick Norton. The "real" Nick Norton—parents deceased, no siblings or spouse—had disappeared ten years earlier after graduating from an independent law school that had merged with another independent law school. Both institutions had been experiencing financial difficulties, and the merger had been bumpy, including some difficulties with blending their online records. It was the perfect opportunity for some creative identify theft. After Stevick decided where he wanted to live, he could take the bar and start over as a low-profile lawyer with no future. But he would at least be a lawyer, that was something.

To help create the new Nick Norton, Stevick grew a beard, gained a few pounds, stood slightly hunched and walked with a slower gait. Combined with the tacky clothes Norton wore, Stevick felt sufficiently disguised. Then he took the bar in his new residence state, making an effort to barely pass the exam so as not to stand out. He opened a small office in the low-rent district and slowly picked up a few clients.

After several tense and uncomfortable months getting used to Norton, Stevick decided he wanted one more line of defense between himself and the mob. He didn't entirely trust Edward's ability to keep his new identity secret, and he didn't want to be on the run with no options other than to keep on running. He used every bit of money he could scrape up to buy a new face: a few nips and tucks, a cleft in his once smooth chin, and a streamlined nose. It made a surprising amount of difference. Especially after he took off almost thirty pounds.

Eric Henderson was born.

Obtaining new ID for Henderson through one of Norton's less desirable clients was surprisingly easy. But as he had already learned, a paper identity was only half the battle. Documentation was the form without the blanks filled in; internally becoming a new person was the substance. And it wasn't simply a matter of changing the outer man and adopting a few new interests and habits. To truly begin again, Stevick knew he must completely eliminate all traces of the old identity. When considering the Witness Security Program, he had been told that something as seemingly insignificant as a preference for a particular hay fever prescription could be the way in which someone might trace him. The former identity must be rejected completely. The past was the past. Forever.

Stevick was the past. Norton and Henderson, the future. Norton wore a fake beard and tended toward plumpness around the middle. Henderson was clean-shaven, always leading with his cleft chin, and refused to give up the cigarettes he had become addicted to as a teenager. Norton wore padding to flesh out his appearance, the prosperous lawyer look without the prosperity. Henderson was lean and tough and macho. No gourmet food and sitting around dark courtrooms for him. Norton was idealistic, a man trying to work the system for the benefit of his clients. Henderson was cynical and determined to work *around* the system. On and on it went, down to the smallest detail.

Slowly, piece by piece, Norton and Henderson became separate personalities, both distinct from Stevick. If occasionally one couldn't remember whether he wore reading glasses or chewed gum, those were minor problems. With a little ingenuity and effort, the former Warren Stevick could maintain both new lives. But, just to be on the safe side, there was a virgin set of ID in a safety deposit box rented under still another assumed name. It was intended as a security blanket, nothing more.

Now, for the first time in over two years, I was wondering whether I was going to need that virgin set of ID.

CHAPTER 4
"OUR" APARTMENT

As I drove toward the apartment, the words "stupid, stupid, stupid" bounced around in my head. A person with the kind of enemies Stevick had couldn't afford to do something so incredibly stupid like leaving a label in a backpack. Especially if Caron was determined to hunt down her errant hubby. Greedy, selfish woman. What would she do if she found him and discovered he was broke? And how could I be sure she wasn't a pawn for someone who didn't care two hoots about money and only wanted blood, my blood? That was one thing I shared with both Henderson and Norton.

There was a gray car about a block behind. Had it been there when I stopped at that light by the corner grocery?

I made a right turn. It was a fairly major intersection, so I couldn't be certain the gray car wouldn't have turned anyway. But it did, and it made me nervous.

As I approached the entrance to a shopping mall, I lost sight of the gray car. That didn't make me any less uneasy. There could be several cars involved in a tail. I was probably acting paranoid, but then, I had reason to be paranoid, so I decided to play it safe.

The mall was busy, cars backing unexpectedly out of parking spaces, kids darting between parked cars, shoppers asserting their pedestrian rights-of-way. I pulled into a space and headed directly for one of the large department stores. Once inside I searched until I found a side exit and escaped around a corner. Two more detours and I was at a bus stop. I took a bus three-quarters of the way, then walked the rest.

The apartment was in a row of apartment buildings all needing paint and tenanted by people who either didn't care or couldn't afford to care. It was near the university, so there was a constant turnover in occupancy. For the most part I was able to come and go without having to worry about little old ladies peeking out of curtained windows. Or little old men for that matter.

I had rented the apartment dressed as Henderson but under another assumed name. It's surprising how little ID you need to convince people you are who you say you are. To prove I wouldn't chew the paint off the walls and would pay my rent on time, all I needed was a driver's license displayed in a wallet "obviously" full of credit cards. The manager didn't ask to see the cards, which was a good thing, because the only ID with my rental name on it was the driver's license. I'd obtained that with a birth certificate given to me by a clerk who believed my story about researching my family tree, a voter registration card obtained online, a forged marriage certificate and a tall tale accompanied by a heavy dose of charm directed at a young female clerk at the state department of licensing.

Henderson uses the front door to the apartment building, while Norton uses the back entrance that opens onto an alley. Each parks his respective car at different nearby locations to avoid having the person, car and apartment building linked.

Since I was dressed as Henderson, I went in the front.

The first thing I did was check to see if anything in the apartment had been disturbed. Not that there was much to disturb, but I did have several hiding places for ID. It isn't wise to carry more than one set at a time. If for some reason you're stopped by the police, extra ID could arouse suspicion, as it probably should.

Satisfied that my hiding places were secure and everything was as I'd left it, I headed for the manager's apartment. On the way, I automatically stopped to check the mail. After moving into the apartment, I'd immediately ordered several magazines under my assumed name: *Time, Sports Illustrated,* and *ESPN.* These magazines in turn got me on a lot of mailing lists that generated even more mail. The subscription departments didn't care who I was as long as my bill was paid, so for all practical purposes I became the person I claimed to be, at least as far as the post office, apartment manager, and other tenants were concerned.

Clutching my occupant mail and magazines, I knocked on the manager's door. He answered with a diet pop in his beefy right hand, the television blaring in the background.

"Anyone been looking for me?" I asked. "A friend was supposed to drop some things off, and I'm afraid I missed him."

"No. Not that I know of."

"Late thirties, medium height, conservative dresser?"

"No. No one. Sorry." He glanced impatiently over his shoulder toward the bluish glow from his television.

"Thanks anyway."

"Sure." The door closed so fast I felt like an unwanted salesman. I turned and headed back down the hall.

The apartment was the last one at the back near the alley exit. Directly across from it were storage lockers for the first two floors. Not a choice location by some standards, but alright by me. Down the hall to the right lived an unsociable old man who was so hard of hearing you practically had to break his door down to get him to answer, and when you tried to talk to him, he never quite made the appropriate response. That left only one other apartment in the corridor. Two young men shared it. They had been there a couple of months. I seldom saw either of them. When one of the two answered my knock, it was clear he didn't recognize me.

"I'm from down the hall," I explained, gesturing vaguely. "A friend was supposed to drop some things off, but I'm running late. Any chance he left something with you?"

He shook his head.

"Anyone ask for me?"

He shook his head again, not bothering to ask my name, not looking as though he cared who I was or where I lived. Real neighborly. Just the way I preferred my neighbors.

"Well, thanks anyway."

I went back to the apartment, locked the door behind me, and slipped the deadbolt shut. At least it looked as though there hadn't been any snoopers around. The place was probably safe. Just to be sure, I got out Henderson's bug detector and swept the apartment. You can find most bugs with a physical search, but Henderson liked using the high-tech option.

I spent the rest of the day thinking about what I should do next. I didn't come up with much.

That evening after the traffic had thinned out, Henderson went to the mall and picked up his car. He checked for tracking devices and headed home, as certain as he could be that no one followed him.

Tuesday, Henderson went through the motions of looking for Stevick, just in case Foster checked up on him. It wasn't easy asking questions without creating the impression Stevick was probably in town, but Henderson tried his best to suggest that his presence in the fair city was at most a long shot. "If the client is willing to pay for my time . . .," he'd say with a shrug. Everyone seemed to see the merit in that all-American way of earning a buck. If Foster heard about his approach and questioned it, Henderson could argue that he didn't want to scare Stevick off.

Late Tuesday, Henderson made out a progress report, resisting the urge to write that he hadn't "found himself" yet.

CHAPTER 5
IF IT'S WEDNESDAY—

Wednesday morning, I got up at the usual time, usual for both Henderson and Norton; it's a question of my body's internal clock. I had my usual breakfast of cold cereal, one slice of toast and black coffee. Then, since it was Wednesday, I set about making myself into Norton.

The beard was made from real hair, hand knotted, and had cost a bundle. Under most circumstances it defied detection as a fake. The remarkable synthetic lace material underneath looked like flesh and fit like a second skin. It attached with spirit gum and came off with determination. Any spirit gum left on the face required a special remover formulated for the specific purpose. The whole process was demonstrated in a number of YouTube videos that made it seem a lot easier than it actually was. And although the videos boasted that a beard would remain intact for long periods of time if applied correctly, they didn't mention what would happen if some wild woman tried running her fingers through your beard. Norton thought it might be worth taking the chance, but he hadn't had an offer.

A special padded vest worn under his T-shirt added the illusion of weight. The vest tapered to look natural instead of simply bulky. Just wearing it made me feel heavier.

Next came Norton's work costume: cheap sports jacket, ready-made slacks, colored shirt open at the neck. When he had to make a court appearance he wore a tie that was either two wide or too narrow. He always looked as if he simply put on whatever came to hand that morning.

One last look in the mirror, and Norton was ready.

Stevick had been an orderly person, as fastidious and invariable in his daily routine as a military recruit. Henderson was by nature and profession a free spirit, unconventional, unencumbered, and unpredictable. In contrast, Norton was a casual and haphazard individual, destined by temperament for mediocrity and hence obscurity in the legal brotherhood. He lived off court appointments and a few referrals from a friendly bail bondsman. His personal clients were inevitably petty criminals who couldn't or didn't want to pay for services rendered any more than they wanted to go straight.

Although Norton was not supposed to be methodical, he had fallen into the habit of going to his office about the same time every Wednesday and Friday. He rationalized that even second-rate lawyers stuck to some kind of routine. Deep down, however, he knew that this was nothing more than an attempt to placate the Stevick in him. Norton was, after all, Stevick's closest, if most vulnerable, link with the past. Edwards had strongly recommended against remaining a lawyer, but Stevick had decided to take the chance. Being a lawyer, even a mediocre one, had come to mean a lot to him.

Norton's office was only a slight hike in rent away from Henderson's, just far enough to get out of "raunchy" and into "almost quaint." The building had at one time been the tallest in the city. But now its main distinction was that it had the only operator run elevator in the area. Norton liked the elevator's brass-latticed cage doors and the feeling that each ride was like participating in an historical reenactment.

Sometimes, to demonstrate he wasn't always predictable, Norton went in the side door. Very occasionally he forced himself to stop somewhere for coffee in order to arrive a few minutes late. This particular Wednesday he arrived early and went in through the front door. Lawrence, one of the old-time elevator operators who remembered when almost every building in the city had attendant-run elevators, was standing in the foyer next to an unoccupied elevator. His dark-blue uniform coat with its frayed gold braid on the shoulders looked as dated as the ornate décor inside the elevator.

"Morning, Mr. Norton."

"Morning, Lawrence." It somehow seemed natural in this setting that the operator should call him "Mr." and he should address him by his first name.

"You're early this morning," he commented.

"Ah, yeah. I've got a lot to do today." Dammit. He didn't appreciate Lawrence keeping tabs on him like that. Although it wasn't Lawrence's fault that he had slipped into a routine.

Norton stepped inside the cage and turned to face the front of the car. Lawrence looked up and down the foyer to make certain no one else wanted to go up, then got in and pull shut the retractable door.

"The petition is doing real well," Lawrence said as the floors whizzed past. "It was good of you to do the wording. Made it sound nice and legal."

"It was the least I could do. I'd sure hate to see these old elevators replaced with push buttons."

"Me too."

And *you*, too, Norton silently agreed. I'd hate to see you have to find new work at your age. I know how hard it is to begin again.

They had reached the tenth floor. Lawrence stopped the elevator exactly even with the landing and pulled open the brass door. Next came the wire reinforced glass door designed to keep people from falling down the shaft. Norton wished Lawrence a good day and sauntered off down the hall. Unlike Stevick and Henderson, Norton never hurried. If it had been the sixties, he would have been a flower child. As it was, he was low-keyed and relaxed, a liberal do-gooder, but unambitious lawyer.

He had his key out as he approached his office but found he didn't need it—the door was ajar. Suddenly my thoughts were racing almost as fast as my heart.

The door should have been locked. Norton didn't have an assistant, and the janitor only came on Fridays. No one else except the security guards had a key.

Was there someone waiting inside to surprise Norton? If so, would he or she have left the door open? Did I want to take the chance?

I shoved the keys back in Norton's pocket and knocked lightly on the door. I'm not Norton, the knock said. I'm somebody looking for Norton.

The door came open another few inches, but no one responded. There was no sound from within. I walked on down the hall, forcing myself to go slowly and to not look back.

No one came after me.

Could the door possibly have been left open since last Friday when the janitor emptied the wastebaskets? Maybe it had been opened by one of Norton's clients who had arrived early and went in to make himself comfortable. A locked door wouldn't stop many of his clients.

Rather than entering, I went around the corner at the end of the hall and stopped. This was pointless. Norton was becoming as paranoid as Henderson. He had no reason to fear anyone. Not unless the mob really was closing in. Foster's visit might be only the first in a series of events that would eventually force me on the run again. The problem was that if I didn't find out what was going on, Norton would have to stay away from his office indefinitely. That would in effect make Norton a nonviable identity. If I wanted to hang on to him, I had to go back.

I waited until some people got off the elevator and headed in my direction, timing it so I arrived at Norton's office when they did. As soon as they were past, I pushed the door open and stepped inside, moving quickly to the right so no one could surprise me from behind.

No one tried.

It was hard to see. There were no lights on, and someone had closed the blinds. That really unnerved me. The janitor was under strict orders not to close the blinds. Norton's plants needed light. But someone had closed the blinds.

While I waited for my eyes to adjust, I remained by the door with my back to the wall, tense, expectant.

Nothing happened.

Gradually things came into focus—the bookshelves with their meager assortment of law books, the ancient oak table where Norton did his work, the heavy old-fashioned desk that he used as a barrier between himself and his seedy clients, the row of herbal teas on the filing cabinet next to the electric kettle.

Damn. The light on the kettle was on. If the pot had been on since Friday, the damn thing was probably ruined.

My muscles started to relax. Maybe it was a new janitor or a vacation replacement that had closed the blinds and failed to lock the door. That seemed more likely than the possibility that Norton was compromised. Breathing easier now, I started toward the electric kettle.

It was then that I spotted the body.

He was lying face down between Norton's desk and the bookcase. As soon as I saw who it was, I was nearly as angry as I was frightened. Bernie Hicks, one of the least desirable of Norton's undesirable clientele. Who did he think he was lying on the floor in Norton's office? From the start all he'd been was trouble.

As soon as I registered the fact that Hicks wasn't passed out drunk but most likely dead, a chorus of voices began offering suggestions about what should happen next. Stevick wanted to run. Norton was trying to come up with an alibi. Henderson urged action. As was happening more and more frequently of late, Henderson's strength of personality won out.

With professional calm, he went over to Hicks, knelt down, checked his pulse to verify he was dead, and tried to analyze the situation. There was very little blood, no weapon, and no sign of a struggle. It didn't make sense. Hicks wasn't the type to be killed without fighting back.

Using a Kleenex to keep from putting fingerprints all over everything, Henderson went through Hicks' pockets. There was nothing unusual: a key chain, a hotel key, some loose change and a wallet. The wallet had quite a bit of money in it, several hundreds and a wad of twenties. The deadbeat! He owed Norton two hundred dollars and was always whining about being broke.

It was the ID that was the second shock of the day. There was no driver's license or photos of any kind, but there were two credit cards, a club membership, and a rewards card, all in the name of Warren Stevick! Jesus, what was this?!

First Foster and now— Maybe Stevick was right; I should run.

Still, I hesitated. If I got rid of the wallet, Norton could call the police and tell them he'd found Hicks like this when he arrived. If the wallet was missing, they might suspect robbery. Then again, maybe they'd suspect Norton. One thing was for certain, Norton would never be able to explain the false beard and padding without making himself look guilty of something.

Think . . . I had to think. There must be some simple explanation why Hicks had been killed in Norton's office with Stevick's ID in his pocket.

Sure!

If this was a joke, it wasn't very funny. And if it was a trap, I had better get going, fast.

Still holding the wallet, I stood up. I would remove the ID and flush it down the toilet, keep the money and toss the empty wallet in the garbage. There was nothing more I could do, unless I could think of some way to get rid of the body. And the rug. There was blood on the rug. No, I was stuck with both. "Damn you, Bernie Hicks, what have I ever done to you?"

The words were no sooner out that I heard voices in the hall, male, official sounding voices. The trap, if it was a trap, was closing.

Instinctively, I dropped the wallet next to the body. They weren't going to catch Norton tampering with evidence. I retreated into the bathroom, locked the door, and gave silent thanks to Henderson for insisting that Norton get an office with access to an exterior fire escape. Although why the exit was through Norton's tiny bathroom window was beyond me. Good planning, I guess.

Henderson had also insisted on keeping the window oiled, so it went up without a sound. I climbed out onto the metal grate landing, clumsy but quick. Even with his padding, Norton could move when he had to.

The fire escape only serviced ten of the building's thirty-eight floors. If you were higher up than the tenth floor and wanted to get out in a hurry, you had to jump.

Moments later I was pounding down the metal steps, cursing Norton's hard-soled shoes. At the bottom there was about a ten-foot drop. Awkward because of Norton's bulk, I fell rather than leapt, miraculously ending up in a seated position before tumbling over backwards like a catcher bowled over by a fast ball.

Ignoring the fact that my heels felt as though they had been compressed a quarter of an inch on impact, I got up and hurried off down the alley. No one yelled for me to stop, so I didn't until I'd put some distance between me and the fire escape. Then I turned back to see what was happening. From where I stood, I could just make out Norton's office windows. Even if something was happening inside, I wouldn't be able to tell from this distance. One thing seemed obvious, if someone had killed Hicks to set Norton up, they could have tipped off the police after I'd arrived. That would explain the timing. On the other hand, the voices I'd heard might not have been the police. Maybe I'd ruined my heels for nothing.

Of course, it was also possible Norton had been seen running away. At this very moment they could be getting into position to intercept him. Damn. Bravery was not one of Norton's strengths.

I took a deep breath to steady myself and, ignoring Norton's usual hunched posture and slow gait, moved briskly forward, chin up, padded chest out. Easy, Henderson cautioned. You're a businessman taking a shortcut. There's nothing inherently suspicious about walking down an alley. All you have to do is look confident and act as though nothing is wrong. No one will have any reason to suspect you're actually fleeing a murder scene.

Walk tall, Norton, walk tall.

CHAPTER 6
FAREWELL, NORTON

No one tried to stop me as I emerged from the alley, so I kept right on going. Down the block, across the street, not looking back. Finally, I paused to look in a store window, studying the reflections in the glass. Then I continued down the street, making several turns and one detour through a drugstore. It was time consuming but seemed necessary.

Norton's car was in a parking lot about a fifteen-minute walk from where I was, but I decided to leave it there. The sticker was good until the end of the month, so it might not be discovered until then. Let the police waste time searching for it.

I boarded a bus amidst a crowd of shoppers. It seemed as though everyone turned to look at me, although rationally I knew no one would be on the lookout for Norton yet. What I wanted more than anything was to rip off that damn beard and be done with it. That would give those nosy shoppers something to gawk at. Instead, I found a window seat near the back and stared out the window at the people on the sidewalk.

A woman sat down beside me and propped a shopping bag against my arm. There was something sharp poking me, but I didn't complain. Then a short-haired man in a gray suit got on and passed up several empty seats to take the one right behind me. Was the woman with the shopping bag and the short-haired man working together?

The bus stopped, and the doors squeaked open. The man behind me stood up. So did the woman with the shopping bag. I hesitated. There were too many people in the way of an easy escape. Before I could make up my mind, the woman with the shopping bag was jostling her way through the crowd; the man in the gray suit following in her wake. I began to relax. See, Henderson, no need to get all worked up.

More people got on. No one paid any attention to me. I took a deep breath and tried to focus.

One thing was certain—there was no way Norton could claim he hadn't been at his office that morning. Lawrence would tell the police that he had taken Norton to the tenth floor right on the hour. It was even possible the people Norton had passed in the hall would come forth and identify him. The police might wonder why he had been coming from the wrong direction, but that wouldn't change the fact that he had been there. And he had run away. That spelled *guilty.*

Someone was trying to frame me, either me as Norton or me as Stevick. No, that wasn't accurate. If the frame had been aimed solely at Norton, Stevick's ID wouldn't have been used. The person or persons who had set up the frame either knew or suspected there was a link between Norton and Stevick.

Foster had traced Stevick to the city. If he could do it, so could anyone who wanted to find Stevick. But why set a trap? That wasn't mob style. Why not simply eliminate Stevick and be done with it? Unless someone at the top had a bizarre sense of humor. Or unless they were going to let the police do their dirty work for them.

The passengers were thinning out. If I stayed aboard until the bus was almost empty, the driver might remember me if questioned later. I needed to get going while I was still just another bearded face in the crowd.

When we reached a busy transfer point, I followed two shapeless women in shapeless beige coats off the bus. There were about a dozen people waiting at the bus stop. I pretended to join them, standing with hands in pockets, avoiding eye contact with any of the other waiters.

A bus pulled up and let off some passengers. I mingled with them and gradually drifted off. If the police managed to trace Norton this far, I wanted them to think he'd hopped another bus.

I felt conspicuous walking through residential districts in the middle of the day, so I took a circuitous route, walking fast, like someone with a nearby destination.

It was a long walk. By the time I reached the apartment, my feet were feeling like I'd run a marathon. I went in the back entrance as Norton usually did, and, as usual, I didn't see anyone. It's one of the mysteries of city apartment living that you get to know the other tenants more as distinctive footsteps in the hall or by their particular noise patterns rather than as faces.

Once inside, I could barely refrain from hastily ripping off the beard along with an inch of skin instead of going through the tedious but appropriate process of removal. It wasn't until everything that could be associated with Norton was carefully bagged and hidden that I allowed myself the luxury of a scotch on the rocks.

It was hard to take in and make sense of the day's events. Norton kept worrying about his calendar. There were some appointments and a hearing scheduled for Friday. He was having a hard time accepting the fact that his life as a lawyer was over. After more than two years of developing an independent character, Norton didn't exist anymore. I wasn't Stevick and I wasn't Norton. The question was whether I was still safe to be Henderson.

I poured myself another drink. How long would it take them to determine that Hicks and not Stevick was the corpse in Norton's office? And when they did, would they then make the connection between Stevick and Norton? Would the FBI find out about the murder and work with the police to locate Stevick? Come on, Henderson, use that detective brain of yours. Think!

The liquor wasn't helping. I set the drink aside and went to make some coffee. Henderson didn't care what kind of brew he drank as long as it was strong, but sometimes I longed for a cup of coffee made from Jamaican Blue Mountain beans from the San Marco Coffee Company. The caffeinated aroma of those freshly ground beans was pure bliss.

Henderson's coffee maker turned water brown, but it didn't add much flavor. And it took forever to fill the pot. Feeling impatient, I pulled out the pot and stuck an empty cup under the spout to catch the mud-colored water the machine continued to spit out. There were dark flecks swimming on the surface. Wasn't it bad enough that Stevick had been forced to give up his gourmet blends, and now, just as I had begun to acquire a taste for green tea, I had to sacrifice Norton's preferences as well. All I had left was Henderson drinking bitter coffee out of a Styrofoam cup.

I dumped the beige liquid back in the reservoir to give it a second chance. Then, using Norton's cell, I put through a call to the Water's Edge, the hotel named on the key from Hicks' pocket. When the operator answered, I asked for Warren Stevick.

"Just a moment, sir."

After a short pause I heard the telephone ringing. Two rings later a woman's voice answered, soft and tentative: "Hello?"

It wasn't Caron. I'd half expected that it would be. The really interesting thing was that they had accepted a call for Stevick in the first place.

Without saying anything, I hung up. Later, after ditching Norton's cell phone, I could call back from a number that couldn't be traced. Just in case.

By the time I got back to the coffee it was the color and texture of creosote. I took a sip, my taste buds recoiling in horror. The rest I dumped down the sink to clean out the drains.

Why didn't I just pack my bags and leave? No one would mourn my departure. In fact, only a few people would even notice I was gone. The magazine subscriptions would keep coming, the junk mail would pile up, the telephone solicitors would call, life in this make-believe world would go on. When the manager finally felt obliged to clean out the apartment, the residue of my reimagined lives, he would undoubtedly not even remember the color of my hair.

The same story would serve as explanation for both Henderson's telephone answering service and Al: he'd taken a job in another city. Goodbye folks, that was all she wrote.

Dammit, who was I trying to fool? The truth was I didn't want to run. I hated running. Norton might be beyond saving, but as long as I still had Henderson, I wanted to hang onto him.

The next step seemed to be to call the hotel again. I went to a nearby mall and bought a prepaid disposable cell phone. Ironically, these cheap burner phones always seemed more reliable than their more expensive counterparts. Go figure. As shoppers swarmed past like animals heading for the water hole, I dialed the hotel again, my finger shaking with anticipation. Maybe this time Caron would answer. Maybe the first woman was a friend she had brought along to lend support for the kill.

"Warren Stevick, please." It never hurt to be polite.

"I'm quite certain the Stevicks are out."

"Oh?"

Some people require very little encouragement to tell you all they know. This particular receptionist needed even less than usual. "Are you a friend?" she asked, giving me my next line.

"Friend and business associate. Mr. Stevick and I have an appointment."

"I'm not certain how much I should say . . ." She paused meaningfully, practically begging me to ask for more.

I used Stevick's authoritative lawyer voice to seal the deal. "Do you know where the Stevicks went?"

"Well, I do know where *Mrs.* Stevick is."

"Fine. Talking with Caron would be helpful." I used her first name to assert my right to information as to her whereabouts.

"The policeman who came to see Mrs. Stevick *did* leave his card." Hint, hint.

"Has something happened?"

"I'm sorry to be the one to bear bad tidings . . ." she began.

I hadn't heard such a perfect blend of apology and excitement since the time Warren Jr. came home with a black eye and proudly announced that *he* had won the fight.

"Yes . . .?"

"I'm afraid that Mr. Stevick has, ah, died. Mrs. Stevick is understandably upset."

"My God! How did it happen? A heart attack?"

"I'm not certain, but the card the policeman left says 'Lieutenant Marco Garcia, Homicide.'" She enunciated the last word precisely so there would be no misunderstanding.

After I thanked her and hung up, I put the cell in my pocket and headed out of the mall. I would try again later. I had to know if Caron was somehow involved. Supposedly she had gone with Garcia, possibly to identify the body. When she saw the corpse, would she be shocked, sad . . . or disappointed?

Uncertain what to do next, I stopped for something to eat, Henderson's choice, a tacky fast-food place where you ate off an orange plastic tray on a purple plastic table with bright green plastic plants drooping from overhead planters. The food tasted great. Perhaps I was finally *becoming* Eric Henderson, starting with my palate.

Afterwards, I returned to the apartment, locked the door from the inside, and checked to make certain the place hadn't been searched in my absence. With so few furnishings and possessions it was difficult to tell when things had been disturbed, but I was fairly confident no one had been rifling through my cheap undies or checking out the stack of Mexican and Italian entrees in my freezer. I settled in to wait until it seemed reasonable to call Castaldo. Four-thirty was the minimum time limit I set for myself.

At four-thirty-one I had Al on the line. "This is . . . Eric." I'd almost slipped and said "Warren." The last twenty-four hours had loosened my grip on reality.

"Yeah."

"Just thought I'd let you know that I didn't turn up anything on Stevick. I'm working on the report now. He may have been in town, but he isn't here now. I'd stake my reputation on it."

"Hell, what's a reputation worth, anyway."

"Huh?"

"You may not have turned up anything on Stevick, but Stevick has turned up . . . dead."

"You're kidding." Pause. "Is this official?"

"Just telling you what I've heard."

"What about the wife? Has she been notified yet?"

"She identified him."

"Damn. There goes my fee." She'd identified him?! Caron would know the difference between Hicks and her ex. Was the woman who answered the hotel room phone posing as Caron? But if so, *why*? She couldn't expect to keep his identity secret for long.

"Kind of a coincidence, don't you think?"

I didn't know what to think. "You mean that I'm hired to look for Stevick and then he shows up dead?"

"Something like that."

"How'd he die? I don't suppose it was a heart attack."

"Neat little bullet hole in the head, and a rather sloppy one in his back. We don't know yet which was the cause of death."

"Mob execution?"

"He was found in a lawyer's office."

"Any connection?"

"Off the record, OK?"

"OK, although it would be nice to have a little something to dress up my report. Maybe I can still salvage something out of this mess."

"Most of it will be in the papers anyway."

"So, give me a preview."

"The lawyer's name is Nick Norton. He handles the big stuff like DWIs and shoplifting. Anyway, someone in the building heard shots and called the police but wouldn't leave their name. So, the officer on duty sent over a patrol car to have a look around. They found the body. Someone had gone through his pockets, but nothing seemed to be missing. You know how that goes though, you have to know what *should* have been there in order to know if it's missing."

"So, what did Norton have to say?"

"He conveniently disappeared just before the body was found."

"You think he did it?"

"I don't think anything. They pay me to do paperwork, not to think."

"I see." Henderson waited, sensing Al was building up to something. He was.

"Eric, I hope you understand, but I had to give the lieutenant in charge your name."

Of course he did. "No problem. Think I should call . . . right away?"

I'd almost slipped a second time; I wasn't supposed to know Garcia's name yet.

"Yeah. I told him you'd check in or drop by as soon as you heard the news. His name is Garcia, Lieutenant Marco Garcia."

"I don't have anything to give him. Wish I did."

"Just tell him what you've told me. That should be enough."

"What's he like, anyway?"

"A hard ass, but a good cop. You two ought to hit it off just fine."

"OK, I'll give it a whirl." Feeling irritable, Henderson added, "Get your name plate request straightened out yet?"

Al made a sound halfway between a grunt and a sneeze before hanging up. Henderson assumed that meant "no."

CHAPTER 7
MRS. STEVICK

The instant Henderson saw him he knew the type. His eyes were as dark as an eclipse, the eyes of someone who has come up the hard way and isn't about to take any shit off anyone, especially some hack gumshoe like Henderson. Even his hair looked tough, thick, and unruly. Probably had a chest covered with it too.

He and his office were a matched set. No fuss, no frills. The only personal touch was a calendar from some hardware store tacked up on a side wall. It hung at an angle.

As Henderson entered the room it was clear there would be no handshaking. Henderson therefore kept his hands in his pockets to show he didn't care. *He* didn't, but Stevick did. Gentlemen always shook hands.

Skipping the amenities—maybe he didn't have any in his bag of tricks—Garcia got right to the point. "You ever see Stevick?"

Garcia hadn't indicated that Henderson should sit, so he stood at attention, resisting the impulse to click his heels together. "No, not in person, just a picture."

"Who showed you the picture?"

"An investigator from Chicago. Stephen Foster." Humming a few bars of "My Old Kentucky Home" seemed inappropriate since Henderson wasn't sure how much he wanted to rile Garcia.

"And just why was this Stephen Foster supposedly looking for Stevick?"

"On behalf of Mrs. Stevick. She was trying to locate him."

"It seems she found him without your help."

"That's what I hear." If he kept on sounding snide, Henderson was going to have a hard time keeping himself in check. In fact, he wasn't sure he wanted to. But Stevick was whispering in his ear to "behave."

"Come on, Henderson." Garcia stood up and came out from behind his desk. "Why don't you tell me the truth and save us both a lot of trouble?"

"Huh?"

Garcia's face looked as unyielding as granite, and his thick hands opened and closed as if remembering how easy it had been to get a witness to talk in the good old days. Only there was something wrong with the way the questioning was going. What "truth" could Henderson possibly tell him? The possibilities were chilling.

"Didn't Castaldo tell you about Foster?" Henderson asked. He no longer felt cocky, more scared than anything, but he was trying hard to keep the fear out of his voice.

"Castaldo told me about Foster," Garcia confirmed.

"And . . .?"

"You kept on snooping around after you were taken off the case. I want to know why."

"Taken off the case?"

"Your hearing is just fine."

"Ah, taken off by whom?"

"By 'whom.' My, ain't we elegant?"

"All right. *Who* supposedly took me off the case?" Stevick just wouldn't let Henderson say "taken off by *who*."

"*You* tell *me*."

How could I tell him something I didn't know?

"Well?" Garcia demanded when Henderson failed to answer.

"I was never 'taken off the case.' Foster *still* hasn't contacted me."

"That won't wash."

"Call Foster. He'll tell you."

Garcia didn't move. He was as still as death.

"What possible reason could I have for continuing to look for Stevick on my own?"

Still no response from Garcia. His dark eyes were unblinking, laser sharp. An inner voice told me to quit protesting, but Henderson's mouth kept right on talking. "I make my living finding people who are lost. Usually it's kids or husbands. Occasionally a missing wife. The kinds of jobs the police can't spare a lot of time for." See, Henderson's on *your* side. "I didn't like this one from the beginning. Not when Foster mentioned the mob. But I needed the money, you know?"

The way Garcia was eyeballing Henderson I felt sure he could see right through Henderson's underwear to the real me, whoever that was. From Garcia's point of view, it probably did seem as though there might be some connection between Henderson and Stevick, especially if Foster had fed him a tall tale for some reason neither Henderson nor I could fathom. But I assured Henderson, there was no way Garcia could know the real truth—no way.

The intercom on Garcia's desk broke the deadlock. It buzzed and a red light flashed. Garcia pushed one of the buttons and curtly said, "Garcia." He made his own name sound like a hammer.

"Mrs. Stevick here to see you."

My knees suddenly went weak.

"Tell her to come."

Garcia turned back to Henderson. "For now, we'll say you didn't know Foster had taken you off the case." He paused, his dark bushy eyebrows raised for emphasis. "But don't think for a minute that I'm not going to be keeping an eye on you."

If Garcia intended to keep an eye on Henderson, maybe he'd get to see him collapse when he came face to face with Caron—*if* the Mrs. Stevick on her way in really was Caron.

Henderson turned toward the door.

"If you 'remember' anything, be sure to give me a call."

"Sure." He put one hand on the doorknob, half expecting Garcia to say something more to keep him there until Caron . . . or her alter ego arrived. When he didn't, Henderson went out and started to turn away from the main entrance instead of toward it. Then he caught himself.

This could be the test. He tried to act as though he had been momentarily confused and turned back toward the main entrance.

The first person Henderson saw wasn't Caron. She didn't even vaguely resemble his wife. Instead of aloof and elegant, this woman was attractive in a soft, wide-eyed sort of way, with a hint of pink on her cheeks that he was certain wasn't natural. As she came toward him, he noticed that she was playing with the gold band on the ring finger of her left hand. She barely gave him a glance as they passed.

Henderson slowed down to see which room she went into. As he turned back, he caught a glimpse of Garcia standing in the doorway of his office, looking down the hall in his direction. Maybe the scene had been staged, after all. Sure enough, Garcia was ushering her into his office. Henderson had just seen Mrs. Warren Stevick, widow of *the* Warren Stevick. So, what did that make the Stevick I shared a body with, the living dead? The whole thing was screwy.

Just to make absolutely certain, Henderson had a look around the waiting room before leaving. Except for the officer on duty, there wasn't another woman in sight.

It was, of course, not only possible but probable that there was more than one Warren Stevick. Still, that didn't explain what Hicks was doing with Stevick's ID. Nor did it explain why someone calling herself Mrs. Stevick would identify Hicks as her deceased husband. It seemed to Henderson that it was a ploy with a short shelf-life. But it did give him some breathing room to figure a few things out.

Back at Henderson's office I put through a call to Langdon, Fennerman, and Wetzel. They were closed, as I knew they would be at this hour, but there was an emergency number. I called the number and tried to convince the person at the other end of the line that it was imperative I talk with Foster immediately. She acted suspiciously like someone who had been warned not to put through any calls. She would only take a message.

There were two Stephen Fosters in the online directory for the area, but neither was Stephen *G.* Foster. I called them anyway, but both claimed they didn't know Henderson's Foster. There was apparently no way I was going to get through to him before morning. Unless he called Henderson, and I wasn't holding my breath.

I was sitting there trying to think what to do when I noticed I was making a list, facts in the left-hand column, unanswered questions on the right, and a row of empty boxes just begging to be checked. Stevick was still alive and well somewhere in the recesses of Henderson's consciousness.

When I finished, the questions were by far more numerous than the facts. One question was underlined twice: what did someone hope to gain as a result of implicating Norton in Stevick's alleged murder?

Mentally I started in on another list, a list of what Henderson had working in his favor. At the top was the knowledge that the body was Hicks. That gave him a head start on the police, but just how much of a head start remained to be seen. What I needed to do was to get in touch with the phony Mrs. Stevick and find out what her game was.

Sometimes hotel staff are stuffy about giving out room numbers, so I decided on subterfuge right off. I called Water's Edge and used a nasal accent to ask for room 202. It was doubtful the receptionist would have recognized my voice from before, but, what the heck, it seemed like the sort of thing Henderson would do. A man answered. He wasn't pleased about being disturbed. I had him switch me back to the operator and complained in my irritating nasal way that she had given me the wrong room. She wasn't pleased either.

"What room did you want?"

"Mrs. Warren Stevick in room 202."

After the briefest of pauses, she said, "Mrs. Stevick is not in that room." Her tone was triumphant. It's always satisfying to be right, even in small things.

"That's what the note says," I argued.

"Well, she isn't. She's in room 307."

"Then ring her in that room . . ., please." It's always satisfying to succeed, even in small things, but I kept the triumph out of my voice.

The telephone rang twelve times before the receptionist came back on the line. As I already knew, the woman calling herself Mrs. Stevick wasn't in.

It was time to pay a visit to the Water's Edge.

. . .

I let myself in through a back delivery entrance with Henderson's handy set of picks and sprinted up the stairs to the third floor. No one answered at room 307. I went down the hall and pretended to be waiting for the elevator. Whenever the car stopped at the third floor, I acted as though I wanted to go in the opposite direction. The act definitely had its limitations.

A man got off and disappeared down the hall to my left. The elevator went back to the lobby and came up again. Another man got off. He had a thick neck, a muscular body, and the perfect face for a police mug shot. Actually, I didn't pay much attention to him until he went directly to room 307 and let himself in with a key.

At that point the elevator opened to reveal a couple I had seen only a few minutes earlier on their way up. It was time to shift my base of operations. I got in, rode with them to the second floor and took the stairs back up to the third. From the stairway I couldn't make out the door to room 307, but by pressing my forehead against the little window in the door, I *could* see the elevator.

Twenty long minutes later the thick-necked man pushed the elevator button. Since I was developing a bad kink in my neck and a very nasty disposition, I convinced myself that following him was the smart thing to do. If not smart, then at least more comfortable than what I'd been doing.

He beat me to the lobby, but not by much. He walked to the far end of the parking lot and got into a bright green Chevy. Henderson's car was only a hop, skip and a dash away. By the time the Chevy turned down the main street headed north, I was right behind him.

We came to a residential district and the traffic thinned out. I increased the distance between us. Still, I had no difficulty following. He stopped in front of a small apartment building. I parked about three cars away and waited until he went inside.

Unfortunately, I gave him too much of a head start. By the time I got past the locked front door, he had disappeared. I hung around outside trying to decide whether to wait until he came out again or return to the hotel. I was still trying to make up my mind when he reappeared carrying a suitcase.

Somehow, I wasn't the least surprised when the Chevy started back in the direction of the Water's Edge. The only question in my mind was whether he was moving in with the alleged widow, or whether the two of them were planning a trip together.

At the hotel he left his suitcase in the car and took the elevator up. I raced up the stairs. When I arrived, he was nowhere in sight. After standing in front of the elevator a few minutes, I went back to the lobby and used one of their in-house phones to call room 307.

"Yeah?" The voice was throaty and deep, a good match for his thick neck.

"I'd like to speak with Mrs. Stevick."

"She's not taking any calls at present. Could I take a message?" In spite of the words, he didn't sound like a social secretary.

"I need to talk to her personally. I'm a friend of her husband's."

There was a perceptible hesitation. "Actually, she isn't here right now. I just came by to drop off some insurance papers she needs to sign." He didn't sound like an insurance agent either.

"Well, tell her Bob Hansen called." Bob Hansen was the name of a real estate agent whose signs seemed to be everywhere and were, in my opinion, an eyesore. That would teach him to advertise.

After I hung up, I bounded back up the stairs, my footsteps echoing all the way to China. I arrived just in time to see the elevator doors closing. Damn. I had to be sure, so I turned and raced back down the stairs.

The bright green Chevy was pulling out of the parking space as I burst out the front entrance. At that distance I couldn't tell if there was one or two people in the car.

At a somewhat slower run, I hurried back up to the third floor and knocked loudly on the door of room 307. "Room Service," I announced. No one answered. "Room service," I said again just to be sure.

Henderson had been wanting to try the keycard hacking device he'd picked up from a questionable street vendor. This was his chance. He'd been warned that it didn't work on all locks, but the instant he inserted it in the slot on the door of room 307, the little light turned green. Too late I started worrying what I would do if someone was in there. Waiters didn't enter hotel rooms uninvited. But guests sometimes made mistakes. *Sorry, I shouldn't have had that third martini with dinner.*

As it turned out, no apologies were necessary. The bed was made and the closets empty. The only sign of recent occupancy was the crumpled sanitary strip on the floor next to the toilet. Green Chevy man had come by to clear out. Damn.

Cursing Henderson, I rushed down the now familiar stairway. If I was lucky, real lucky, I might overtake the Chevy on the way to the airport. *If* they were headed for the airport.

I kept my foot down hard all the way there. But I wasn't lucky. My luck had apparently run out three days ago.

CHAPTER 8
THE MOB

E veryone ought to have a friend in the Department of Motor Vehicles. I wish Henderson did. Whenever he wanted information, he had to go through channels, and sometimes those channels meandered like streams through a country meadow before someone finally took pity and dropped a request into the computer. Then the computer took a coffee break. That's why Henderson had been known to ask Al to put his name on an occasional request form. Once or twice he'd even come up with a successful scam for speeding things up. This time I decided to try what Henderson would refer to as an alternative strategy.

It was barely 8:00 a.m. when I pulled up in front of the thick-necked man's apartment. The manager answered my rather insistent knocking, but it was obvious he hadn't been up long, about as long as it took to walk from his bed to the door, I'd guess. He was barefoot and had on an old flannel robe that wasn't securely tied and gapped where it hung crooked.

"No salesmen allowed in the building," he mumbled, rubbing his thumb and forefinger up and down the bridge of his nose.

"I'm not selling anything." Couldn't he tell I was dressed like an office employee on the way to work? "A fellow came out of this building a few minutes ago and drove off in a bright green Chevy.

Medium height, broad shoulders, flattish nose." Henderson used his hands to illustrate the description. "After he left, I noticed this package next to where he was parked. Thought it might be his." Henderson held up the package in evidence. It was a pretty good performance overall.

The manager looked from me to the package with a suspicious glint in his eyes. Perhaps there weren't too many honest people in the neighborhood. "You can leave it with me," he offered, reaching for the package.

Henderson jerked it back. "I just want to know his name so I can check with him. If it isn't his, well, then I guess it's mine."

This avaricious display eased the manager's suspicions. "Simco," he said, stifling a yawn. "Dan Simco. His name's on the mail box." He started to close the door, then gave me an unflattering onceover and added, "I wouldn't mess with him if I was you." With that he shut the door.

The mailboxes in the lobby indicated Simco lived on the second floor, apartment 201. Later I'd take a look inside, but first I had more pressing matters to attend to.

Back at his office Henderson checked in with his answering service. Several clients were getting anxious about progress on their respective cases. I made a notation on his calendar to return their calls. There was no message from Foster. Henderson had already called him twice that morning. First, they said he wasn't in yet; later they had to see if he was free. He wasn't. But he would call back the first chance he got. Uh huh.

I made a full pot of coffee to prepare myself for the ordeal ahead. Then I got a lined legal pad and placed it next to the computer. My first call was mainly for warm-up; I didn't really expect Mrs. Stevick to be in her hotel room. When she failed to answer, Henderson called Castaldo.

"Can you do me a small favor?"

"Depends. How small?"

"I'm not asking for something for nothing. What do you want in return, a big screen TV maybe? A nice mink stole for the wife? I know a guy who can make you a real deal."

"I'll put it on your tab. When you owe me a Jaguar, I'll let you know."

"Importation of exotic pets . . . isn't that against the law?"

"You shouldn't try to be cute, Eric. Leave the cute stuff alone. It's like bad booze; it doesn't go down well before noon."

"Man to man then, how about that favor?"

"Why not . . .?" Al sighed. "I need a break from this paperwork."

"No name plate yet?"

"Just tell me what you want."

"What I want is anything you have on a Dan Simco. Ever hear of him?"

"You must live right. I don't even have to look that one up. His arrest record I know by heart: assault, disturbing the peace, more assault, sometimes with a deadly weapon, sometimes not. Strictly hired muscle. Doesn't even pretend to use his brain. We've been keeping an eye on him for some time. One of these day's he's going to go too far and we'll put him away for good."

"Work for anyone in particular?"

"Not that I know of, but I can ask around. See if there's anyone he's been doing stuff for of late. What's your interest in him?"

"Husband got beat up. Won't tell his wife what happened. She wants me to find out. Simco's name came up."

"Concerned wife. That's nice."

"What she really wants to know is where all their money has been going of late. Maybe hubby is into gambling or drugs. Something like that."

"Sounds messy. You'd better be careful."

"Don't worry, I won't take on Simco. Just dance around him a little."

"Stay on your toes or you'll wind up dancing a dirge."

One pot of godawful coffee and two hours later, I wasn't much wiser than when I'd started. Between my online research and numerous telephone calls, I'd ascertained that no one named Simco or Stevick had taken a plane from the city on Wednesday evening. Of course they could have used assumed names. Or they could have taken either a train or a bus. People often purchased bus or train tickets at the last minute and paid in cash. I did get a list of departure times and destinations, but so many fit the timeframe that it was next to impossible to draw any sound conclusions.

If I'd had an army of employees at hand, I could have checked parking near bus and train stations, but Henderson didn't even have a sidekick. If they'd hopped a bus or train, the Chevy could be in any one of numerous downtown garages. A search just wasn't feasible.

One last call and that would be it for now. I switched the phone to my left ear and tried the Water's Edge one more time. Mrs. Stevick still wasn't answering her telephone. I asked if she'd checked out and was put through to the main desk.

"Mrs. Stevick is still with us," the clerk assured me. "Sometimes guests prefer not to be disturbed." Hint, hint. Smug bastard.

I was still holding my burner cell when an annoying ringtone started playing. Like the proverbial Pavlovian dog, I responded, pressing the phone to my ear and saying "hello" several times before I realized I was answering the wrong phone. Fortunately, the default ditty on Henderson's cell goes on interminably, so I managed to answer the right phone before Garcia hung up. He wanted to see Henderson again, in person and on the double. Swallowing both pride and irritation, I grabbed Henderson's raincoat and headed out into a Pacific Northwest downpour.

It's an axiom of Northwest living that the harder it rains, the farther away from your destination you have to park. I ended up over three blocks away from the station. Water streamed down my forehead, ran into my eyes, and dropped off my chin onto my shoes as I tried to figure out how to punch the right buttons for the time needed on the parking meter and not end up contributing a month's wages to the city for parking. Someone always managed, perhaps deliberately, to scratch the plastic over the directions so as to make them unreadable.

By the time I reached the station I was sopping wet. I left a trail any rookie could follow as I made my way to Garcia's office without stopping to ask permission.

Garcia didn't look up when I stepped inside his office and stood there dripping on the floor. Plink, plink, plink. Like a leaky faucet. Instead, he continued studying some papers on his desk, as if he was too busy to be bothered acknowledging Henderson after insisting that he hotfoot it over to his office posthaste.

Finally, Henderson got tired of the power play and decided to make himself at home.

He took off his coat and shook it out, trying to splatter a few drops on Garcia's desk in the process, before neatly folding it across the back of a chair. His pants were damp from the knees down, and his shoes made a squishy sound when he wiggled his toes. He sat down and waited for Garcia to acknowledge his humid presence. Garcia better have a damn good reason for calling Henderson down here, I thought. Then again, I almost hoped he didn't.

"Got a new story today?" Garcia asked without looking up.

"Still the same old story . . ." Henderson was tempted to add, ". . . a fight for love and glory." Then again, maybe the better response was that "there are eight million stories in the naked city."

Garcia's head came up, his black eyes fastened on Henderson's. "Come clean with me now and I'll see that you get a break."

"Why don't you lean on Foster? He's the one telling tall tales."

"I've checked Foster out. He's with a reputable firm."

"So am I."

"Come on, Henderson, what reason does Foster have to lie about this?"

"By the same logic, what reason do I have to lie about it?"

Garcia's expression suggested that although he didn't know the reason—yet—Henderson just wasn't in the same league as Foster. Solo practitioners were sleazy and untrustworthy; it went with the job. Obviously he hadn't met Foster in person.

"I could hold you as a witness," he threatened.

"A witness to what?"

"I could hold you as a witness," he repeated.

"At least I'd get free room and board."

"It wouldn't be no picnic."

"I don't expect the Ritz."

"You protecting someone? If so, they'd better be worth it."

Yeah, *I* was worth it.

Garcia stared at Henderson for a few seconds, then seemed to make a decision and dismissed him with a wave of the hand. Was that it? Just proving he could get Henderson to jump whenever he wanted him to?

Henderson shook the wrinkles out of his wet coat, leaving a line of tiny water droplets on the floor.

"You'll be hearing from me," Garcia warned as Henderson squelched out of Garcia's office.

It was still raining, a steady blanket of water like in a car wash. I raced for the car, weaving like a soldier dodging enemy fire. It didn't do any good. I'd have been left for dead on the battlefield. Cheap raincoats and cheap shoes are to rain gear what the bow and arrow was to an M-16. It was about time Henderson got over his hang-up about umbrellas not being macho.

Cursing the rain and life in general, I sped toward the airport. Let Foster tell Henderson to his face how he had personally taken him off the Stevick case the same day he'd hired him. The weasel. If he didn't cough up the truth and offer to straighten things out with Garcia, Henderson would see to it that Foster's dentist got some business.

Airport security was happy to accept Henderson's phony ID, and the airline gladly accepted his VISA. They didn't care who he really was or whether he might be trying to leave the state to avoid arrest. If I wanted to, I could keep right on going after Chicago, me, and VISA, all the way to the ends of the earth. I wondered if it was raining there.

My plane didn't leave for an hour. To pass the time I bought a hotdog that was sweating on the outside and artic cold on the inside, a cup of coffee so black and so strong that it quickly began seeping through the seams on the paper container, and a lukewarm turnover with contents allegedly related to the apple family. Although in my opinion, the relationship was at least twice removed. Even Henderson's stomach didn't understand what it had done to deserve such abuse.

The flight produced more bad coffee, a soggy roll, and a headache.

Since the flight attendant was old enough to be Mother Tums, it came as no surprise that she had a roll of them in her purse. I took one along with two aspirin and a glass of water so full of chlorine I was certain it had been piped in from Mark Spitz's swimming pool. I pictured the Tums floating around in my stomach like a miniature life cushion.

By the time we arrived in Chicago my headache was only a weak throb and the hotdog a burpy memory. At least it wasn't raining. It was overcast and cool, typical Chicago for the time of year. All of a sudden Stevick started remembering, and I had an overwhelming urge for some kielbasa, real kielbasa, not the kind you buy wrapped in plastic in the deli section of the supermarket.

I took a taxi downtown. The airport shuttle cost less, but I wanted to get this over with. No sense hanging around Chicago thinking about the past. This was one time cheapo Henderson would have to splurge.

It was tempting to ask the driver to take a detour through the former neighborhood for old times' sake. Maybe I would get a glimpse of the kids. No, they would be in school. Besides, someone might get a glimpse of me, someone who recognized Stevick in spite of all the physical changes. It was a chance I couldn't take. No detours. No kielbasa. Just a quick trip to see Foster and I'd be on my way "home."

Langdon, Fennerman, and Wetzel was located near the stratosphere in the IBM Building in downtown Chicago. With its plush carpets and commanding view of the city, it might have passed for a moderately successful law firm if it had not been for one violation of image: not even a middling law firm would use counter top cabinet pigeonholes for paper messages. What did they think they were, a 1960s hotel?

After a perfunctory greeting, the receptionist accepted without question my story about Dean Gerberth recommending Foster. What did it matter there was no Dean Gerberth, there was a Stephen Foster, wasn't there? And, I was in luck, Mr. Foster happened to be available. Yes, she could give him my name, Victor Mature. Norton—may he rest in peace—had been a classic films buff, not that I had any intention of being particularly "mature" about what I was going to say to Foster.

The receptionist gave me directions to Foster's office. When I found it, I paused, relishing the moment. Then I gave his door a two-finger rap and entered before he had a chance to respond. The instant he saw Henderson, Foster rose up out of his chair like a ptarmigan taking to the sky. Only he couldn't fly. And the way his mouth was working with no words coming out, it also seemed as if he'd lost his ability to speak.

"Don't get up," Henderson said, motioning him to sit back down. "I just came for a little man to rat talk." Henderson closed the door firmly behind him for emphasis.

Foster sank back into his chair and found his voice, well, maybe not quite *his* voice, but a squeaky facsimile. "You can't come barging in here threatening me like this."

"No one is threatening you. Just keep your hands where I can see them and everything will be fine."

His eyes darted to the intercom on his desk.

"I wouldn't do that if I were you."

"That's a threat. You can't tell me that isn't a threat."

"If you make a wrong move I'll break every bone in your lying body. That's a *promise*, not a threat. Now move back from your desk."

Apparently, the look on Henderson's face convinced him Henderson meant business. After a brief hesitation, Foster pushed back his chair and rested his hands on his knees. "What do you want?"

"Push your chair back another foot or so. That's a good boy. Now then . . ." Henderson pulled up a chair just a wild man's leap away and stared Foster down, watching his pale face slowly turn a remarkable magenta, a shade lighter than panic purple. "OK, Foster, I want to know who ordered you to lie about taking me off the case and why. That's all. Tell me that, and I'll walk out of here and you'll never see me again."

"I didn't lie . . ."

Henderson stood up and moved menacingly toward the man. Foster recoiled. Fearless Fosdick he wasn't.

"Well, maybe I fudged the truth a bit," he admitted.

"Lieutenant Garcia has me down as a suspect in a murder investigation because of your little 'fudge.'"

There were droplets of moisture forming on Foster's upper lip. "We're both reasonable men. There's no reason why we can't settle this thing without resorting to violence . . . is there?"

"It depends on how quickly you come across with the information I want." Henderson went around behind Foster and hulked. Foster started to turn toward him, but Henderson whirled the chair back in place. Real rough stuff. Foster's face was fast approaching panic purple.

"I've always felt resorting to violence was unnecessary in our profession." It was part statement, part plea.

"Not all private investigators are tough guys." Henderson spit out the words and moved in front of Foster again. "Just some of us." He didn't thump his chest, but they both knew who he meant.

Foster swallowed hard, his Adam's apple bobbing up and down erratically.

Henderson glared at the cowering Foster. If he didn't tell Henderson what he knew, Henderson would beat the crap out of him. Wouldn't he?

"I would have called you, but I was scared. He said I should lay off the case. He threatened me. *Really* threatened me. Like, you know, those guys don't kid around."

Those guys? Suddenly Henderson didn't feel so hot. It must have been that damn hotdog. "You think *I'm* kidding around?" Maybe he was kidding himself most of all.

"Hey, you know what those guys are like."

"You can name them out loud; the boogieman isn't going to get you for that."

Foster glanced around as if worried that his office was bugged. "The mob," he murmured.

"How do you know?"

"Hey, it was clear."

"Did he wear a pin in his lapel that said 'Mafioso'?"

"No, but, you know, he looked like, well, like a criminal."

"Striped suite, brass knuckles . . ."

"You think I'm making this up?"

"Did you check him out?"

"I'm not crazy. You don't mess with the mob."

"That written in the good book?"

Foster shook his head as if it had been a serious question.

"So, someone threatened you. You don't know who he was or how to get in touch with him. But you *assume* he was a bad guy because of the way he was dressed. What specifically did he tell you to do?"

"He told me to drop the Stevick case."

"What did he say about me?"

"You?" Foster seemed genuinely surprised. "He didn't mention you."

Henderson almost hit him then. His fists ached for the feel of Foster's weak chin. "You fool," he said. "You damn fool. If he didn't mention me, then why in hell didn't you call and tell me to quit?"

Patches of fright white appeared on Foster's flushed face. That only made Henderson angrier. "Well?"

"I . . . I didn't think of it."

"And when Garcia called you, what did you tell him?"

"That I'd told you the case was finished."

"Why?" Henderson practically screamed the word. Foster jerked back as if he'd been struck.

"Because . . . because . . ."

"Look, you dumb shit, I want you to get on that telephone and call Garcia right this minute."

Foster shook his head "no."

"Why not, for God's sake? What difference can it possibly make to you?"

"The mob," he whispered hoarsely.

"The mob got what it wanted. They don't give a damn about me."

"Garcia will want to know why I lied."

"Tell him you made a mistake and didn't want your boss to find out."

"I can't do that."

"Why not?" Henderson grabbed Foster's shirt front and lifted him part way out of his chair. The little twit was really getting to him.

"Garcia will check. He'll find out. The mob . . ." Foster's voice cracked, and he seemed to be having difficulty swallowing. Henderson released him and he flopped back into his chair like a rag doll.

It made no sense. Foster was scared shitless, but he wasn't about to give in. Maybe deep down he knew Henderson wouldn't beat the crap out of him. Maybe he suspected that in many ways Henderson was just as impotent as he was.

CHAPTER 9
DING DONG, STEVICK IS DEAD

My plane got in at 9:33 p.m. It was still raining, although it wasn't coming down quite as hard, just enough to make life thoroughly miserable. Sometime during the day Henderson's clothes had finally dried, but they were creased and shapeless, an old man's shabby outfit, and his shoes had developed a pulpy quality, like walking on fungus. Those damn shoes.

As I passed a row of newspaper machines that had somehow managed to survive the declining newspaper market, the name "Stevick" caught my eye. Headline news. That was certainly worth a dollar. If I'd had the right change. I shook the handle and the door plopped open. I took my free paper and read it under the ceiling light in Henderson's car.

According to the article, continued on page A5 after only a brief introduction, Stevick was indeed dead. The writer hinted at mob connections and mentioned several other crimes in the area that were suspected of being mob related. There were no facts, just speculation, much the same speculation that kept running through my head. Still, they managed to get two good-sized columns out of the story. There was even a picture of the front of Norton's office building. In newsprint black and white it looked like the kind of place murders happened.

I read the article through twice, searching for some indication that the police knew or suspected the body wasn't Stevick's. If they *did* know, they weren't telling reporters. Maybe they were sitting on the information for some reason. Or maybe their computer had decided on its own to keep the information secret. The beginning of an AI takeover. Nothing in this case made sense.

The first thing I did when I got back to the apartment was to pour myself a drink. The brand was Henderson's choice, but for once Stevick wasn't complaining. It was fiery and potent, that was enough. Drink in hand I ran bath water, feeling suddenly nostalgic. It often happened like that. Some small act would bring back a pleasant memory of the past. In this instance it was Caron serving me a drink while I soaked in the tub at the end of a long day. Life had been good then.

As I undressed, I noticed I had developed a rash around both wrists and at the back of my neck from wearing wet clothes all day. That made me mad all over again. Enough is enough, Henderson. Maybe they made umbrellas with carved wooden handles, a raging rhinoceros, or a man-eating tiger. Even Hemingway would approve.

The water was steamy hot and soothing, but my muscles weren't fooled. They knew this was only a momentary respite. There was work yet to be done, the kind of work that was supposedly second nature to Henderson, but a source of anxiety for Stevick, Norton, and me. Whoever "me" was at this point. The liquor was for Henderson, the bath for all of us.

Afterwards I dressed in one of Henderson's many work outfits: dark double-knit slacks, dark pullover sweater, dark rubber-soled shoes. The modern after-hours burglar. No after shave, just a hint of masculine musk. To complete the outfit, I tucked a pair of dark, custom-made leather gloves in the pocket of Henderson's dark water-resistant jacket. Rubber gloves are easier to work in but harder to explain to a police officer. Not even surgeons wear them home.

It was the kind of job that made Henderson almost thankful for the rain. People tended to stay indoors on dreary, wet nights. Rain also provided a sound cushion. Of course it kept the perpetrator from hearing at peak efficiency too, but when you are breaking and entering, the advantage was with the one committing the crime.

Since it was seldom wise to plunge right in, Henderson staked out Simco's apartment from the cover of a row of shrubs and waited. The assignment dampened his clothes and his spirits, pointedly illustrating the difference between "water-resistant" and "waterproof." How anyone could enjoy singing in the rain was beyond him—they would just get their teeth wet.

After standing there about fifteen minutes with raindrops slowly dribbling down the inside of his jacket collar, Henderson decided he didn't care who was hanging around on the second floor, he was going in.

Using a standard BLT—not the sandwich but a bypassing lock technique—he let himself in the back. He'd learned about lock picking from a book he'd sent for by Eddie the Wire. His professional lock picking tools came from an online company that specified the tools were to be used strictly for legal purposes. Sure.

Entering Simco's apartment was a snap. There wasn't even a safety bolt. In some ways that was discouraging. Anyone with something to hide ought to have a better lock setup.

After making certain the curtains were drawn, Henderson switched on a light. Why fumble around in the dark when Thomas Edison had made things so easy? Then he had a look around to get a feel for the layout and to make certain he didn't have company in some back room. If Simco was there, Henderson certainly didn't want to disturb his beauty rest. He needed it.

The place was Spartan but comfortable. There wasn't much furniture in the living room, but the chair and couch were soft looking and roomy. The big, unmade bed in the back room passed the fingertip test, and the unmatched towels in the bath were thick piled, not made with zero-twist Egyptian cotton yarn like Stevick was used to, but plush enough. Throughout the apartment there was no attempt to coordinate colors or styles, unless comfort could be considered the theme.

In the middle of the living room floor, behind the heavy wood coffee table, Henderson literally stumbled over a set of barbells. Art nouveau no doubt.

Henderson usually began a search by going through the contents of a desk or wherever letters and papers were stored. Simco didn't seem to have a place for such things, but there was a pile of magazines and envelopes next to the butter dish on the kitchen table, so that's where he started.

He browsed the magazines first. Simco seemed to like muscles and women, in that order. He apparently especially liked women *with* muscles. A feature article on women body builders had been folded open and propped against the toaster.

The envelopes contained mostly bills and advertisements. *This is your last chance to enter our sweepstakes contest. This is your very last chance. Buy now and save two dollars. This is absolutely your very last chance. FREE BOOK of your choice with every ten-year subscription.* On and on. Junk mail and magazines. As Henderson and Norton both knew, they *did* confirm one's existence.

After looking through everything on the table, Henderson turned his attention to Simco's refrigerator. Some people consider the refrigerator the safest place to keep their valuables because refrigerators can supposedly survive a fire. They are not, however, burglarproof.

Simco's refrigerator was old enough to be a real color, a shade of pea-soup green. No mechanical ice dispenser. No separate freezer drawer. No double doors. Humming softly as it performed it's basic, no-frills function. Inside, its prized possessions included two six-packs of Coors Light, a puckered quarter of lime, a pile of molded cheese slices, and an opened bottle of quinine water. There wasn't even any ice in the plastic ice cube trays in the freezer compartment.

Next Henderson went through the cupboards. There were very few staples and even fewer dishes. If Simco entertained at home, he probably didn't feed his women before asking to feel their muscles.

Henderson moved on to the living room.

It was a desert. He couldn't even find anything to search. He groped around under the chair and sofa cushions and came up with a couple of lint balls and a dime. There wasn't even that much on or under the coffee table. The wall-to-wall rug was older than Stevick and Henderson combined and not as well preserved. Henderson worked his way around the perimeter of the rug, looking for a gap, but came up with nothing. He had about given up on finding anything in the living room when he noticed the pad on an end table next to the couch. He didn't expect to find anything. It was too obvious. Too cliché. Yet . . . there it was.

He had to blink several times to convince himself he wasn't seeing things. There actually was the outline of a notation that had been made on the now missing top sheet. Almost as clear as the original. He didn't even need to shade it to read what it said. Simco's fingers were apparently as muscular as his neck.

The scenario too was clear. Simco had been sitting on the couch, either talking to someone in person or on the phone. They had given him an address, and he had written it down, packed his bags, and taken off.

Henderson gave the rest of the apartment a cursory search. There was no computer, no personal letters, no pictures, no address book. But he did develop a sense for Simco's lifestyle. He never cleaned anything, had a penchant for wide cowboy belt buckles, and didn't read any magazines that weren't primarily pictorial. Some of the latter probably came in plain brown wrappers and steamed themselves open.

Clutching the note pad address as if it were a check for a hundred thousand dollars, Henderson took one last look around, switched off all the lights, and with a profound sense of relief, slipped back out into the night.

The address was for some place on the peninsula. You had to take a ferry to get there, and late at night the ferries didn't run that often. It was cold, so I didn't want to stay in my car while waiting in the ferry line. Instead, I spent over an hour in a musty room lined with wooden pew benches and vending machines. It took another twenty minutes to unload and reload the ferry, and almost a half hour for the crossing. Once there, things went from bad to worse.

It was dark, country dark, without mercury-vapor bulbs and 7 Eleven stores to mark the way. And it was raining so hard I couldn't read the road signs. Stevick would have used the GPS on his iPhone, but Henderson was reduced to reading a map with an expiring flashlight, cursing all the people who had gone to bed instead of staying up to give him directions. Where were the insomniacs when you needed them? I drove blindly into the inky night. It felt more unsettling than poetic.

The rain didn't let up; I was starting to feel like I was trapped in a dystopian joke. Low on gas, dispirited, tired, and lost, totally and completely lost, it seemed like the only sensible thing to do was to pull off the road and take a snooze. So, that's what I did.

After a fitful sleep, I awoke to a gray morning and found I was parked next to a field where a lone cow kept company with a lone tree. Across the street was an abandoned house. It had once been a nice place, the kind of home where you expected to see a couple of kids swinging from an apple tree in the front yard while an apron wearing mother baked cookies in her sunny kitchen. All-American, the backbone of the country. Now the windows were boarded up, the roof sagged with rot and moss, and the front steps had collapsed in the middle. America's slipped disk.

Looking at myself in the rearview mirror, I saw another sad sight, a "before" ad for a shaving commercial. I ran my tongue over my teeth a few times, combed my hair and rubbed my eyes. So much for my morning toilet.

In spite of a few aches and pains from being scrunched in a car seat all night, life seemed a lot better now that I could see where I was. Still, I didn't know where was *was*, but it was at least visible. I started the car and headed on down the road. Around a bend I came across a café, the parking lot filled to capacity. I was saved.

Breakfast was good, a hearty trucker's meal of scrambled eggs, bacon, toast, and hash browns washed down with lots of hot coffee served by a smiling waitress in an orange and white uniform that didn't quite reach her knees. It seemed a safe bet that she had been a cheerleader at the local high school not too many years back. She walked with a springiness that suggested boundless energy and good feet. Henderson couldn't help envisioning all that energy unleashed on a king-sized bed, those strong toes moving up and down his thighs. Animal.

After breakfast I felt almost human. My neck was stiff though. If

Henderson was going to make sleeping in cars a habit, he ought to invest in a van.

My waitress recognized the name of the road I was looking for right off, informing me, "That's way out in the sticks."

"Nearby?" I asked.

After two beats she laughed at my joke. "About twenty minutes from here." She grinned and said, "Unless you're a conservative driver."

Henderson accepted the challenge with a smirk. Who, me, conservative? They call me Wild Man Henderson. You ought to see me . . . Cool it, Henderson, you're on a case.

"Could you draw me a map?" I asked meekly.

She leaned over the table and began drawing directions on the back of a paper placemat. Three buttons on her uniform top were unbuttoned. Two firm, down covered breasts were trying to escape. And, from the looks on the faces of the men at the table across from us, the view from behind also had its advantages.

Even her drawing was erotic, two small hills followed by a long stretch of straightaway, a dip in the road, then a right past a clump of evergreens. It wasn't easy keeping Henderson under control.

"You can't miss it," she concluded, standing up. She was at least partly right; I hadn't missed much.

I left a generous tip and made a hasty exit with my virginity intact. Exactly eighteen minutes later I turned onto the tree-lined road I'd been looking for. There was nothing conservative about me. I began humming the theme song from Rocky.

The trees on both sides of the road were so dense that I almost missed the narrow dirt driveway. Slowing down, I caught a glimpse of a house half hidden among the evergreens a way back from the road. It didn't look like much, but it was definitely occupied. Smoke streamed out of the chimney, gray-white, probably from a wood stove. More important, there was a bright green Chevy parked right out front.

I drove on past, then swung back for a second look. As I made the U-turn, I watched in my rearview mirror to see if anyone was interested in the maneuver. Henderson's was the only car in sight. Besides, if it was a trap, there was no need for a tail; all they had to do was wait for me to show up. Ready or not, here he is, a fearless sleuth ready to take on the hired muscle. Step aside Dirty Harry.

The road was narrow, about the width of two large trucks, with a ditch alongside. It was a quarter of a mile before I found a convenient place to pull off and park. There was absolutely no way I was going to manage a stakeout from the car. It would have to be done on foot. That meant greater risk of discovery and a slower getaway. But it had to be done. At least it wasn't raining.

As I hiked back along the road, Stevick and Norton protested in unison. For once they were in agreement. They wanted me to make an anonymous call to the police and return to the safety of the apartment. What did it matter that Nick Norton was suspected of murder? There was no reason why he ever had to show his bearded face again. And Stevick was supposedly dead.

Henderson won out, and I cut through the woods right next to a "No Trespassing" sign, approaching the house from the side. The ground was damp and soft. Henderson's shoes instantly sucked up the moisture like thirsty sponges. Designed obsolescence. If you want a good sponge, on the other hand, you can't find one.

I wasn't exactly the last of the Mohicans and felt obvious as hell darting from tree trunk to tree trunk in Henderson's burglar clothes. Either Simco was on the lookout for me or he wasn't. If he was, no amount of subterfuge would do any good. If he wasn't, I could probably be as subtle as a Russian tank battalion and still sneak up on him. All the same, I couldn't shake the uneasy feeling that I was a duck in a shooting gallery at the county fair. Here he comes again, folks, just wait until his head bobs back up and you can nail him right between his little ducky eyes.

When no shots were fired, I found a nice tree with an excellent view of the side and front of the house and began my vigil. All the curtains were pulled and there was no activity other than the rising smoke. To my city boy's ears it was uncomfortably silent. No car noises, no hustle and bustle, no general din. Just smoke silently spiraling upward.

The first ten minutes or so were all right. Then I started to get cold. I'd stand first on one wet foot, then the other, trying to keep my circulation going. It seemed obvious that if I had to wait too long I wouldn't be able to walk, let alone run, if someone spotted me. Maybe that was part of their plan.

Somewhere in the distance a dog barked. At least I assumed it was a dog. Did they have wolves this close to the city? Did wolves bark? Dammit, I wasn't the rugged outdoor type. I didn't know shit about bears and hypothermia or how to live off the land. So, what was I doing playing Daniel Boone in some godforsaken place that didn't even have a Starbucks every two blocks?

I was about to move to a new location just to prove to myself that I could still walk when I heard a sound. Instinctively I ducked down and drew Henderson's gun. Moments later Simco came out the front door. Without so much as a glance in my direction, he got in his Chevy and drove off. I remained crouched down out of sight until my knees protested. Then I made a decision. Sometimes a man's gotta do what a man's gotta do.

There didn't seem to be any easy entry into the house. No open windows, no French doors, no inviting second story balcony. Just a back door and a front door. It was one or the other.

I cut back through the woods and stepped out onto the road. Then I walked up the driveway to the front door and knocked. It was the simple, direct approach.

There was the sound of movement inside. A curtain moved at the window on my left. After an eternity the door creaked open a few inches, about the width of a gun barrel.

CHAPTER 10
WHO ARE YOU?

"What do you want?" The female voice was as neighborly as the chain visible in the space between door and jamb.

"My car broke down about a half mile from here. And my cell battery is dead. Any chance you have a telephone I can use?"

A single, disapproving eye peered through the crack. Standing there in his burglar outfit with a two-day growth of beard, Henderson didn't exactly feel he was putting his best foot forward. If she *was* alone, he could hardly blame her for being skeptical. But he needed to get inside. If she didn't cooperate, Henderson would be forced to break through the chain lock like some modern Prometheus.

"Just a minute." The door suddenly closed. There was the clank of metal against metal. Then the door opened again, this time all the way.

Without makeup and wearing casual clothes, the phony Mrs. Stevick seemed younger, younger and more blatantly female. Her jeans left no doubt as to the shape of her bikini underpants, and her blue turtleneck jersey boldly declared her membership in the braless generation. With a touch of lightener, her hair might have been blond. It was pulled back from her face and tied with a blue scarf that was a perfect match for her baby-doll eyes.

"Come on in."

"Thank you."

Keeping his hand on the gun in his pocket Henderson cautiously stepped through the doorway. There didn't appear to be anyone else in the room. In the corner a portable color television silently broadcast a daytime talk show. On the coffee table in front of the couch was a stack of newspapers and a diet Coke.

She motioned toward a beige landline telephone on a small table in an alcove separating the living room from the kitchen. An antique. Henderson went quickly over to it, and, keeping his back to the wall, dialed a number at random. The phony Mrs. Stevick kept her distance. Was it because of his unkempt appearance or because she was giving someone in a back room plenty of space to launch an attack?

From where he was standing Henderson figured he could cover both the kitchen and the living room, but if more than one person rushed him, he'd have to be both quick and lucky. Damn lucky.

Ignoring the insistent "hello, hello" on the other end of the line, Henderson waited an appropriate interval, then hung up. "No one there."

Her chin came up slightly, and her eyes darted toward the door. Thinking about trying to escape? Or anticipating help on the way?

"I'll try someone else."

This time he faked a conversation with a dial tone to try and put her at ease. It worked. He too began to feel calmer.

"Someone's coming to pick me up," he said. She'd heard the conversation so he didn't need to tell her that, but it seemed to make things official. He smiled. She gave him a tentative smile in return. Henderson's male ego began to swell with warmth; there was something defenseless and vulnerable about her, like a doe in a meadow being stalked by a hunter.

"I'm glad you were able to get hold of someone," she said. "We're a long way from anything out here." Her smile wavered as she realized what she'd said.

"Being out in the country has its advantages," Henderson quickly reassured her. For some strange reason it seemed to him that he sounded like Vincent Price. She must have thought so too; she backed away as the smile disappeared completely.

"Do you live nearby?" she asked, sounding wary.

"I'm here on business." Damn. Why had he said that? Businessmen didn't wear casual black clothes and forget to shave. He should have said he was on his way back from a funeral or a wake or that he couldn't be outside after the sun came up. Heh, heh.

"Oh?"

"Yesterday. I finished up yesterday. I'm on my way home."

"What do you do?"

She was slowly moving toward the door. In another minute or so she might break and run, the doe bolting back into the woods, out of range.

"I'm a private detective."

He couldn't have surprised her more if he'd claimed to be a Martian. One hand flew to her throat in the classic female-in-distress pose. Her mouth came open and her eyes seemed to double in size. If it was an act, she was good, really good.

"And what do *you* do, Mrs. Stevick?"

"Why . . . why did you call me that?"

"That's the name you gave the police."

She moved decisively toward the door. "You'd better leave."

"Stay right where you are."

She froze, one hand on the doorknob, and turned those soft blue eyes on him. "Who are you? What do you want?"

"As I said, I'm a private detective. The question is, *who are you?*" Now he sounded like the hookah smoking caterpillar in *Alice in Wonderland.* Whooo are youuuu?

"I . . . I can't say. Please leave." Her lower lip began to quiver.

"Look, I want to be long gone before your friend Simco returns. Just tell me your real name and why you pretended to be Caron Stevick, and we'll forget I was ever here."

"I want you to leave." Her voice was firmer, but hardly commanding, a lamb ordering the wolf to go away.

"If I leave, you leave with me."

Her hand went to her throat again. The phrase "you must pay the rent" went through Henderson's mind.

"No, please. I can't do that."

"Why not?"

"I just can't, that's all."

Henderson took a step toward her.

"Please," she begged in a little girl voice. He felt a tug at the old heartstrings. He was going soft, like a dish of ice cream left in the sun.

"When's Simco coming back?"

"He went for some groceries. He should be gone about an hour."

"Good. It shouldn't take you nearly that long to tell me what I want to know."

"Who are you?"

"That's *my* line."

Her cheeks suddenly flared red. "You trick me into letting you in and then you expect me to cooperate without giving me so much as one good reason why I should."

From her point of view, it *did* seem he was being unreasonable. "Someone's in trouble," he explained. "I'm trying to help them. Is that good enough?"

Her eyes went from cobalt to robin's-egg blue, but she didn't say anything.

"Are you sure *you* aren't in trouble? Simco isn't someone to fool with, you know."

"He's taking care of me."

"Some people he 'takes care of' are never seen again."

"What do you mean?"

"You know who he works for, don't you?" Henderson tried to insinuate that *he* did.

"Yes . . ." She blinked a couple of times. "Do *you*?"

"Let's not play games. We both know Simco is dangerous. I also know that you posed as Caron Stevick and identified a body as being that of Warren Stevick, your alleged husband. If I turn you over to the police, you are going to have a hard time explaining all that." He paused to let it sink in. "Your other option is to tell me what I wat to know. Then I'll forget I ever saw you."

"You say you're trying to help someone who's in trouble. That doesn't tell me anything. Why should my identity make any difference?"

"Haven't you wondered who your employer is trying to blackmail with the alleged murder of 'Stevick'?"

"No one is trying to blackmail anyone."

"Then what are you up to?"

"I can't tell you. It's a secret."

Henderson gave a Bogart snort of derision that sounded like he was having nasal problems. She wasn't impressed.

"I can't tell you," she repeated firmly.

The way he saw it, he didn't have many alternatives, and whatever he did, he needed to do it soon. He could kidnap her and hold her until she was willing to talk. Or he could push her around a bit, maybe even slap her a few times. Another possibility was to call the police and turn the whole matter over to Garcia. Kidnapping, assault, or self-incrimination. Some great choices.

They heard the car engine at the same instant. Henderson's heart started thumping like the pistons on a GMC diesel, and the phony Mrs. Stevick's hand moved upward again, this time all the way to her mouth.

"Oh my God," she exclaimed.

"Simco." The name escaped my lips like the air leaking out of a tire, a tiny hissing sound warning that something bad was about to happen.

"You've got to get out of here," she said. "He'll kill me if he finds out I was talking to you." She motioned him toward the back of the house. "Quick. Now!"

At the back door he took out one of his cards and thrust it at her. He was pretty sure that she was in almost as much trouble as Norton, maybe more, and he didn't want to see her hurt. "If you need help, give me a call." That was his exit line.

CHAPTER 11
NOT TOO SMART

The first thing I did when I got back to the apartment was to change from one costume into another: goodbye burglar, hello private eye. Then, after a hasty lunch of bologna on dry bread—I was out of butter and mustard—I drove to police headquarters.

Al's desk was clear, and he was staring at the wall when Henderson went in. The old nameplate was still on his desk, turned face down.

"No luck yet?"

"Luck, what does luck have to do with it? It's a simple government business transaction. I fill out the form and the fools dink around with it. You'd think I was asking for a new jail."

"That's your problem. You need to think big. Why don't you ask for a pool table or a couple of original oil paintings to contemplate in your spare time?"

"All if want is a f-ing nameplate."

Henderson leaned back in his chair, feeling weary. He was getting too old for this sort of life.

"You look beat," Al said.

"I feel beat. Beaten down, bruised by life, an aging shell of a man."

"That bad?" Al shook his head. "You must still be nosing around about Simco."

"And if I am? You got anything?"

"I can tell you this much: if you plan on messing with him, you ought to rest up, get in shape, clean your gun maybe. Word has it he's into carving, and not for art galleries."

"Sounds like a real charmer."

"I've been asking around."

"I appreciate that."

"You might not when you hear what I've got to say. Simco's graduated recently. He's into some heavy stuff, a couple of untimely deaths may have been his work, but nothing we can make stick. It's my guess he's about to take a fall. Just don't let him take you with him."

"His employer?"

"Still basically freelance, but he's done quite a bit for Frankie Gillis lately. You might start there, unless you're interested in living long enough to collect a pension."

"Investigators on their own don't have pension plans, or two nickels to rub together for that matter."

"Well, Gillis may be strictly the minor leagues, but he's a real hothead. Dangerous as hell. Likes to throw his weight around."

"Drugs and child porn, right?"

"Those are at the top of his list, but if it's illegal or disgusting he's your man."

"Thanks, Al."

"I'm not sure I'm doing you any favors getting you mixed up with Gillis."

"I don't intend getting 'mixed up' with him. I'm just 'interested.'"

"It's the kind of 'interest' that can land you in the hospital. Or the morgue. Watch yourself, Eric."

As I left the station, Al's warning lingered in my mind. He'd become more and more solicitous of late. He never used to be like that. Thinking too much; it wasn't a good idea in our business. It could make you worry about every little decision. If Henderson let himself start thinking too much, he'd never even stick his head out the door in the morning.

I stopped at a nearby office supply store and ordered a nameplate for Al. Maybe that would cheer him up. Solid oak base with a brass plate. Classy. I paid in advance—just in case—and arranged for them to send it to him at the station. If anything happened, Al would have something to remember me by.

Next stop, Buffy's. It's the kind of joint Stevick's mother warned him against when he was entering his teens, unsavory, uncivilized, and probably unhealthy. The three big "uns." Boyhood fascination with such hangouts had long since given way to something bordering on aversion, but it was one of Henderson's regular stops, a place where you could buy information, or, for that matter, just about anything you were interested in buying that wasn't part of a normal store's inventory.

The first thing you saw when you entered Buffy's was . . . nothing. Only after your eyes adjusted to the Cimmerian atmosphere of perpetual darkness could you make out the eight pool tables randomly positioned in the long, rectangular room. To the left was a door leading to a tavern that could also be entered directly from the street. You weren't supposed to carry drinks from the tavern into the poolroom because of some archaic law that was still on the books, but everyone did, walking right past the sign that cited the city ordinance violated by doing so.

Stevick had learned to play pool at a YMCA recreation center when he was about eleven. He'd kept at it all the way through college, perfecting his skills in law school. Now Henderson played in places like Buffy's. That's spelled with a capital "B" and rhymes with "P." *Mothers of River City! Heed that warning before it's too late!*

It was a bit early for the usual crowd, but, as Henderson had hoped, Fred was there, playing by himself at a table near the back. A thin, bent man, probably younger than he looked, chronically unemployed, and always on the lookout for a way to make an easy buck.

"Wanna game?" Fred asked.

"Might as well."

"Straight pool?"

"Sure."

"Buck a ball or ten spot a game?"

"Let's go for the game." That was the cheapest for Henderson. More often than not he lost, sometimes fair and square, sometimes for reasons of diplomacy. But he always put up a good show to make Fred feel he was earning his money. Fred never told Henderson anything that wasn't common knowledge in Fred's circle of acquaintances, but since Henderson wasn't otherwise privy to such information, he was happy to pay for it.

Two games and twenty dollars later, they broke for a beer. Fred didn't offer to pay, not even for his own. He knew what was coming.

"Haven't seen much of you lately. Thought maybe you'd moved on."

"Been busy."

Fred drank down most of his beer and wiped his mouth with a dirty looking sleeve. Henderson stubbed out his half-smoked cigarette on the floor. He wished, not for the first time, that Buffy's didn't ignore the city's no smoking ordinance in public places. You almost *had* to smoke there to fit in.

"Your pool ain't improved."

"Need more practice."

"Wanna couple more games?"

"Maybe later."

Fred finished his beer and pushed the empty glass toward Henderson. Henderson went for a refill. When he returned he asked, "You seen Dan Simco around lately?"

"Simco? Nah. He doesn't hang out here."

"You know him though."

"Dan's been around for a while."

"Works for Frankie Gillis, doesn't he?"

Fred kept his eyes on his beer.

"How about a fifty on the next game?" Pretty obvious, Henderson. Don't be too eager.

"Put it on the table, and I'll think on it."

Henderson put a fifty-dollar bill on the table between them.

"Gillis don't like no one butting in on his territory."

"I'm not interested in Gillis, just Simco."

"Simco don't like no one period."

"So I gather."

"What you want with Simco?"

"I want to know who he's currently working for."

"He works for Gillis some."

"Think he's doing a job for him now?"

Fred picked up the fifty and put it in his pocket. "That's an advance, see. This info should be worth double."

"It depends on what you find out."

"Takes as much time to ask around no matter what you find out."

"Business hasn't been all that great of late," Henderson complained.

"Information costs, man, you know that."

Henderson folded. "All right. Another game, fifty more when you come across."

Fred grinned, showing a gap in a row of yellow stained teeth. "No way you beat me, man."

"No way," Henderson agreed.

After Buffy's, Henderson made two more stops, drank too much beer, and spent considerable time in grimy restrooms emptying his bladder and reading immature graffiti. He paid out another fifty, learned nothing I didn't already know, and was beginning to wonder if there wasn't a better way to get the information he wanted. Something simple. Like maybe an ad in the personals. *Dannie boy, who you working for now? Love, an interested party.* That sort of thing. He doubted Simco had a LinkedIn profile.

During the evening Henderson had actually won several games against pretty fair players. Of course, his opponents had been half crocked, but then, so had he. I still was for that matter. The world looked like it was on the other side of an aquarium, wavy and blurred, and my head didn't feel properly attached to my neck. Nevertheless, with the confidence of the truly sloshed, I had no doubt I could pass a breathalyzer if pulled over by the police.

Halfway up the stairs to Henderson's office I almost turned back. I couldn't seem to remember why I was headed there. Bed sounded a lot better. Then I decided, what the hell, maybe someone had slipped a payment or a new client under the door. I might as well have a look.

By the time I registered the fact that there were two men leaning against the wall across from the office it was too late to do anything but either run like hell or try to bluff. Since I could barely walk, I opted for the latter. I would walk on by as if I'd never heard of Eric Henderson, Private Investigator extraordinaire.

It didn't work.

One of them, the big one—there always seemed to be a big one—stepped in front of me. "You Henderson?" His head was too small for his body, and his eyes were set close together. You almost had to be cross-eyed to look him in the eyes. His companion, on the other hand, had a small body and a large head. Maybe they'd got confused getting dressed that morning.

"You Henderson?" he repeated.

I wasn't *that* drunk. "No, Foster, Stephen Foster." I tried to step past him.

"He's Henderson," the little guy with the big head said.

"Excuse me." I moved to the left. "My office is down the hall."

The big guy moved to the left too. "Let's see some ID."

"ID? Since when do you need ID to walk down the hall?"

"Since *I* asked."

"Oh." That seemed like a convincing reason, given his size and my state of inebriation. "In that case, what do you want with Henderson?" I wasn't sure how clearly I was enunciating, but he seemed to get the message. He grabbed me under my left armpit and twirled me around until I faced Henderson's office door.

"Open it," he ordered.

"I didn't say I was Henderson."

"Open it."

I fumbled in my pockets for Henderson's keys. I had trouble finding one that would fit the lock. The two thugs were just beginning to think I wasn't Henderson after all when one of the keys slipped into the little slot and the damn door opened.

Once inside, the little guy stood with his arms folded across his chest, barring the exit. Like a prison guard. Or Cerberus at the gate to hell.

The big one pushed Henderson up against the wall and frisked him.

"Hey, what's this all about?" Henderson asked. He hated the fact that he sounded peevish rather than menacing.

"Shut up."

"Who are you?" Then, trying to sound in control, Henderson asked, "What the hell do you think you're doing?"

The side of the big guy's hand chopped into Henderson's neck. Henderson's knees started to buckle, but he was jerked upright. "Stand up and shut up." The big guy definitely had a way with words. He took Henderson's gun and wallet and started looking through the cards in the wallet. "Looks like you're Eric Henderson."

"You can read."

"Smart guy, huh? Well, I don't like smart guys."

"I didn't think you would."

He tossed the gun and the wallet on Henderson's desk and spread his feet in the attack stance of bulls and bullies. I half expected him to paw the ground with one foot. "Why were you asking around about Gillis?" he demanded.

"I'm on a case. I don't care about Gillis. I just want to find Dan Simco."

The big guy turned to the little guy. "He wants to find Dan. Ain't that a laugh." He turned back to Henderson. "Simco could take you just like that." He snapped his fingers. In the quiet room it sounded like a gunshot.

"I just want to talk to him."

"What do the two of you have to talk about?"

"I'm on a case."

"You said that already. Who's your client?"

"I can't say."

"Come on. The boss said I should use my 'dis-cre-tion' how I handle this. It's up to you."

"I'm a private investigator. I can't go around giving out clients' names and expect to get work. That's why the title is 'private' investigator."

"At least now you're capable of working."

He had a point.

"Come on, we don't have all night."

"Stephen Foster," Henderson said. Why should he protect the little creep? "He's an operative out of Chicago. I'm working for him."

"What's he looking for?"

"He's, ah, interested in Warren Stevick's murder. It's an insurance matter. That's all. Nothing to do with Gillis." Pure inspiration, Henderson. Who said drinking dulled the wits.

My stomach churned as the two exchanged looks. Beer and fright were a bad combination.

"Anything more you want to tell us?"

Was this the point where Henderson was supposed to ask for a last cigarette? "No, that's it."

They exchanged looks again. Then the little guy nodded. There was something about the gesture that made me think Henderson should have asked for a priest.

The first blow caught me in the solar plexus and took my breath away. It also brought up a thin stream of beer. I didn't try to fight back; I knew it wouldn't do any good.

The second blow took me on the side of the neck again. I dropped like a parachute with a hole in it. When I didn't get up, he kicked me. I moaned and pretended to be in mortal pain. The next kick caught me in the kidneys and ended all pretense—I *was* in mortal pain.

"Make it quick," the little guy urged.

"He won't fight back."

"He's a pansy. Let's get this over with and get out of here."

A toe nudged me from behind. I moaned again.

"Oh shit. You're right, the fucker's a fucking pansy."

He kicked me one more time for good measure, a sharp-toed, powerful jab below my right shoulder. Then the two of them left, their footsteps fading as they headed off down the hall.

I stayed where I was on the floor. Although it seemed impossible, I thought my stomach actually felt worse than the rest of me. The next thing I knew I was spewing up my lunch. Then came breakfast. Last night's dinner. My stomach slowly made its way back in time until all that was left was a green, watery bile. With each spasm I came a little closer to hell.

Why is it when you want to pass out you can't? I lay there, barely conscious, but definitely aware of what was happening, revolted by the smell, desperately wishing I had the energy to move to a new location. My pants were wet. I could smell urine mixed in with the vomit. Disgusting. Nothing like this had ever happened to Stevick. It was that damned Henderson's fault. He was a loser, a real loser. He thought he was so tough, but he was nothing more than a motherfucking pansy.

CHAPTER 12
ACHES AND PAINS

I didn't remember finally dropping off, but I must have. I woke up with my cheek resting in a pool of barf and blood. Even if every bone in my body had been broken, I would have tried to get away from that cloying mess. As it was, my arms and legs seemed only nominally functional, almost as useless as flippers on a beached whale.

Inching my way forward, I finally found a relatively clean spot and rested until I had the energy to try to get up. Every square inch of my body hurt, although I sensed that there were a couple of places worse off than the rest. It's hard to tell for sure with indiscriminate pain. Using the desk for support, I pulled myself to my feet and managed to stagger a few steps in order to collapse in a chair.

Take it easy, Henderson, I said as my head sagged forward and my eyes automatically closed. You're alive; that's something to be thankful for. Although it would have been far more pleasant to have awakened in a king size waterbed next to a naked lady.

After several minutes of recuperation and self-pity, I raised my head and opened my eyes. The first thing I saw was Henderson's gun, right there on the desk next to his wallet. Next, I noticed the door to the office was ajar. So much for security. Although the smell would probably keep most people, even some animals, away. God, did I ever stink!

As soon as I could manage it, I made my way over to the door and locked up. Then I hobbled into the john. The mirror told me I didn't look a lot better than I felt. There was dried blood on my forehead and down the side of my neck. Ironically it wasn't the blood but the mustard brown splotches that bothered me the most. They were randomly splattered from chin to toes. And the stench of upchuck and urine hovered about me as if it had soaked into my epidermis. It was too bad I couldn't bundle myself off to the laundry—extra rinse and don't spare the starch.

My hands trembled from cold and effort as I stripped and washed up in the tiny sink. Fortunately, Henderson had a sweat suit hanging from a hook on the back of the bathroom door. It was for when he felt like running. That didn't happen very often. Stevick had never engaged in regular exercise, and Henderson had a hard time remembering how much he enjoyed it. At least it was a change of clothes.

In spite of all the cuts and bruises, I felt better after I was cleaned up. But the smell in the main room was overpowering. Someone was going to have to do something about that, and the only person available for the job was me.

Unable to keep from gagging, I mopped up the mess on the floor with Henderson's soiled shirt. Afterwards I threw it and the rest of Henderson's clothes in the wastebasket and covered the top with a makeshift lid of cardboard backed tablets. The smell lingered, but in a less identifiable form.

Exhausted, I sat down, positioning the chair so I couldn't see either the wastebasket or the stain on the floor. Movement had loosened my muscles and reassured me that, miraculously, nothing was broken. But I didn't feel anywhere near normal. In fact, I wasn't entirely convinced I would ever feel normal again.

The message was clear. Gillis didn't want Henderson snooping around in his affairs. Although Henderson wasn't enough of a threat to justify more than a moderate assault; still, if I valued my life, Henderson should stay as far away from Gillis as possible.

I sat there and thought about the problem, trying not to breathe through my nose. I didn't think it was broken, but it hurt like hell. Finally, I mustered the energy to get up and leave.

Out on the street several runners chugged past, breathing hard, arms pumping. They took in Henderson's sweat outfit at a glance, then turned away, whether from embarrassment at his poor condition or the smell, I couldn't say.

No one followed Henderson on the way home. Apparently, they didn't care if he was dead or alive. Even I was gradually losing interest.

I parked closer than usual to the apartment and drew on my last reserves to get out of the car, across the street, down the dim hall, and inside. It was like hitting the wall for a marathoner, and uphill all the way.

My world had become a movie with an out of sync soundtrack, every motion, every reaction slightly delayed. Even the pain in my head. Here it comes again, almost, almost, NOW. What I needed was a nice bowl of chicken soup, Mother's chicken soup, good for whatever ailed you. No, that was Stevick. Chicken soup wouldn't work on Henderson. He wasn't Polish. He wasn't anything.

After considering my condition for several pain-filled minutes, I decided I was more thirsty than anything else. I drank two glasses of water, one right after the other. My mouth still had that sour aftertaste that I associated with childhood illness. What was it Stevick's mother used to give him after he had thrown up? I couldn't remember. Anyway, there wasn't any real choice in Henderson's apartment. I fixed myself a sandwich with what remained of the bologna and bread and forced my stomach to accept the offering. The stomach gods were appeased, somewhat at least.

Next, I took a much-needed bath, staying in the tub until the water turned cold. That eased the tension in my muscles, but at the same time it seemed to heighten the aches and pains overall. I climbed out of the tub and surveyed myself in the mirror. From the shoulders up I didn't look all that bad. There was a slight swelling and the hint of a bruise on my left temple. There was also a nasty red spot on my neck. In a couple days I would have some whopping black and blue marks, but they would be mostly hidden by clothes. As long as I didn't move too fast or breathe too deeply, I'd get by. Not bad for a man who'd descended into hell and lived to talk about it.

The big question was what to do next. I'd already muffed my best bet—getting information from the phony Mrs. Stevick. Asking around any more about Simco had definitely been ruled out. And until the police went public on Hicks, I didn't dare mention his name to anyone.

Out of sheer frustration I called Henderson's answering service. There were several messages. Most of them were from disgruntled clients, soon to be *former* clients if Henderson didn't do something to earn their fees. There was also another invitation from Garcia. He wanted to see Henderson. Would he ask about the bruises? Or would he just smile? Sadist.

When Henderson got Garcia on the line, the lieutenant asked, "Where've you been?"

"Doing my thing."

"You're supposed to keep in touch."

"You want I should report in every hour? Maybe you'd like me to ask permission before going to the john."

"Don't pull that kind of crap with me."

Being a wise guy never seemed to pay the percentages for Henderson. Turning polite, he asked, "Do you want to see me?"

"Yeah, yesterday. Now get your butt down here on the double."

Then again, being polite never got him anywhere either.

To show Garcia he couldn't push Henderson around, I flamboyantly stabbed the off button on my phone. The motion caused a stabbing pain to shoot up my arm and settle somewhere between my shoulder blades. I would have to avoid raising my arm above shoulder level for a while. That meant no saluting, no waving bye-bye and no punching out anyone taller than me.

As Henderson headed downtown, one of his inner voices protested: Don't give in so easy, it said. Show a little spunk. Be a man. Just because that big guy caught you off guard doesn't mean you have to kowtow to every Tom, Dick, and Garcia.

I stopped at a fast-food place for something to eat. After that I went grocery shopping and picked up some essentials that Henderson liked. Together, Henderson and I delayed long enough to make a point before arriving at police headquarters.

Garcia too had a point to make. He kept Henderson waiting for over forty-five minutes. Henderson drank two cups of lukewarm coffee out a machine and tried to ignore the headache he could feel gathering like storm clouds somewhere over his left eyebrow.

When he was finally granted an audience, Henderson didn't bother with small talk. He plopped himself down in the nearest chair and asked, "You don't happen to have any aspirin, do you?"

"So *that's* how you've been spending your time."

"Something like that."

Garcia reached into a drawer, pulled out a white plastic bottle and tossed it to Henderson. "On the house."

"Thanks." Henderson worked up some saliva, popped two in his mouth and swallowed. Nothing happened. A bitter, chalky taste spread across his tongue and started down his throat. He began swallowing hard, but that only made it worse. As he raced for the door Garcia said,

"To your left."

When Henderson returned, the lieutenant was sitting there twirling a pen between thumb and forefinger. "Whenever you're ready . . .," he said in a tone that suggested Henderson better be ready instantly.

"Sure, I'm ready. Shoot."

"Don't tempt me." Garcia cleared his throat. "All right, what do you have for me?"

"You called *me*; I didn't call *you*."

"You're the one that's holding out."

"Haven't we already gone over this once before?"

"We're going to go over it again. And again. Until you decide to tell me why you kept on investigating Stevick after you were taken off the case."

"I told you before, Foster lied." Henderson paused, trying to come up with an explanation Garcia might accept. "Or maybe he *thought* he'd called me off, maybe he'd intended to, but he didn't. All I can tell you is that as far as I was concerned, I was still on the job."

"You want to tell me what you were doing last night asking questions about Frankie Gillis?"

Henderson groaned. "Does everyone in town know about that?"

"I take it Frankie didn't approve?" He motioned toward Henderson's forehead.

"Very observant."

"You walk like they gave you quite a going over."

"That obvious, huh?"

Garcia nodded.

"It only hurts when I laugh."

"Sure. Want to give me an explanation? One that holds water?"

"It's another case, that's all. It's what I do for a living. Track down runaways, find out where kids are getting drugs, trace missing husbands, tail adulterers. That sort of thing."

"And it's a coincidence that Gillis is involved in the child porn racket and that Nick Norton had several clients who've recently been arrested on sex charges. And it is still another coincidence that one of these clients had an appointment to see Norton the morning Stevick was found dead in Norton's office."

All this was news to Henderson . . . and to Norton. Hicks had been arrested once on sex molestation charges, but his most recent problem had to do with a parole violation involving a failure to show up to a required appointment with his parole officer. Besides, Hicks didn't have an appointment with Norton that morning.

"Who did Norton have an appointment with the morning Stevick was murdered?"

"I think you already know."

"No, I don't. That's the truth."

"Come off it, Henderson. If you didn't get a peek at Norton's calendar, then how did you make the leap to Gillis?"

"Like I told you, it's another case. This city is filled with child molesters and sickos. *You* ought to know that."

"I don't suppose you want to name your client."

"Not unless you force me to."

Garcia accepted that as a challenge and began staring Henderson down with those powerful eyes of his. Henderson wondered how many criminals had confessed rather than sit there and be stared at like that.

"I'm being honest with you. It's another case. Totally unrelated."

Still staring, Garcia spoke in a slow, menacing voice, "I can make life in this city very hard for you, Henderson. Don't you forget it."

"I know. But you've got to believe me when I tell you I want to get this cleared up as much as you do." No, that was wrong. The expression on Garcia's face told Henderson that Garcia didn't have to believe anything he didn't want to believe. He was the alpha male by virtue of position. He called the shots.

"Very, very hard." Finally, Garcia broke eye contact and looked out the window. "I talked with Castaldo about you again. He seems to think you're OK." As if talking to himself, he added, "Maybe you're telling the truth." He turned back to Henderson. "*Maybe*. But don't go getting in my way. You understand?"

"I understand."

"All right. You can go now."

Henderson got up and started for the door. He had his hand on the doorknob when Garcia spoke again.

"Just a minute."

Henderson froze, silently cursing Columbo.

"This guy Norton had the appointment with was a con named Bernie Hicks. Ever hear of him?"

Using his pain as an excuse to move slowly, Henderson turned back toward Garcia. He barely had enough time to compose his face. "I don't think so. You say he's involved in child porn operations in the city?"

"May be. He works for Gillis."

"Then he could be connected to the case I'm working on. Is it okay if I talk to him, or is he off limits?"

"Just keep your nose clean."

"Mama taught me to always carry a handkerchief."

"Very funny." He waved Henderson away.

What in hell was Garcia up to? All this bullshit about Norton's calendar. And telling Henderson about Hicks, leaving out one small fact having to do with the state of his health. Was Garcia trying to set Henderson up? Damn – no wonder I had a headache.

If nothing else, Garcia had given Henderson an excuse for checking up on Hicks. It was almost as if he wanted Henderson to look in that direction. Whatever his game was, I might as well play along. Either that or pull up stakes and run. At least I had the advantage of knowing quite a bit about Hicks already since I was privy to Norton's confidential discussions with his former client. But first I had to get rid of this damned headache.

Back at the apartment I took another two aspirin, this time with water, and set my alarm for seven. At seven sharp that damned thing went off. Alarm clocks never let you down when you want them to. I dragged myself out to the kitchen only to remember that the groceries were still in the trunk of Henderson's car. That damn Henderson; I was getting sick and tired of his carelessness.

Irritated, but relatively headache free, I decided to go out and get something substantial to eat. I drove to a Mexican café Hicks had once recommended to Norton, a place where I could hopefully combine business and pleasure.

The café turned out to be directly across from a popular hangout for gay teens with a row of window tables that provided a perfect view of the comings and goings across the street. Bernie had probably spent most of his time in the café ogling the young boys in their tight-fitting jeans and their T-shirts with slogans like "Closets are for clothes" and "Normal: it's just a dial on the washing machine." I hoped it wasn't his only reason for liking the place. I was hungry.

When I went inside and saw the plastic flowers hanging from the ceiling, I almost turned back. A large plastic parrot swung on a gilded hoop over the cash register. Paintings of bullfighters on black velvet decorated the walls. Dammit, Bernie, what had Norton ever done to you?

Before I could make up my mind to leave, a dark-haired woman with a row of blouse buttons longing to burst came over and asked if I wanted to sit inside where I couldn't smoke or in the atrium where I could. Stevick started to speak, but Henderson interrupted to say he preferred the atrium. Liar.

The atrium was twice as large as the inside seating. Technically I wasn't sure that the smoking area met the standards set by the state, but I could hardly complain since I had chosen to be seated there.

The menu had a corner missing, and there was a red stain down the middle that looked more like blood than wine. But for my piece of mind, I was going with "wine." I scanned the page and chose the special with rice and beans, hoping that its quality and not the fact that they wanted to get rid of it was what made it "special."

The dark-haired woman returned, wobbling on toeless high heels, really tall heels with a web of leather strands spiraling out from an ankle strap like some sort of cage. Only her toes were free. Free with toenails painted bright red to match the Mexican design in her flared, short skirt. In spite of the color coordination, the shoes seemed out of place with the rest of the outfit, and uncomfortable for someone on their feet a lot, but then, what did Henderson know about fashion? He was just an ordinary gumshoe doing a job, a lecherous, ordinary gumshoe hoping against hope that one of those damn buttons would pop while he was looking.

The meal turned out to be surprisingly good. It almost made me forget the plastic décor, but it wasn't quite good enough to drive the bosomy blouse from Henderson's mind. When she brought dessert, Henderson made himself look her in the eyes when he asked if she knew Bernie Hicks. She had a nice face, a few laugh lines around her eyes, and a pleasant smile.

"Describe him." There wasn't even a trace of an accent. Hot Latin blood at least once removed. No wonder the buttons refused to cooperate.

"Medium height, slight build, brown hair, about forty."

"That could be a lot of men."

"He chain smokes, likes to tell off color jokes, and he makes a kind of hiccupping noise when he laughs."

"*Him.*" The way she said the word made Henderson certain they had the same guy in mind. "Sure, I think I know who you mean. Rotten jokes. Lousy tipper."

"Seen him lately?"

She cocked her head to one side and moistened her lips with a red tongue tip while she thought. "No, not for a while," she concluded.

"Anyone around who might know how I can get in touch with him?"

She took a deep, thread popping breath. The middle button was on the verge of dropping off. One more breath—

"I doubt it. But you might check the bar and grill on the corner. I think he used to spend quite a bit of time there."

That ended the discussion. Some other lucky customer would reap the benefits of time and fortune. Henderson finished his coffee and left a large tip. "He's a lousy tipper" makes a pisspoor epitaph.

The bar and grill on the corner was packed. It took almost ten minutes to get a seat at the bar, shoulder to shoulder with two other patrons. Three beers later Henderson finally managed to get the middle-aged bartender with his scraggly goatee to stand still long enough to ask his question.

"He owe you money?" the bartender wanted to know.

"No. I have a job for him."

He looked Henderson over carefully. His eyes said he didn't believe Henderson, but he admitted to knowing Hicks. "Haven't seen him lately though."

"Know anyone who might know where I can find him?"

"I could ask around for you. Want to give me your name and leave a number where you can be reached?"

Henderson handed him a card with a twenty tucked neatly alongside. "For your trouble."

The bartender slipped the bill into his pocket without a word, then read Henderson's card. "Humph," he said, caressing his goatee. Henderson couldn't tell if that was approval or dismissal.

"Bernie and I have worked together a couple times in the past. He usually keeps in touch. Anyway, I appreciate your help."

The bartender moved off to wait on other customers. Henderson hung around long enough to finish off his beer before moving on.

Three stops later Henderson's headache was little more than an unpleasant memory. And he was getting a good buzz on. He had to be careful or he was going to forget why he was going from place to place. The current spot had a long, dark saloon bar that looked like it could have been used in an old-fashioned western film. He was sitting on a high stool facing a good-sized mirror that hung on the wall next to a row of glasses. It just so happened that from where he was sitting he could see the entrance reflected in the mirror. And it just so happened that he was looking in the mirror when the big guy with the small head and the little guy with the big head came in.

They didn't look around but went directly to a dark booth in the corner with a view of the entrance. Had they seen him? Did they already know he was there? Did he want to find out?

"Want another beer?" the bartender asked.

Henderson thought he'd better not waste time. "Do you happen to know Bernie Hicks?"

"Is that a brand?"

"No, a person."

"Then I don't." He stood there a moment saying nothing. Then, "Want another beer?"

"Sure."

Henderson waited until the beer was set in front of him, then he got up and headed to the restroom. It was in the opposite direction of the two guys. If they had seen him or were following him, the beer was supposed to say: *See, he's coming right back.*

There was a window in the men's room just like he'd hoped, only it hadn't been opened during the last century, and it wasn't about to be during the next. Besides, it faced a brick wall. Some architect's idea of a joke.

Seeing all the urinals seemed to affect my bladder, so I stopped to take a whiz. When I heard footsteps approaching, I didn't know whether to zip my fly or get out Henderson's gun. After all the beer he'd had to drink, apparently I couldn't do both at the same time.

I had my hand in my pocket and my zipper stuck halfway when the man came in. I didn't recognize him, and it was obvious he would never pass a sobriety test. While I struggled to free my zipper, he sprayed the wall with urine, grinning all the while as if he was somehow marking his territory.

Back at the bar Henderson conspicuously asked for change. Then he went to the only remaining pay telephone this side of the Mississippi and pretended to make a call. The telephone put him within sprinting distance of the main entrance.

His exit was hasty but well-timed. The instant someone blocked his view of the booth in the corner, and vice versa, he slipped out. Once outside, he didn't hang around to see if anyone missed him.

CHAPTER 13
SURVIVOR

If they had been waiting at Henderson's car, I don't know what I would have done. Given up, perhaps. My body needed an overhaul, and my psyche wasn't in such great shape either. It would have been a kindness to end it all. Instead, when no one appeared, I got in Henderson's car and headed for the apartment, my shoulder pulsing with pain each time I had to shift gears. Damn stick shift. And damn Henderson for thinking it was macho to have a car with one.

Things just weren't falling into place like they were supposed to. If I wanted to avoid becoming a statistic, Henderson needed to get to the bottom of things fast. Although I was no longer sure there was a bottom. The situation seemed to be rapidly becoming more complicated. Garcia, Gillis, perhaps the mob or some mob-like bad guys, they were all out to get me. And once Caron found out the body didn't belong to her husband, she too would be after blood, Stevick's blood, *my* blood. It felt like I was slowly being boxed in, and it was beginning to look as if the box might turn out to be a coffin.

What I needed was inspiration. A new slant on things. Or a tried-and-true approach. Something old, something new. Anything.

Searching the furthest recesses of my mind for options, memories of a motivation seminar Stevick had attended when he first joined his law firm came back to me. The instructor had emphasized that it was important to concentrate on assets instead of shortcomings if you wanted to succeed. At this point anything seemed worth a try, so I mentally started in on a list of Henderson's assets: secondhand gun, underdeveloped muscles, male ego that needed constant refueling, minimal knowledge of investigative techniques, and a brain that sometimes stalled in a crisis. It wasn't much, but people with less had changed the course of history, so who was I to complain? Someone whose butt was on the line, Henderson replied. That's who. Only in the cloistered atmosphere of three-piece suits and leather briefcases would someone get away with pushing optimism like a non-prescription drug. Life on the outside wasn't that simple.

Henderson was right; I had to face facts. There were only two options: either I could push back when pushed and hope like hell I was stronger than they were, or I could run. If I chose to run, I'd better run soon and fast. So . . . why wasn't I running?

I argued with myself—and with my other selves—all the way back to the apartment, unable or unwilling to make a decision. Once there, I did what any sensible man would have done under the circumstances: I made a beeline for the whiskey bottle.

It was nearly empty. If you're so smart, Stevick said to Henderson, then why do you keep trying to drink yourself into oblivion? I peeled my fingers from around the bottle and went to make some coffee. Caffeine instead of liquor, at least I wouldn't die in my sleep.

There was barely enough coffee left to make half a pot. The next time I went out to the car I really did have to remember to bring back those groceries.

While waiting for the coffee I went over what had happened that evening one more time. Was I certain the big guy and the little guy had seen Henderson at the bar? No. Was I certain they had been looking for him in the first place? No. They could have stopped by for a nightcap, one more coincidence in a string of coincidences. On the other hand, they could have heard Henderson was still around and asking about Hicks. Maybe they knew the dead Stevick was Hicks even if the police didn't.

Damn it, why have a virgin set of ID ready and waiting if I wasn't going to use it at a critical time like this? Henderson, you jerk, you don't have to prove your manhood by getting us all killed. Use your brain for once, and maybe you can keep your teeth, and your life, for what it's worth at this point.

I took my coffee into the other room and poured in a liberal shot of whiskey. Deep down I knew what was wrong, but I didn't want to face it. I was boxed in by more than outside forces; I had reached the point where I didn't have either the energy or the inclination to make still another fresh start. It was all very nice to dream of beginning anew, but when you've actually done it several times it loses much of its appeal. It's damn hard to give up everything and begin again. Damn hard. A clean slate has absolutely nothing written on it.

What I wanted was something to build *from,* something solid and constant. At least when my mother had taken me and skipped out on my father when I was a youngster, I'd had *her* to hold onto. And she'd had me. Looking back, I realized how difficult it must have been for her, giving up friends and family and building a new--and what she hoped would be a *better*--life for us. We had moved from place to place, changing our family name so many times I'd had a hard time remembering which was my real name. Her one concession to the past was finally choosing a Polish surname and settling in a Polish neighborhood. I suppose it was a way of reestablishing roots. Her father had emigrated from Poland when he was only fourteen. He had died before I was born. And now she was gone. And Stevick too, in theory, at least. And for all practical purposes, his children were lost to me. Even Norton had to be metaphorically buried. All I had left was Henderson, and, as imperfect as he was, he was at least familiar.

People suffering from middle age crisis didn't know how lucky they were. A fling or an affair or a change of scene, and they could return revitalized to family, friends, and routine. As for me, when I dared to think ahead, all I could envision was more disruption, upheaval, and danger, liberally mixed with ennui.

I poured myself another drink, without coffee this time. What the hell. A man about to risk his life shouldn't be denied what might be his last drink. If I wasn't ready to give up Henderson, then he had no choice but to keep investigating, nosing around where he wasn't wanted, until he had some answers. Or until we were pushed right out of existence.

Even with the aid of alcohol, coming up with a plan of action wasn't easy. My mind felt like silly putty, working first this way, then that, ever seeking its true shape. Finally, I decided to try and save two lives at once by concentrating on the phony Mrs. Stevick. She was undoubtedly up to her pretty little ear lobes in trouble. Someone, probably Gillis, had her on their payroll. But she obviously wasn't a trusted employee. Otherwise, there wouldn't be a guard. And it seemed entirely possible that once her usefulness ended, she would be given her pink slip by Simco.

I gulped down my drink, opened a new bottle, and kept on drinking until I dropped off into a restless sleep. Sometime during the night I made my way to the bedroom, but I didn't manage to get undressed. The next morning, I woke up feeling sweaty and with a bad taste in my mouth. It took the combined willpower of Stevick, Norton and Henderson to keep me from having a drink to clear my head.

The walk to Henderson's car for the groceries helped. My muscles were still stiff and sore, but already my body was beginning to remember what it had been like B.B.G., before the big guy.

Too late I remembered all the frozen food Henderson had bought. Everything had thawed, soaking the bottom of the sack. When I lifted it out of the trunk the bottom gave way. Cans clanged, plastic bags plopped, the contents of previously frozen cardboard containers, drooled and spit, and Henderson swore. A jar of peanut butter landed on the big toe of my left foot, brick heavy. I snatched it up with an angry oath and flung it back into the trunk.

Several items had rolled under the car. I had to use a tire pump to bat them out from under. Then I tossed most of the stuff back into the trunk, saving out a misshapen loaf of bread, a dented container of coffee, a limp pound of bacon, and what was left of a carton of eggs. Henderson could clean the mess up later. It was, after all, his fault.

After a fairly decent breakfast, I set out on the day's agenda. The wind was blowing from the north, a cool, clear day. On the ferry I got out and strolled around the decks, pretending I was on a ship, muscles contracting and releasing with the movement of the water. Caron and Stevick had taken a cruise to the South Pacific once. They'd had to fly back to save time, but the trip there had been a wonderful, lazy time for the two of them. One of the few vacations he remembered that was truly relaxing.

Once back in my car, reality descended, and I was again mulling options. Soon there would be short, gray days and lots of rain, too much rain. Maybe it *was* time to move on. I could relocate to a sunnier clime. While I was at it, I might as well make my next identity someone a little more cheerful and optimistic than Henderson who moped around all the time feeling depressed about who he was. Maybe a less stressful way to make a living would help, something where I could put in the hours and leave it behind at the end of the day. Before, I'd wanted to hold on to the skills I'd had in my previous life; maybe that had been a mistake. There were lots of low-paying jobs that I might find satisfying. I just had to find the right thing.

When I arrived, everything looked exactly as it had on the last visit. The Chevy was parked in the driveway. Gray-white smoke spiraled upward from the discolored brick chimney. Everything seemed peaceful. Was it a secluded, happy love nest, or a prison for one?

I parked down the road like before and cut through the woods past the "No Trespassing" sign. If I kept this up, I would have a neat trail leading from the road to my surveillance spot. Maybe I could build a treehouse and watch from there. Stevick had always wanted a treehouse when he was young. Once he'd even started to build one, but they'd moved before he had time to finish it.

The curtains were pulled like before, so there was no way to tell what was going on inside. All I could do was wait. This time I'd brought along a couple candy bars to pass the time, but what I really wanted was a thermos of coffee. Or, better yet, a chilled thermos of martinis.

After maintaining my post for an hour, my circulation had slowed down almost to the stopping point. In order to get my blood flowing again I stomped around and flapped my arms up and down. That helped convince me I was still alive and boosted my circulation to a lively dribble. If Simco didn't come out soon I wasn't sure how long I could make it.

Maybe I needed a different approach. For instance, what if Henderson tried to take him by surprise? Let's say he succeeded, then what? He'd been beaten up for asking questions; if he started interfering directly, he could really get on someone's shit list. Bad idea.

The day wore on. I got progressively colder and more cynical. My periodic efforts to keep myself warm produced less and less heat. I began to fantasize about dying. They would find Henderson's perfectly preserved body in the spring when the ground began to thaw. Everyone would then have what they wanted, compliments of Mother Nature. Unless Henderson could come up with a better way to keep an eye on that godforsaken house.

He couldn't.

More time passed. The Chevy sat there leering frog-eyed through its bulging headlights. Gross. Insolent. How I hated that car. And the house. And the puffs of smoke coming from the chimney. I hated everything.

When I first heard the barking, I wasn't concerned. Probably some dogs romping in the woods, I thought, chasing squirrels or raccoons, whatever it is dogs chase in the woods. Then, as the barking drew nearer, I began to get angry. Why didn't they go do their doggy thing somewhere else? This was *my* tree, *my* hiding spot. Let them find their own.

The barking stopped suddenly, and I relaxed. Moments later I saw them loping toward me, three of them, big dogs of indeterminate origins, the kind of ungainly creatures you can keep only if you live in the country.

They sniffed their way over to me. "Scram," I hissed. "Get away from here."

They backed off a few feet, tails wagging uncertainly, ears flattened against their heads.

"Shoo," I whispered, waving my hands for emphasis.

That did it. Their tails stopped moving. Then one barked and the others joined in, a cacophonous trio of howling, yelps and growls. I had no choice but to quickly withdraw.

Unfortunately, it was too late.

The sound of a door closing reached me above the din. I turned just in time to catch a blur of movement at the edge of the tree line. Damn. This wasn't part of the scenario I had in mind.

One of the dogs trotted off in the direction of the house. The other two continued to plague me. I was on the verge of panic. I could hardly claim to be a hiker dressed as I was. And although it was unlikely Simco knew any of the neighbors, claiming to be one didn't ring true either. Besides, Simco might recognize Henderson. My only chance was to try and hide.

As I headed for cover, I saw Simco dart out from behind one tree and swiftly take shelter behind another. There was no doubt in my mind that the glint of silver was a gun. It was war games among the trees, winner take all. Christ! This was for real.

At least the dogs had drifted off, disinterested now that they had given Henderson away. I crouched down, gun drawn, waiting. The woods suddenly seemed silent as a tomb, an analogy I didn't much care for.

Moments later Simco made another move that Henderson almost missed. He was good, fast and efficient. A hunter perhaps? Or a soldier. What difference did it make; in either instance, being at home in the woods gave him the upper hand.

Simco was working his way to Henderson's right. Maybe he intended to sneak up on me from behind. My only option was to try and track his movement and hope Henderson came up with a clever way to escape before Simco attacked. Come on, Henderson, *think*.

A shot zinged into a tree close to my left ear, amazingly close. Simco had either pinpointed my location to within a few inches or had been damn lucky. And he had apparently decided that I was an enemy, even without knowing for sure who was in the woods spying on his house. Although an innocent neighbor wouldn't have tried to hide.

I crouched down lower, trying desperately to blend into the backdrop of trees and bushes. Something moved in the bushes almost directly behind me, and instinct or luck kept me from turning toward the sound. Straight ahead I glimpsed Simco as he changed positions, moving still closer.

After that I lost track of him, following Simco's progression intuitively, sensing rather than seeing him close in. I could almost feel the earth pressing into Simco's knees as I imagined him kneeling behind a tree, planning his next move.

The nearer he came, the more Stevick and Norton wanted to break cover and run. Henderson, on the other hand, had no doubt that would result in more than one bullet in the back, so he forced us to hold our ground.

In the end, Henderson didn't wait to fire until he saw the whites of Simco's eyes. Instead, he relied on guesswork. When his calculations placed Simco about one hundred feet away, he made his move. He raised his gun, took aim at this invisible target, and pulled the trigger. The bushes seemed to leap up as if trying to get away. Then everything was quiet. If Simco had been hit, he wasn't letting on. He was tough. Or else he was trying to fool Henderson into thinking he'd been hit.

I desperately wanted to make a break for it, but Henderson forced me to wait. He still thought Simco was there somewhere behind the row of bushes and that he now knew for sure where I was hiding, if he hadn't before. I had fairly good cover, an old maple with a trunk that flared at the bottom. Unless Simco approached from the side or the rear. Unless—

It seemed possible that a barrage of gunshots would smoke Simco out into the open, but that could also attract unwanted attention. An occasional shot might be mistaken for target practice, or a kid taking potshots at birds. But a series of shots . . . I couldn't chance it. And if Simco was smart, neither could he.

In addition to worrying about being shot, I was also getting numb from cold. To keep my fingers flexible, I had to keep working them. As for my toes, they didn't have any feeling left. My only consolation was that the same thing was probably happening to Simco. I could picture us eventually getting to within spitting distance of one another, pointing our guns, but neither of us able to pull the trigger.

Somewhere in the distance I heard an engine start. Moments later a car passed by. I hadn't realized we were that close to the road. It was unreal. Two men stalking each other like a couple of guerrillas, while only a few hundred yards away normal people were going about their daily lives, safe in their ignorance of the drama unfolding among the trees.

A bush quivered. It was slightly behind and to the left of where I estimated Simco was hiding. Was he circling around again? Getting in position to shoot or trying to escape? Whatever he was up to, I couldn't wait to find out. I had to act while I was still capable of action.

Stiff and awkward, I scooted to a new position.

Nothing happened.

Another bush wiggled, this time closer to the house. Maybe he was going for reinforcements or another weapon. Or maybe he *was* wounded and he was retreating. If I rushed him now, Simco might surrender and tell Henderson everything he wanted to know in return for assistance. Then again, he might shoot Henderson.

As I watched, Simco, or whoever or whatever was moving in the bushes, continued in the direction of the house. Trailing along, charging recklessly from one tree to the next, I almost convinced myself that Simco was running away . . . when he attacked. If he hadn't miscalculated Henderson's position by several yards, the round of shots would have finished me off.

The instant Simco stopped firing, I rushed him.

We went down in a tangle of branches and sticker bushes, rolling over and over, each trying to get a grip on the other. Simco was a lot stronger than me, but, as I kept telling myself, less desperate and determined.

Simco managed to get off one last shot before I wrenched the gun out of his hand. I had dropped Henderson's gun during the assault, so all I had were my bare fists. Trying to think like Henderson, I swung at Simco's head with my right fist but only got in a glancing blow. Then Simco rammed me in the stomach with his head. It felt as solid and heavy as a cannon ball. Still reeling from the impact, I chopped Simco on the back of the neck like I'd seen action heroes do in the movies. That only seemed to make Simco madder. He kept right on grabbing and ramming and kicking. Why do the bad guys always kick?

Even though the stakes were high we fought like two kids having it out on the playground. It wasn't a fight to be proud of, just two men mucking about in the dirt, each struggling to win any way he could. Even *I* managed to get in a few good kicks.

When I rolled over and saw the gun right there within reach, I quickly snatched it up. I had no intention of using it for anything more than a threat, but Simco wasn't in the mood to listen to threats. Bull strong, he was hell-bent on beating Henderson to a pulp. And he was slowly succeeding.

As Simco grabbed my throat with his beefy fingers, I pulled the trigger with only one thought in mind: getting Simco to let go. Simco flopped back, releasing the bear hold he had on my neck. I felt instant relief and a flash of triumph. Then the blood gurgled out of Simco's mouth between his parted lips, and an animal slaughter smell assaulted my nostrils.

The gun still pointed at Simco, I got to my knees, gagging, waiting for him to get up and come at me again. But he didn't. Except for the blood streaming down the side of his face and out the hole in his chest, Simco was still.

There was another wound in his left thigh. That must have been from my earlier shot. Simco had been crawling away, just like Henderson had fantasized. If I had stayed where I was, that would have been the end of it.

I don't know how long I stayed there watching Simco's blood drain out before Henderson finally prodded me into action. If he hadn't come after you with a gun, Henderson argued, then you wouldn't have shot him. And don't think he would have wasted any tears on you if things had ended up the other way around with *you* dying on the ground in front of *him*. He meant to kill you. Only *you* killed him instead.

You're a heartless bastard, I told Henderson.

I'm a survivor, he countered. And if *you* want to survive, you'd better get the hell out of here.

Feeling more like a loser than a winner, I got up. Simco was dead, but I wasn't. I only wished I was.

It took me a few minutes to focus on the fact that the gun in my hand was Simco's. At least I hadn't used Henderson's gun for the fatal shot. I wiped it clean on his jacket and dropped it on the ground next to his body.

I located Henderson's gun not far away. There was nothing I could do about possible hair and blood samples I might be leaving behind.

Nor could I do anything about the bullets Henderson had fired from his own gun. There wasn't time. I had already delayed too long.

The logical thing was to hightail it back to the car and make a hasty getaway. That wasn't what I did though. Maybe chivalry isn't dead after all.

I might have saved myself the bother. The car I'd heard earlier had probably been the green Chevy. The woman I had risked my life to help hadn't worried about anyone's welfare but her own. Not that I blamed her. But I was feeling in desperate need of reassurance and regretted not getting any credit for her escape.

The front door of the house had been left open. I went inside to have a quick look around. She had taken her clothes with her. She wouldn't be coming back.

I stole an overcoat to hide my disheveled clothes and cut back through the woods, careful to avoid the spot where Simco lay dead. Then I got in Henderson's car and left.

I guess I'm a survivor after all.

CHAPTER 14
LIFE INSURANCE

I t seemed that all I was doing of late was cleaning myself up. Out, out damn spot. Me and Lady Macbeth would never come clean. Simco's bloody face was branded on my soul.

Outwardly I appeared unchanged. A few scratches, some additional bruises, that was all. And Henderson wasn't wasting any time mourning Simco's passing. He was busy trying to figure out the best way to dispose of the evidence. He had already dropped his gun in the water on the way back on the ferry. But Simco's overcoat would have to go too. And this time I couldn't leave my soiled clothes in some office wastebasket, because this time the blood wasn't all mine. Besides, out of sight, out of mind, hopefully.

I put everything in a shopping bag with a smiling Santa face on the side, something I'd saved since last Christmas, and drove around looking for a place to dump it. The more I drove, the more nervous I became. Sure, I'd removed all the labels and checked the pockets. I'd even groped the lining in case Simco had hidden something there. But what if I'd missed something? Henderson wasn't infallible. Worse yet, what if I was stopped by the police before I'd unloaded the coat?

There are undoubtedly as many hiding places in the naked city as there are stories, but for some reason, I couldn't find even one. Nowhere seemed safe. Even if the clothes couldn't be traced, I didn't want the police finding them right away. Nor did I want to risk trying to burn them. Someone would surely see me doing that and call the police. No, I had to find a dumping spot. What I needed was some public place where the chances of discovery were slim and the possibility of someone seeing and remembering the dumpee even slimmer.

When I spotted a Salvation Army contribution box in the back of a grocery parking lot, I was certain I had found the perfect depository for Simco's overcoat. The coat was, after all, still serviceable; someone might as well get some use out of it.

I waited until no one seemed to be looking my way before pulling alongside the dark blue box. Then I took the coat out of the bag and tossed it in with the other donations. I half expected an alarm to go off, but none did. Slowly, I made my way through the parking lot and turned onto the busy street in front of the store.

When it was all over, I felt both let down and upset. Getting rid of everything hadn't been as liberating as I'd anticipated. There was no longer any physical link between Henderson and Simco; still, I couldn't get the memory of the blood running out of his mouth and pooling beside his head out of my mind.

It was dark. The city had become a world of lights—street lamps, signs, headlights, houses with bright interior—all staring back at me. Inside those houses were people going about normal evening routines, kids tucked into quilt-covered beds, dogs gulping down their dinners, adults relaxing with a glass of wine. A world I was never to know again.

Maybe I should get a dog. That would give me a reason to go home at the end of the day. We could take walks together, keep Henderson in shape. Not a dog like those smelly, drooling creatures that had ruined my vigil in the woods, but a quiet, loyal friend. A dog I could talk to.

All at once I felt drained. Why was I fighting so hard for survival? What did I have that was worth saving?

Henderson didn't have an answer. And Stevick and Norton had already lost everything.

I kept on driving. Maybe all I needed was a good night's sleep, and not perchance to dream.

. . .

I woke up in the middle of the night thinking about Simco. Shivering, I pulled the covers up around my face. It didn't help; I was cold to the core. Cold and very much alone.

After a while I got up and poured myself a drink. I tried to read, but Simco's presence hovered over me like a malevolent ghost. Only I didn't believe in ghosts. I didn't believe in much of anything anymore.

Shortly after four I went back to bed. Sleep came almost instantly, but it didn't last long. By seven I was wide awake again, awake but not rested. I got up, made myself eat some breakfast, and tried without success to make a list of things to do. Keep busy, Henderson advised. This was no time to sit around and think. Not when the only thing I seemed capable of thinking about was Simco.

The first thing I did was call Henderson's answering service. There was only one message: someone named Henry Widmark wanted an appointment. He would be at the office at ten o'clock. That gave Henderson enough time to clean out the car and buy some more groceries to replace the food that had spoiled. It wasn't much, but it was activity.

At a quarter to ten I was in the office waiting for Henderson's new client to put in an appearance. Henderson was well aware that there were a number of other clients he'd not been doing much for of late, but starting on a fresh problem seemed a better way of taking my mind off the recent past. I had more or less decided to let the Norton/Stevick situation rest for a while. If someone was out to destroy me, let *them* make the next move. I was tired of making myself available by being on the offense.

Ten o'clock on the nose I heard footsteps followed by a crisp knocking. I got up, slipped out into the hall through the empty office, and peered around the corner into Henderson's future.

Henderson's new client was a snappy dresser in a fashionably cut dark suit and a light blue shirt with a stiff looking collar. It came as no surprise that his silk tie was a stylish but not flashy red hue, and his pinstripe mustache ran impeccably parallel to his precise upper lip. In short, his appearance spelled money and tidy little problems. The perfect client.

I let him in the main office door, apologizing for taking so long. He sat down cautiously on the test chair. Perhaps he recognized it as an antique. When it didn't collapse, he relaxed slightly, his shoulders remaining squared, back straight.

"Henry Widmark of Capital Insurance," he announced as he handed Henderson his card. Then, as an afterthought, "We got your name from Stephen Foster."

My stomach did a flip-flop and my collar suddenly felt too tight. "Oh?"

"I understand you have already done some work on the Warren Stevick case and are familiar with the background and problems surrounding his disappearance and death."

"He died before I located him," Henderson said as calmly as he could manage. Would Stevick never go away?!

"Yes, that is what I want to talk to you about. We represent the widow. She has a considerable amount of life insurance on her late husband, but there are a few questions that must be answered before she receives payment."

Dear sweet Caron. Even after Stevick left she had kept up the premiums on his life insurance policy. A wise business move, or merely wishful thinking?

"I wonder if you would mind telling me what it was you were asked to do by Mr. Foster?" Widmark's tone was neutral, but Henderson sensed there was something behind the question. He wondered what Foster had said about him. Could it possibly have been complimentary?

"Didn't Foster tell you?"

"I'd rather hear it from you, if you have no objection."

What objection could Henderson have? He certainly didn't give a damn about protecting any confidences. "None at all," he said finally. "It was a simple case of tracing a missing husband. Stevick bought a present for his son at a local store. Foster wanted me to use that as a starting point to track him down for his wife."

"Have you given any thought as to why he was killed?"

"Some. I don't have any answers, if that's what you're getting at."

Widmark hesitated. "What is your impression of Stephen Foster?"

So, it *was* a question of what Foster had said about him. Well, obviously if Widmark liked Foster, he wasn't going to be impressed by Henderson. With a smile Henderson replied, "That he is a sniveling weasel who would sell tickets to his mother's funeral."

For a second Henderson thought Widmark was going to smile, so did Widmark. But he quickly regained his composure and came to a decision. "If you are available at this time, we would like to hire you to pursue the matter."

Henderson cleared his throat. This was hard to swallow. First he was hired to find himself, now it sounded as though he was being asked to investigate his own death.

"I have some time in my schedule. But it depends. What do you want me to do?"

"This is a somewhat delicate matter." Widmark puckered his lips as though experiencing an unpleasant aftertaste. The tidy mustache humped over the wrinkles. "Let me come directly to the point. We want your assignment to be perfectly clear."

"Perfect clarity is always nice."

Widmark continued as though Henderson had not said anything. "We must be absolutely certain that Mrs. Stevick is in no way involved in the death of her husband. Once that is established the company will be happy to fulfill its contractual obligations. If, however, Mrs. Stevick played some, ah, role in the events surrounding her husband's death, then the company has no responsibility to honor her policy."

How ironic. Henderson had told Gillis' henchmen he was working on an insurance matter in connection with Stevick's death, and here was someone hiring him to do just that. Premonition? Or bad karma?

"Why do you think she might be involved?"

"I want to make it clear that we are *not* assuming any involvement on her part. Mrs. Stevick did, however, hire a private investigator to search for her husband, and he was traced to this city prior to his death. Most likely a coincidence. But there is a large amount of money involved, so we need to be absolutely certain before we proceed. After all, it was a homicide. Do I make myself clear?"

"Perfectly."

"Fine. Can we assume you'll give this assignment priority?"

"You may assume. Tiptop priority."

After we settled on fees and Widmark wrote a generous check as an advance, I walked him to the door, then closed and locked it behind him. I had an overwhelming urge to tell someone about the hilarious joke the fates were playing on me. *"You won't believe this."* *"No, really, that's what actually happened."* *"Ha, ha, ha."* *"Pass the whiskey bottle back in this direction."* *"Isn't life a hoot?"* Only there wasn't anyone I could tell, no one to laugh with, no one to commiserate, no one to reassure me that everything would be all right. With Norton gone, all I had was Henderson. And most of the time he was pretty poor company.

How nice to be as self-assured and confident of your place in the order of things as Mr. Henry Widmark, part of the "we" of Capital Insurance. His life was surely as neat and tidy as his mustache, well-balanced meals on time, regular bowel movements, sanitized sex during the full moon. No surprises, just day after day of comfortable and predictable living.

So, having accepted his job offer, where did Henderson begin? That is, where would he have begun if he hadn't already done so? And how did he go about billing Widmark after the fact? Henderson might as well be paid for my suffering.

First, Henderson Googled Widmark and made a few telephone calls to confirm his identity. Then he paced back and forth for about twenty minutes. Finally, he decided to look in on Al. Al was about the only person Henderson enjoyed being around, even given the limitations of their relationship. It was too bad Al was tied to a desk these days. Their past occasional drinking bouts at the end of Al's shifts had been the next best thing to friendship.

Al was rearranging his office furniture, shirtsleeves rolled to the elbows, face flushed, when Henderson went in.

"Fall housekeeping?"

"I took your advice," Al said, eyeing the empty space along the wall.

"My advice?"

"Yeah. I ordered a couch, real leather, dark brown."

Henderson didn't remember mentioning anything about a couch. "Instead of a nameplate?"

Al rubbed his back. "I'm still working on that. No, this is instead of a new jail. I don't need a new jail." He looked around. "What do you think of right here?"

"That's a good place for a real leather couch."

"I *could* move my desk, I suppose." He pointed to the corner. "Then the couch could go over there." Squinting, he considered the proposition. "No, I kind of like my desk where it is now."

"Facing the door so no one can sneak up on you."

"It might not be good to have someone see the couch the instant they enter the office."

"Especially if you're taking an afternoon siesta."

Al bristled. "It's not for napping. I want it to, well, all sorts of police types have couches—Barney Miller, Patrick Jane, Frank Reagan, all sorts."

"Those are fictional characters, Al."

"But they had couches." His voice trailed off, embarrassed.

"*I* could use a couch in here," Henderson offered. "Right now, for instance, instead of sitting on this hard chair, I could be stretched out, feet up. Sounds great."

Al rolled down his sleeves. "It'll look good in here. Give the place a relaxed atmosphere."

"The crooks can think of you as 'father' instead of as 'captain.'"

"Sure." Al frowned. "OK, what's up?"

"I have a new job."

"What was wrong with the old one?"

"I mean a new client."

"Oh."

"Aren't you going to ask about it?"

"So, I'm asking."

"I've been hired to investigate Stevick's murder."

Al groaned. "No, please tell me you're joking. Garcia has it in for you the way it is. I don't know why, but the mention of your name makes him turn red in the face."

"I need the money, Al. Insurance companies pay their bills. I even got an advance. And I already know a little about the case. All I have to do to earn a nice, fat fee is to show that either the widow had a hand in hubby's death or she didn't."

"Have you told Garcia?"

"I'm on my way there now. Just stopped in to build up my courage."

"He isn't going to like it. In fact, I get the distinct impression he doesn't much care for anything you do."

"I've noticed."

"He seems to think you're not telling him everything you know."

"That would take a long time."

Al shook his head and smiled.

"Just give me courage, Al, that's all I ask."

"I'm afraid I don't have any to spare at the moment."

"I'll settle for information then."

"Like what?"

"Like what's been happening with the investigation into Stevick's death?"

"I don't have all the inside scoop, but . . . one does hear rumors."

"Do rumors come cheaper than scoop?"

"Bargain special, one day only."

"Sold."

Al leaned forward, his voice animated like it always was when he finally talked shop. "Rumor number one: since Norton hasn't shown up, Garcia is beginning to suspect Norton may be another victim instead of a murderer."

"Hmmm." I liked the sound of that.

"Number two. You aren't the only one who's been asking questions. Some guys with Chicago accents have been nosing around. Makes you wonder whether the mob's right hand knows what the left is doing. A power shakeup maybe, with Stevick somehow involved."

"Hmmm." That I didn't like the sound of. Although it would put Caron in the clear.

"Number three. The local bad guys are having a few problems of their own. Gillis lost one of his men, someone whose name you might recognize." Al paused, pointedly waiting for me to ask who.

"Who?" My stomach was suddenly queasy.

"Dan Simco. Small world, isn't it?"

And closing in.

"You going to comment?" Al asked.

"I'm waiting for you to tell me how it happened."

"He was shot. In the woods over on the peninsula. Near a rented house. Some kids found him."

"Kids?" Henderson hadn't thought about that possibility.

"Neighbors seemed to remember some shots earlier, but they didn't pay much attention. Then these two kids were cutting through the woods on their way home . . ." Al made a face. "Bastards. Leaving a corpse like that. One of the kids was pretty shook up."

Al was right—I was a bastard.

"So," he concluded, "who are you putting your money on? Norton, the mob, or the wife?"

"Well, we know for sure the butler didn't do it."

"That's assumption, not fact. Just because you haven't come across a guilty butler yet doesn't mean you won't."

"I'll keep that in mind." Henderson stood up. "But first I have to gird my loins and face Garcia." He sidestepped past the space where the couch was going to be.

"See that they stay girded," Al called after him.

CHAPTER 15
THE WRONG BODY

Garcia surprised Henderson. Instead of objecting to Henderson's new assignment, he offered encouragement. It crossed Henderson's mind that Garcia was hoping he'd act as a lightning rod while Garcia stood around waiting for lightning to strike. That probably meant the police weren't making much progress with the case. Still, that didn't explain why they hadn't figured out that the body was Hicks, not Stevick. Did Caron know that another Mrs. Stevick had made the identification? Henderson left the station with Garcia's blessing and a sick feeling in his stomach.

Later, when Henderson called his answering service, there was another message: an invitation to stop by and have a drink, but not on the house. One of the bartenders Henderson had talked to about Hicks had some information for him. Maybe this was the break we'd been hoping for. And with Widmark's advance, I could afford it.

It was still fairly early for most of the regulars. The place was deserted except for a lone man on a stool near the end of the long bar. He looked as though he'd just crawled in from some alley, one littered with garbage. It was too bad I'd already disposed of Simco's overcoat; this guy could have used it.

The bartender was lounging against the counter, a toothpick moving back and forth between his thin, pale lips. Henderson couldn't help admiring the way he handled the toothpick. It was a decidedly masculine act, like chewing tobacco or scratching your crotch.

"Beer," Henderson said as he gently settled his butt on the stool. He was still feeling discomfort from the beating he'd taken.

The bartender drew a schooner and set it in front of him. Foam was oozing over the rim. Henderson turned the glass to a clear spot and took a drink. The beer could have been better, but Henderson wasn't fussy. He could probably drink real horse piss and not notice.

"I got your message."

"That's what I figured."

"Got something for me?"

"Maybe."

If he was confident enough to hold out for more money, he might actually have something worthwhile. Henderson put a twenty on the counter. "Keep the change." Big spender. If it was worth more, he'd cough up a few extra bucks.

The bartender eyed the twenty a few seconds, then shrugged and pocketed it. "Rumor is that Hicks has disappeared."

"Maybe that's why he's so hard to find." You sure didn't get much for your money these days.

"He won't be missed."

"I wanted him for a job."

"No one around here will miss him. It seems your friend is a snitch."

"A snitch?"

"That's right. And in this part of town it ain't too healthy to turn in your friends."

"Bernie wouldn't give a cop the time of day." Henderson wanted his money back.

"Maybe not. But to the Feds he sings on command. At least that's what I heard."

"Your source reliable?" It *was* possible. But that still didn't explain why Hicks had turned up dead in Norton's office with Stevick's ID in his pocket."

"Sure." He raised his eyebrows and asked, "You want another beer?"

"No. That's enough. Unless you have some more information for me."

"That's all I have."

Henderson drained the glass. "Well, thanks. I appreciate it."

"Any time."

As Henderson left, he glanced one last time at the hunched figure at the end of the bar. The man wasn't all that old, but at this rate, people would be thinking of him as "gramps" before he hit fifty. See, Henderson, some people are even worse off than you. So quit feeling so damned sorry for yourself.

Out on the sidewalk, I didn't know which way to turn. The fact that Hicks may have been a snitch for the FBI wasn't exactly the kind of break I'd been hoping for. I was back to square one. No, that wasn't accurate. With Garcia's stamp of approval Henderson was free to pursue normal channels of investigation. Perhaps it was about time he got some firsthand information on the body.

The medical examiner's office was a hop, skip, and expiring breath away from the vast medical complex on the hill, just blocks from downtown. I often wondered whether the hospital and morgue were connected by an underground tunnel, maybe one with massive, creaking doors and winding passages. Or maybe there was entry though a huge laundry chute. Quick and efficient.

When you first enter the examiner's suite of rooms it resembles county offices everywhere--beige walls, standard office furniture, a calendar with pictures of puppies for the current month thumbtacked to one wall, and a framed print of a wooded scene in golds and browns hung on another. All very familiar. Then you notice the faint odor of disinfectant that lingers like cheap perfume or fried chicken at the local franchise.

The receptionist, another typical piece of government equipment, asked in an officious tone if Henderson had an appointment. He gave her his best smile and his card. She had a scented candle on her desk, cinnamon or mint or soy sauce--he couldn't tell which. Since he doubted it was legal for her to have an open flame in a government building, she must have really hated the smell of death and disinfectant to chance breaking the rules. Or maybe they were just for show and smell.

Fortunately, Dr. Vernon was available. Henderson had met him on a number of occasions, none of them memorable. The doctor had no reason to either like or dislike Henderson, unless he'd been talking to Garcia. I hoped he hadn't.

The office was spacious and neat. Dr. Vernon was seated behind a large wood desk in a very expensive looking stainless and leather chair. Tall, lean, and somber. He hadn't the slightest trace of Quincy's emotional belligerence or Temperance "Bones" Brennan's naïve determination. Rather, he looked like a high-paid executive in some large corporation. Only the hint of antiseptic in the air and the skeleton suspended from a metal stand in the corner reminded visitors that the doctor dealt with bodies rather than stocks and bonds.

"It was kind of you to see me, Dr. Vernon."

"Things are slow today."

"That's, ah, good, I think." Henderson smiled. Dr. Vernon didn't.

"I like to keep busy."

"Yes, of course." Well, don't look at me, I've already done my share for the week.

"What can I do for you?"

"I've been hired to look into the death of Warren Stevick." When Dr. Vernon didn't react to the name, Henderson continued. "He died last Wednesday. I believe you did the autopsy."

"Yes. I remember him."

"Can you tell me the results?"

"Death by gunshot wound."

"Can you be more specific?"

"You wish to know about the bullet track, type of weapon, condition of the wound, time of death, that sort of thing?"

"Yes, that sort of thing."

Dr. Vernon was apparently bored enough to share what he knew to kill some time. He didn't bother with the usual confidentiality spiel but simply got out a manila folder and went through the report using a minimum of jargon. Both shots had been fired at close range, the one through his head had penetrated the brain and resulted in death. Not much to report actually.

"What about fingerprints," I asked.

"We of course took them for our report, but it wasn't necessary. We had a positive ID from his wife."

I decided it was not smart to ask more about the fingerprints. Although I was surprised that with the body of a mob informant that they hadn't put them through the system. Having them and checking them out were obviously two different things. Unless they knew the body wasn't Stevick's, and the police were withholding that critical piece of information.

Dr. Vernon closed the file and leaned back. His brief respite from boredom at an end. Unless I had more questions. Which I did.

"When Mrs. Stevick identified her husband, was she emotional?" Perhaps I shouldn't have asked, but I was curious whether the phony Mrs. Stevick was going to be up for an Emmy.

"I thought you were an investigator, not a reporter."

"I *am* a private detective. I've been hired to determine whether the wife was involved in her husband's death. It's an insurance matter."

"I see." Dr. Vernon stroked the arms on his classy chair and considered the question. "Anything I tell you would be guesswork."

"I understand. Strictly off the record."

He put the tips of his fingers together and held them in front of his chest, a studied, reflective pose. "She appeared nervous, very nervous."

"Broken up nervous? Or just nervous?"

"Just nervous."

"Did she cry? They'd been separated for almost two years, you know. She was probably more shocked than anything."

"Yes, I read that in the paper." He focused on a spot on the wall behind Henderson. "No, I wouldn't say she was particularly broken up by his death. Of course people express their emotions differently. You see all sorts of reactions in my business."

"Did she have any trouble identifying him?"

"No, his facial features were intact."

"I mean, maybe he'd changed in the two years. Did she say 'that's him' the instant you pulled back the sheet?"

"She had no trouble recognizing him. I guess he hadn't changed that much."

"What about funeral arrangements?"

"The police are holding Stevick a while. I assume Mrs. Stevick will contact me soon about where to send the body."

If no one discovered the mistake, would Caron bury the wrong body? Had she even questioned who had made the identification? Had *anyone* suspected that Mrs. Stevick wasn't really Mrs. Stevick, wife of the alleged deceased?

"Anything else you noticed about her?" Henderson was fishing now *and* testing whether Dr. Vernon was at all concerned about the identity of the body.

"Good legs, although a bit thin. I prefer rounded contours above and below."

Henderson couldn't help smiling. "I should think you'd get rather blasé about bodies in your line of work."

"I assure you I'm still capable of appreciating the female form. Although I prefer it at a warmer temperature than what I usually see around here."

"I should hope so." I forced a smile.

Dr. Vernon smiled back, a dignified and somewhat grandfatherly smile. "Would you care for a drink, Mr. Henderson?"

"As long as it isn't formaldehyde."

"All liquor pickles your brain eventually." He went over to a cabinet and pulled back a door. Inside were several bottles and a row of upside-down glasses on a white cloth. He removed two brandy snifters and a bottle whose label Stevick immediately recognized from his halcyon days. My heartbeat quickened.

"I don't usually drink during the day," Dr. Vernon observed, "but as I said before, it has been rather slow around here."

I accepted the brandy, took a deep breath, and moved the glass gently to allow the brandy also to breathe. Then I took a sip, holding the liquid briefly in my mouth, savoring. Henderson, you cheap bastard, this is what liquor is supposed to taste like.

The doctor's face brightened. "I see we share an appreciation for a good label, even before dinner."

Henderson was suddenly on guard. His taste buds weren't supposed to be able to distinguish the difference between fine brandy and rotgut, and here he was acting like James Bond at a tasting party. "It's been a hard day. I needed a drink."

"Are you familiar with this?" Dr. Vernon indicated the bottle that had brought Stevick to the surface.

"No. I don't think so." Not wanting to overdo it, in case the opportunity to share a drink with Dr. Vernon arose again sometime, Henderson quickly added, "It's good though." He took a big swig. Liquor razed his throat and hit his stomach like a land mine. Creep, why don't you just thump your chest and burp to make your point?

Dr. Vernon smiled and thoughtfully sipped his drink.

"I can't afford this kind of booze on my salary," Henderson said. "I'm more of a six-pack fan."

"I see."

That's what Henderson was afraid of, that Dr. Vernon saw right through his act. "I suppose Garcia told you I'd be coming by."

"He did mention that if you showed up, I should make any information you wanted available."

"That was nice of him. He's always so helpful." The sneaky bastard. And just what kind of feedback was the urbane Dr. Vernon going to give Garcia about the visit?

"I'm afraid I don't share your perception of Lieutenant Garcia. At times I find him difficult to work with."

Aren't you being a big obvious, Dr. Spy for Garcia? Well, Henderson wasn't about to be tricked a second time.

"He's always been fair with me." Henderson took another ungentlemanly gulp of brandy that removed a second layer of tissue from his throat. What a waste. But gulping was Henderson's style.

"I suppose one might characterize him as a fair man, depending on whose perspective you have in mind."

Sitting around philosophizing about Garcia might be Dr. Vernon's idea of fun, but Henderson had better things to do. He finished off the brandy with a shudder and stood up, vocal cords quivering from the assault. When he opened his mouth and tried to speak, nothing came out at first. He had to swallow several times. "I've got to get going." It was someone else's voice, but at least it was audible.

"So soon?" Dr. Vernon sounded sincerely disappointed. It really must have been a slow day.

"I've got a lot of ground to cover yet today." And miles to go before I sleep.

"It *is* nice to keep busy," he said wistfully. "Do come again."

"Hopefully in a vertical position," Henderson joked.

Dr. Vernon didn't laugh. Apparently, *any* visitor was welcome in his book.

CHAPTER 16
LIGHTNING STRIKES TWICE

Monday evening came and went without anything exciting happening, the lull before the storm. Although I didn't know it then. Tuesday morning the storm broke.

I had barely settled in at Henderson's office when there was a thunderous knock on the door. Before I could slip out through the adjoining office, the lock splintered and Henderson found himself staring into the chest of a man monster who had mob written all over him, probably embroidered on his shorts, unquestionably tighty-whities.

"Won't you come in?" You might as well be polite when the person you're addressing is going to do whatever he wants to do anyway.

A short fellow followed the monster's wake. Oh god, not another big guy and little guy! Henderson wasn't sure he could face it. Big and little, muscle and brains, only he suspected this big guy had more muscle than the little guy had brains—no one had an IQ *that* good.

"You Henderson?"

"Yes, I am." Today at least. You Godzilla?

"I'm Smith," the big one said. "And this here is Jones. We wanna talk with you."

His Chicago twang was music to Henderson's ears, funeral music. Of course, it *was* possible that all they really wanted was to talk.

"Fine. Take a seat." A good host, Henderson got another chair for Jones. Smith had already taken the test chair, like an ape squatting on a tree stump. When Jones sat down on my spare chair his feet didn't touch the floor.

"What can I do for you?" Henderson asked. Peel a banana maybe?

"We hear you're investigating a murder. Man name of Stevick, Warren Stevick."

"Yes, I am." Keep it simple, Henderson. Let them do the talking.

"Well, we are too," Smith said. "Thought we might pool our information."

Jones nodded. He hadn't uttered a sound yet. Maybe he was a puppet.

"I don't usually 'pool' information of that sort."

"We can make it worth your while."

"Oh?"

"Yeah. You tell us what you know, and we promise not to beat the crap out of you."

It seemed a reasonable offer.

Suddenly Smith laughed, a deep belly laugh that didn't quite reach his eyes. "That was a joke," he explained.

"Oh." Some people can tell a joke, others can't.

"Of course," he continued, "it might be better for your health if you cooperated. Wouldn't it, Jonesy?"

Jones nodded again, the perfect straight man.

"This *will* be an *exchange*," Henderson emphasized. He didn't want to seem like a pushover.

"You don't think we expect somethin' for nothin'?"

"Well." Henderson smiled broadly, showing off his capped teeth. "I don't have much use for insurance companies anyway. I mean, it's hard to consider an entire insurance company a client, if you know what I mean."

From the looks on their faces, they neither knew nor cared what he meant. He didn't let that discourage him though. The trick was to *appear* cooperative, a safety precaution, like getting inoculated against a disease. In this instance, a disease that could prove fatal.

"So," Henderson said cordially, "what do you want to know?"

"What you've found out?"

"That covers a lot of ground. When you're working for a big insurance company, you don't spare the expense. It's all billable time, you know." Henderson realized he was still smiling, and since no one else in the room was, he erased the smile and replaced it with a look of sober sincerity. "I assume what you really want to know is whether I've made any progress."

Smith and Jones nodded in unison.

"The answer to that is, unfortunately, 'no.'"

Smith frowned, an awesome sight. Henderson hurriedly went on to explain.

"What I *do* know is this: Stevick had apparently been in the area several months, since his son's birthday. At that time he bought a present at one of the local stores. What he was doing here I haven't been able to find out. Nor have I discovered any connection between him and Norton." Henderson offered a silent prayer of thanks when there was no reaction to that assertion. "Most of the people I've talked with think the mob finally caught up with him." Should he have mentioned that?

Smith and Jones glanced at one another. Then Smith leaned over and whispered something in Jones' ear. Jones appeared to whisper something back. None of this was particularly reassuring, but at least they weren't whispering behind his back.

"Like I said already, an insurance company, Capital Insurance, hired me. If the wife didn't do in her husband, she gets a nice, big death benefit. So far, I have no indication that she was involved. That's my only interest in the matter."

"What about the police?" Smith was apparently spokesman *and* muscle.

"The police don't exactly take me into their confidence, but as near as I can tell, they're stymied."

Smith didn't respond. He slowly and deliberately looked around the office as if seeing it for the first time. Finally, his eyes came to rest on Henderson. "If I thought you wasn't telling us everything . . ." He didn't need to finish his sentence with words, his rippling arm muscles did it for him.

"What reason would I have to hold out on you?"

Smith chose to ignore the question. "Ready Jonesy?" They both stood up. "We'll be in touch."

"Hey," Henderson said. "I thought this was supposed to be an *exchange* of information."

Both men stared at Henderson in surprise. Henderson, you pushy bastard, why can't you learn to keep your big mouth shut?

"Sure," Smith said. The word exploded from his mouth like a gunshot. "I'll be glad to give you something in exchange for what you told us."

Please make it a fist and not a bullet, I silently begged. Or kill bigmouthed Henderson but leave me alone.

When he got close enough so Henderson could see the nicotine stains on his incisors, he delivered his quid pro quo: "The mob had nothin' to do with Stevick's death."

The next thing I knew, the two were marching out of the office, Jones literally on Smith's heels. I had to pinch myself to make certain I was still alive. No bullet hole between my eyes. No knife handle sticking out of my chest. Just Smith's bad breath lingering in the air over Henderson's blotter. Surely in the hereafter there was no such thing as bad breath.

Whether Smith had "mob" embroidered on his shorts was still in question. But it was possible that Smith had been telling the truth. The mob could have sent them to find out what had happened to Stevick, nothing more. But if so, then who had gone to all that trouble to set up Norton?

If Henderson didn't get hopping, it was beginning to look as though the whole mess was likely to blow up in my face. The minute the police discovered the body was Hicks—if they ever did—they would no doubt start thinking Stevick killed Hicks and planted his own ID to thwart discovery by the mob. And the mob would then be double pissed at Stevick, first for testifying against them and then for making it look as if they were to blame for his death. Yes, if and when the mistake about the body came out, everyone would be after Stevick's blood, and a pint of his was the same as a pint of Henderson's.

I paced back and forth for about fifteen minutes before finally deciding I had to do something, anything. The only thing I could think of was a trip to Norton's office. I already knew what was there, but it *was* the scene of the crime. And it was billable activity.

It seemed strange going to Norton's office as Henderson instead of as Norton. Henderson had never been there before, yet he knew the place intimately. Even so, he stopped at the reader board in the lobby to look up Norton's office number. In case someone was watching. Amazingly, Norton's office was right where it had been when I was posing as Norton.

Even though I felt confident Henderson didn't look anything like Norton, he didn't want to face Lawrence, the talkative elevator operator, so he took the stairs. It was quite a hike, but I told myself it was good for Henderson.

Since Garcia would have been mighty surprised if Henderson was caught using one of Norton's keys—surprised and suspicious—Henderson picked the lock. It was a cinch since he'd known in advance what to expect. In just a few minutes he was inside.

There was a pile of mail on the floor under the mail slot and a few spots on the rug where the body had been. Other than that, everything looked like it had the last time I'd been there, although the plants were looking sad. They could use some water.

At least Henderson didn't need to worry about fingerprints; he and Norton had that much in common. But just in case Garcia discovered Henderson had paid the office a visit, he used gloves to go through the mail.

Most of it looked like the usual: bills, a few advertisements, a check from a client. Well, actually, the check was a bit of a surprise. One of Norton's clients actually paying his bills. Astounding. Reluctantly, Henderson dropped the check with the rest of the mail back on the floor, everything except one plain envelope with no return address.

It was a dilemma. Technically the police had no right to interfere with Norton's life or to keep an eye on the mail inside his locked office. Officially he was only wanted for questioning. Still, a murder had been committed in his office, and his rather abrupt departure after that made him either a suspect or another victim. Henderson had no doubt that the police, in particular Garcia, would not hesitate to take a few liberties in their efforts to locate Norton. And that might include keeping an eye on his office and its contents. But lightning rods have some rights too.

It was handy knowing right where everything was. Henderson got out Norton's letter opener and tried to open the envelope without making it obvious the letter had been tampered with. When that failed, he got impatient and slit open the end of the envelope. What the hell. Norton had a few spare envelopes he could use to replace it. Unless the police had already looked at the letter and resealed it, they might conclude that it had been shoved under the door instead of sent through the mail.

As he read the letter he felt as though he'd entered the eye of the storm. He had to read it through at least three times before he thoroughly comprehended what it said: someone was willing to buy some information from Norton in exchange for evidence that would clear him of Stevick's murder.

There was no date on the letter, but it was postmarked two days after the murder. Perhaps the writer had tried to call or email Norton and, when that failed to get a response, had resorted to writing to him. There was no name, but there was a number to call.

Had the police seen the letter? Was this the reason for Garcia's change of heart toward Henderson? Was he hoping Henderson would do something to draw out the person who had written the letter? It didn't take Henderson long to make up his mind. He stuffed the letter in his pocket, let himself out, and walked boldly back to his car. No one tried to stop him. Either he was intended to find the letter, or he was one step ahead of the police.

He bought another burner phone and made the call from the street. The phone rang quite a few times before a voice message came on. "Leave a number and I'll call you back." He punched in his burner phone number and decided to catch some lunch while waiting for a return call.

The call came just as he was taking his first bite of a Rueben sandwich. The voice was gruff and to the point: "Yeah?" I identified myself as Norton. "What took you so long?"

"I have found it necessary to avoid my office of late. For reasons with which I believe you are familiar."

"I can help you with that."

"That's what the note said."

"I'm willing to give you the gun that killed Hicks in exchange for certain information."

I felt as though someone had reached out and grabbed me around the throat. The voice had said *Hicks*.

"Did you hear me? I'm willing to give you the gun in exchange for information."

"I heard you." I was fast losing my appetite.

"You see, I know all about you, Norton. Now I can do one of two things with that gun. I can either make certain it's found in a place that would prove you committed the murder, or I can deliver it to you, and you can give it to the police. Then they can trace the fingerprints of the real killer."

"All the police want me for is questioning."

"Then why did you run away?"

"I didn't run away. I've been out of town on business."

"Bullshit! Your life doesn't bear looking into too closely. You know that, and I know that. The police may be a little slow, but eventually they'll stumble on some things I'm sure you would rather keep secret."

"All right. Let's suppose it would be more convenient if the killer was discovered. What do you want from me?" I kept my voice low. It seemed advisable to not let other customers hear me using the word "killer."

"Information. A few names. Some details." He paused. "Like who you're afraid of back in Chicago, and why."

"I think you have me confused with someone else. I've never lived in Chicago." That hand was back, constricting my vocal cords.

"Don't waste my time . . . Stevick."

I'd feared it was coming, but it nevertheless left me speechless.

"Think it over. I'll call you back at this number tomorrow, about the same time. By then you'll realize my offer is your only way out."

"What if I can't take your call tomorrow at this time?" It seemed pointless to deny I was Stevick.

"Then call me back and leave a message. I'll call when I can." The dial tone droned in my ear.

Damn. From the moment I'd found Stevick's ID on Hicks' body I'd known someone had made the connection between Norton and Stevick. But how? Had they stumbled across Norton's secret by accident? And if so, why weren't they asking for money instead of information? Smith claimed the mob wasn't involved, and if he was telling the truth, he was obviously speaking for the existing power structure. Maybe someone seeking a shortcut to the top had traced Stevick to Norton.

One thing was for sure: if I gave my mystery man the information that had driven Stevick underground, the people Stevick had run from would pull out all the stops to find and destroy him. Somehow, I had to come up with a plan to unveil my opponent without revealing anything. I asked for a box for my lunch and returned to the office.

They say lightning doesn't strike twice in the same place, but on that stormy Tuesday, they were wrong. Henderson had been back at his office less than five minutes when he was zapped again, this time by a telephone call from a very frightened woman.

"I wasn't sure I should call," she said.

"I told you if you needed help that I'd be available." Henderson, a knight in tarnished armor.

"I . . . I ran away from Simco.

"Do you know he's dead?"

Softly, she replied, "I was afraid of that."

"Do you know who shot him?" Henderson held his breath waiting for her reply.

"No, I don't. But *I* didn't do it."

"I didn't think you did."

"The police, what do they know?" she asked.

"I'm not sure."

"Have you, well, have you talked with the police?"

"Yes, but I didn't mention you."

"Oh, thank you."

"Of course they didn't ask me. You see, I didn't mention anything about our little visit the other day."

"That was wise."

"Wise?" It seemed a strange thing for her to say.

"You can't trust anyone. *Anyone.*"

"Look, are you in trouble?"

"I'm not sure."

"But you think you are. That's why you called me."

"No, I called to warn you."

"To warn me?"

Henderson seemed to be having difficulty following her logic.

"They know about you."

"They?"

"I can't say any more. I just wanted you to know that you're in danger. Simco mentioned your name on the telephone. I overheard him. You need to be careful."

"What about you? Can you tell me who you are?"

"No, I can't say any more."

"How can I get in touch with you?"

"Don't trust anyone. Do you understand? Anyone."

She hung up.

CHAPTER 17
CELL PHONE CLUE

Her name was Leanne Adams, but she went by Lolly. She was not, however, to be confused with the James Bond hottie the name conjured up. Henderson's Lolly wasn't like that at all. She didn't have moist red lips with the words "take me I'm yours" on the tip of a succulent pink tongue just waiting to plunge itself into his mouth. No, his Lolly was dry lipped, tough, and hard to get along with. In the vernacular of her employees, "a real bitch." But she liked Henderson.

She was a former telephone employee who now worked for an IT company, a professional who knew her way around the backdoors of the technical world, especially when it came to telephones. He'd picked her over several women who *should* have been named Lolly and several hotshot males who it would have taken more time, effort, and money to enlist. His Lolly knew he was using her, but she was also a tiny bit flattered. Out of that relationship a good measure of mutual respect had slowly evolved.

Henderson called her after he'd gone as far as he could on his own in tracing the telephone number from the letter left in Norton's office. He'd been fairly certain it was a burner phone, so he wasn't surprised when he couldn't track it through normal channels. But he knew it was possible to find the location, if not the person, behind the call. So, he'd contacted Lolly and asked her to take a shot at it. In exchange for dinner at a restaurant of her choice.

When Henderson stopped by to pick Lolly up for dinner, he almost felt dressy in his best cheap suit. She was coming straight from work and had on a dark tweed business suit with out-of-date padded shoulders that made her look like a villainess in a children's book. The evil stepmother or a wicked witch in disguise. Take your pick.

They went to one of those pricey waterfront places Stevick might have patronized if he had lived in the city. Henderson couldn't afford it, but he felt Stevick owed him a decent meal under the circumstances.

"This will cost you," Lolly warned as she sat down at their reserved corner table for two shielded from the other tables by a couple of potted plants and a rather ornate silkscreen. "I'm hungry."

"And thirsty?" Henderson smiled. Lolly ventured a tight grin in return. While she studied the menu, Henderson gave the waiter their drink order. It didn't take her long to decide.

"Lobster," she announced with pride. No price was listed next to the menu item. It was based on season availability. "With saffron rice and a small Caesar salad. And, of course dessert. I'll decide on that later."

"Of course."

The waiter brought their drinks. Henderson ordered, including a very nice bottle of wine in keeping with the occasion. Even Henderson was allowed to show a little class now and then.

"Business before or after dinner?" Lolly asked.

"How about before? Then we can concentrate on enjoying the rest of the evening."

"Fine." She took a piece of yellow notepad paper out of her purse. High tech recorded on low tech. "As you already guessed, I'm sure," she said as he handed him the paper, ". . . it's a burner phone. Not an easy task, but I managed to pinpoint the caller's location from data history . . . and with a bit of luck." She gave him a wide triumphant smile. "There were a couple of other calls made from the same location, including one I caught live. People are so predictable." She pointed to the piece of paper he had unfolded. "That's the address. I assume it's enough information to cover the lobster."

"Just what I needed," Henderson said, pocketing the paper after a quick look at the address. "Now for the enjoyment." He gave her a big smile. "You know, don't you, Lolly, that sometimes I make up numbers just to have an excuse to go out on the town with you."

"Go on." She blushed and looked down at her drink.

"Seriously, I can't tell you how much I appreciate both the information and the company."

"Well, I admit providing a PI with information is a lot more exciting than what I normally do at work." She cocked her head to one side and looked him in the eyes. "You're not going to do anything illegal with that information, are you?"

"Me?" Henderson feigned shock. "Never."

"I wrote the note left-handed just in case," she said. "Just in case."

It was dark when Henderson dropped Lolly off at her car and headed for the address she had given him. He'd already checked and discovered it belonged to a small fitness center at a strip mall just south of downtown. It was in a one-story building sandwiched between an Edward Jones financial services center and Central Bark, a dog grooming shop. "Get Physical" was the name printed on a sign above the door of the fitness center. All three businesses were closed for the night. Anyone currently "getting physical" was apparently doing it elsewhere.

There was no one around, but you can't break into a place that fronts on a busy street, at least not from the front—unless you wanted to get caught. I went around back and checked out the alley. There were the usual dumpsters and dim lighting . . . no cars, no people, not even a stray dog. Sorry, Lolly, I know I promised, but this situation is too good to pass up. And, after all, you ordered lobster.

The problem was matching doors from the alley with the right business. Not every business has a back door, and there's no rule that says a business has to have only one back door. I was prepared to count and punt. But as it turned out, I didn't have to. Central Bark's back door had a picture of a dog painted on it. At least it resembled a dog. It was a black and white animal leaping in the air to catch a round object that was either a Frisbee or a Martian ship. There was nothing written or painted on any of the other doors, but from there it was easy enough to figure out that the next door down was my target.

Henderson was wearing a baggy sweatshirt with no logo on it and a baseball cap he'd picked up at the Goodwill. He kept them in the car for occasions like this. The team named on the brim of the cap probably wouldn't approve of it being used to hide the wearer's face from cameras, but it was less suspicious than a ski mask. This one had a broad brim that drooped slightly in front. Maybe the previous owner had used it for a similar purpose.

There were no obvious cameras in the area and no numeric keypad next to the door. It looked straightforward. There might be a silent alarm system, although I doubted it. It was unlikely there was a hot market for used gym equipment. There was, however, a lock with a mushroom tumbler, the kind developed in the late fifties. Henderson could tell by the way the plug rotated slightly when he applied tension and attempted to raise the first pin stack. It was a common locking device that more people would use if they realized how hard it was to crack. Henderson had spent countless hours practicing on the model. Even so, it seemed to take forever to get inside.

The door opened onto a back room that appeared to be mostly used for storage; there were stacks of unmarked boxes and pieces of exercise equipment lining the walls. In one corner there was a pile of towels with "Get Physical" printed on them. Next to door was what looked to Henderson like a medieval torture devise. He moved quickly past it into the next room.

Next, he found himself in a small kitchen with a microwave, coffee maker, dish washer, and a small vending machine filled with junk food. Just what you needed in a fitness center. What he was looking for were the locker rooms. Assuming the owner or an employee of the gym wasn't the person he was looking for, then it was probably a member. Someone who didn't want to have a burner phone on his person.

When he found the men's locker room he was surprised to see several rows of lockers. From the outside the place hadn't looked that big. Maybe there were a lot of people who paid for membership but didn't use the facilities. That seemed likely. Good intentions; little follow-through. A lucrative business model for the center.

Before getting down to business, there was one thing he needed to do. Just because an alarm hadn't gone off didn't mean he was entirely in the clear. Someone might have seen him and called the cops. Or someone might show up after hours. You never knew. It was always smart to be prepared with an exit strategy.

The first places he checked for accessible escape routes were the restrooms. The door to the women's had the image of a skirt-wearing figure on it. I wondered how many women wore skirts to the gym-- maybe they came straight from tennis practice. Inside, the tiny space was windowless. The men's restroom was also small, but it had a window he might be able to squeeze through in a pinch, if fueled by panic. He checked to make sure it opened—it did. The bad news was that it would land him only a few feet away from the back door he'd come in through. Still, if no one was covering the alley, it might give him enough time to get away.

There were no other means of escape other than the front door, and that would put him right under a streetlight. Not the best situation, Hopefully, he wouldn't need to leave in a hurry.

He went back to the locker room, took out his burner phone, and dialed the number from the note. When he heard a muted melody coming from somewhere nearby, he couldn't help but smile. Not that it had taken much imagination for Henderson to come up with this plan. But he was nonetheless pleased.

Before he could determine which locker the phone was in, the ringing stopped, and a voice said, "Leave a message." He hung up and dialed again. This time he made it to the right locker, well, one of two possibilities. He couldn't tell whether the phone was behind door number 327 or 328. One or the other. Both had combination locks.

Henderson had learned how to break a combination lock in under 60 seconds by watching a YouTube video. It involved putting pressure on the shackle as you rotated the dial, doing a little math, and guessing right. Sixty seconds later, or maybe just a little longer, I was staring at a locker with sweats hanging on a hook under a shelf. And there, in the middle of the shelf was a cell phone. Bingo.

Now all Henderson had to do was figure out who paid for the locker. Possibly someone using a phony name. Or he could wait and see who showed up to call him tomorrow. One way or the other he was going to figure out who the mystery man was.

Unfortunately, the office was right behind the reception desk and had a glass wall facing the storefront. Anyone passing by would see him in there. Even though there didn't seem to be any traffic in the area at this time of night, Henderson decided against searching the office for the locker owner's name. He would have to find another way or go with plan B.

Even though Henderson had erred on the side of caution, by the time he was done, I had a bad case of the jitters. Neither Norton nor Stevick had ever become comfortable with Henderson's professional tactics, especially the illegal ones. At the same time, we were all feeling good about being one step away from discovering the caller's identity.

Back at the apartment I was too wound up to go to bed right away, so I poured myself a drink and sat there in the dark thinking about my life, or what was left of it. I certainly didn't have much to show for my years on this planet. No money, no friends, and no real family to speak of. Caron had seen to that. She'd made Warren Jr. and Tammy think I didn't care a whit for them, so why should they waste any tears on me? Damn her anyway. All she'd ever really cared about was Stevick's position in life and his earning potential. If only I'd realized that back when.

The more I thought about it, the more it seemed to me that I was no better off than Lolly. We were both loners doomed to empty lives, out of step with other people. We couldn't even confide in each other, not even when we recognized common needs. "I tell you everything that is nothing and nothing that is everything." I'd read that somewhere once. Probably on somebody's Facebook page. Or maybe scrawled on a bathroom wall.

At least Lolly didn't have to worry about finding a gun pointed at her chest some dark night. Or having monster man leap out of the shadows. No, she didn't have to worry about threats to her physical well-being, but that didn't make her life much better than mine. When

Donne had written "no man is an island," he hadn't had either me or Lolly in mind.

CHAPTER 18
AT THE ZOO

On the way to the office, I stopped at a Dunkin' Donuts and picked up a couple maple bars and some coffee. From there it was only a block to Henderson's office. Between the Donut shop and his office I managed to lose about fifty cents worth of coffee. I spilled another thirty cents worth on the hall carpet trying to unlock the side door without putting anything down.

Once inside I checked to make certain there were no urgent messages. Then I turned on Henderson's computer and googled the website for "Get Physical." While it was downloading, I took the lid off my coffee. Droplets from the inside of the lip promptly drooled all over some papers on Henderson's desk. There was nothing at hand to mop up the mess with, so I smeared the liquid around with the back of an envelope and pushed everything to one side. Henderson was a slob; why should I worry about his desk?

The maple bars were sickeningly sweet. Stevick would have hated them. But Henderson and I kinda liked them. Only I was getting grease spots on the computer screen. Too bad, Henderson.

I had one sticky finger on the number for "Get Physical" when the telephone rang. "You said if I needed help to call." The barely audible voice was unmistakably that of the phony Mrs. Stevick.

"Just name it."

"Can you meet me somewhere?"

"Anywhere." The ends of the earth, your place or mine.

"How about the zoo?"

"The zoo?"

"Yes. The front entrance by the rose garden. In an hour."

As I hung up, I found myself humming an old Simon and Garfunkel tune, "It's all happening at the zoo." Not at that very moment perhaps, but in an hour.

I gulped down what remained of my coffee, licked the maple icing off my fingers, and wrote down the telephone number for "Get Physical." Henderson was closing in.

Still humming, I locked up and left, not on the cross-town bus but in Henderson's rickety car. I really did need to get that rattle fixed one of these days.

The walk from the zoo parking lot to the entrance was lined with maple trees. Wind whipped dead leaves, scattering them in random directions, and the air smelled faintly like a preview of winter. A couple of squirrels chased each other among the fallen leaves, their jerky, silent film movements a testament to high energy and a sense of comedy. One stopped to glare at Henderson as he went past. Perhaps he was a lookout for the mob.

Henderson arrived ten minutes early. There was no one around except for a middle-aged man in the ticket booth reading a newspaper. Henderson had to wait fifteen minutes before she showed, walking rapidly in flimsy high-heeled shoes. Dr. Vernon was right; she *did* have nice legs.

When she saw Henderson she hesitated, then with a determined stride totally incongruent with her impractical shoes, she hurried toward him. Cheeks flushed with color from walking, she looked youthful and wholesome, not at all like a person involved with organized crime and a homicide.

"Do you want to drive somewhere?" Henderson asked. "Or would you prefer to go inside and walk around while we talk?"

She glanced over her shoulder. "Inside I think."

Henderson paid for the tickets. They would go on the expense account. He dared Widmark to challenge it.

Once through the toll gate she seemed to relax. They proceeded at a comfortable strolling speed until they reached the lookout station near the savannah. They stopped there, leaned on the railing, and watched giraffes nibbling leaves that had been placed high up in an otherwise barren tree.

"They're so beautiful," she said. "So beautiful and so . . . free."

"They're in a zoo," Henderson pointed out. "That's not exactly freedom in the strictest sense."

"Free from worry," she explained. "They don't have to fear being hunted down in here."

"But *you* do?"

She shuddered and pulled up the collar of her dark blue jacket. "Yes. And you do too."

"Are the same people after both of us?"

She nodded.

"And you know who they are and why?"

Again she nodded, slowly, as if trying to make up her mind whether she wanted to talk to Henderson or not. "Maybe I shouldn't have come."

"How do you expect me to do anything to help if you won't tell me who the bad guys are?"

She turned her guileless blue eyes on him. He really did feel an urge to help her.

"How much do you know?" she asked.

"Not a hell of a lot."

They started along the path again. She took Henderson's arm to steady herself as they went over a plank bridge. He began to recite what he knew to encourage her to fill in the blanks.

"I can only guess at some of the reasons why you were willing to perjure yourself by identifying the body as that of Warren Stevick. I also know that Dan Simco is, or *was* freelance muscle who frequently worked for Frankie Gillis, and that Gillis is not directly linked to organized crime. But I suspect the mob is involved in some way." He turned toward her and stopped. "Are you, that is, are *we* running from the mob?"

"No." Her surprise seemed genuine.

"That's a relief. Those fellows can get nasty."

They started walking again. They were coming up on the penguin exhibit. A half ring of realistic stones riddled with tiny caves stretched out behind clear looking water. Off to their left, two penguins were squabbling, or playing, it was hard to tell which. Another penguin was standing there, unmoving, looking out from his world into ours. Probably bored. But with his life or ours, I could only guess.

"I've always liked penguins." She sounded pathetically like a kid on holiday who knows her days of leisure are numbered. They pressed against the chain-link fence and watched a couple of penguins watching them. Both shows were pretty dull.

"I wish we could see them being fed," she said.

"We could check out the schedule, find out when it happens."

"That's OK."

They stood there for several minutes without speaking. Finally, Henderson said, "Look, I hate to be pushy, but we didn't come here to stare at the animals. At least *I* didn't. You tell me our lives are in danger . . . don't you think I have a right to know why?"

"I . . . oh . . . I just don't know."

"Who are you afraid of? And why did you run away from Simco if he was your 'protector'?"

"He was. That is, that's what I thought he was. You see, I don't understand everything that's going on. All I know is what I've been told."

"So, *who* told you all you know?"

She glanced over her shoulder again, then scanned the penguin habitat as if expecting to find some enemy lurking in one of the tiny caves. "I'm afraid if I tell you anything, well, they could kill me."

"You're acting very much like a person who is afraid someone is out to kill her no matter what you do or don't do."

One of the penguins began waddling around and motioning with its flipper wings as if agitated. "See," Henderson said, "he thinks you should tell me."

She smiled.

"That's better. Now, why don't we walk some more while you tell old Uncle Eric what's troubling you."

"Let's go see the gorillas," she said.

That was okay by me. I was becoming increasingly concerned about a man in a loose jacket who seemed to be rather out of place hanging around in front of the Reptile House. Henderson suspected that the man belonged inside.

"You might begin by telling me your name."

She stumbled on something, and he had to act fast to keep her from falling. "These damn shoes," she muttered. "They aren't very good for this sort of terrain."

"Your name," he repeated.

Smiling shyly she said, "Faith, Faith Devine."

"That your real name?"

She laughed. "No. That was the name I took when I joined a commune where I thought I was going to find myself."

"And did you?"

"I found I wasn't really a 'Eunice,' that I didn't have to be, that is."

"So now you're a 'Faith.'"

"No offense to my great aunt, but it's better than being 'Eunice.'"

"Yes, I agree. Sorry, great aunt Eunice." Henderson reached out and took her hand. She seemed surprised but didn't withdraw it.

"Anyway, that's where it all started, at the commune. You see, we all used drugs. In fact, a couple of the members were into the importation end. When the crackdown came, all of us were caught up in the sting. But I lucked out. At least I wasn't put in prison. I've had to earn my right to freedom though. That's how *he* puts it."

"He?"

"My contact. At the Bureau."

It took Henderson a few seconds to take in what she'd said. "The FBI?"

"Yes."

He wasn't sure he had heard her correctly even then. "The Federal Bureau of Investigation? *The* FBI?"

"Yes."

"Are you saying that you've been working for the FBI?"

"Un huh."

"*They* hired you to pose as Mrs. Stevick?" Was it possible?

"Well, they didn't exactly *hire* me; it was more of a command performance."

"Why?" If she could answer that one, he would consider believing her.

"They didn't tell me. They never really explain why they ask me to do things. I assumed it was to find the murderer. Now I'm not so sure."

Henderson steered her into the viewing area for the gorillas. Even though the animals were behind glass in the alcove, there was a musty barn smell. Maybe it was piped in to add a touch of atmosphere. Only two gorillas were making themselves available for visitors. One was asleep, and the other was watching television. It looked like a rerun of the Survivors.

"Let me see if I have this straight. You were working for the FBI. That means Simco was working for them too. And now you believe Simco was going to eliminate you when your, ah, usefulness ran out."

"It's crazy, isn't it? I mean, the FBI doesn't go around murdering people."

They stood staring at the gorilla watching television. He didn't even glance at them. Was he fascinated by the contestants or the habitat? Maybe he wanted to be a participant. That would add a touch of drama to the competition.

"Are you sure Simco wasn't pulling a double agent act and working for more than one employer?"

"I don't know for sure. But I don't think so."

"Then you really do think the FBI is out to get you." It was a statement. "Maybe you'd better tell me why."

"It was something I heard, something Simco said on the telephone when he thought I was asleep. But I was listening, with a glass, through the wall. It really does work." She looked at him for confirmation. "He mentioned you, and me. He said he would make certain neither of us was ever seen again. 'Just let me know when with the broad,'" she mimicked. Suddenly she stopped talking and began to shake. Henderson took her by the arm and stepped closer. The man with the baggy jacket had come into the area and was staring at the sleeping gorilla.

"That only proves Simco was taking orders from someone, not necessarily from someone at the FBI."

"I guess." She sounded like she wanted to believe him but couldn't.

"After you ran away, they, whoever they are--you think they've been trying to find you?"

"Uh huh. I called my old apartment. A friend is staying there while I'm away. She said there have been people asking questions. I couldn't go back there. I . . . couldn't go anywhere. I got a room in a motel, but last night I thought somebody followed me there, so I sneaked out the back. I didn't know who to turn to."

"You were right to call me." She looked as if she was about to cry. Henderson gripped her arm firmly and said, "Now listen carefully and don't panic. There's a man following us right now."

She let out a tiny squeak, half gasp, half shriek.

"Quiet. Don't speak. Don't turn around. Just act normal. We're going to walk out of here and go to the nocturnal House. I'll take care of him there."

She managed to get herself under control and let Henderson guide her outside and across a small plaza. As they angled toward the Nocturnal House, Henderson sneaked a quick glance back. The man was coming out of the gorilla viewing area, looking in their direction.

Inside the Nocturnal House a ramp led to the second floor where the animals were displayed in a nighttime environment. The theory was that by the time you reached the top of the ramp your eyes have made one of several adjustments needed to see well in the dark. A half hour is required to adjust completely.

Henderson sent Faith on ahead and waited for their friend at the entrance. He sincerely hoped that the tail was the first one to come through the door. Rather than some unsuspecting visitor. If he jumped the wrong person, they would probably think they were being attacked by some crazed creature of the night, a vampire, or the Hound of the Baskervilles. He could always yell "Trick or Treat" and run.

His eyes were slowly getting used to the darkness, but it was still difficult to see more than faint outlines of shapes. When the door finally opened, Henderson was momentarily blinded. The instant the person was inside, Henderson aimed his fist where he thought the man's stomach ought to be and charged forward. Contact! His second blow caught the man on the side of the head. He went down on one knee, but didn't collapse.

Almost simultaneously Henderson felt the man grab him around the knees. As he fell, he landed another blow to the back of the man's head. That seemed to stun him. Before he could recover, Henderson took out his revolver and let him have it with the gun butt, what he probably should have done in the first place instead of worrying about who he was attacking. Better to say sorry and all that. Of course, once you knock someone out, an apology looses its punch.

This time the man was definitely down for the count. Henderson was in the process of disentangling himself when Faith screamed.

They were almost to the exit by the time Henderson caught up with them. He was conscious of dark forms fluttering and scurrying behind the glass walls. Bats dropped from the wire fence covered ceiling and swooped around. Sloths and opossums and snakes, all on the move, drawn to the excitement of the hunt.

"Drop it," the man holding Faith said. Faith wasn't struggling; the man had a gun aimed at her head.

Was this where Henderson was supposed to acquiesce and wait for another chance to take the enemy by surprise? Then why was he backing away with his gun still in his hand?

"Drop it," the man said again, louder.

If he shot Faith, Henderson would take him out. But he wasn't going to let the man shoot both of them without a fight. Henderson retreated further into the darkness until he could barely make out the two shapes under the dim exit sign.

Retreat turned out to have been a mistake. Apparently, the gorilla Henderson had already clobbered had arisen from the dead. Henderson sensed his presence milliseconds before I felt the blow to the back of my head.

CHAPTER 19
A MEETING WITH THE BOSS

"He's *drunk*, can't you see that?" It was clear from the emphasis she gave the word that she considered coming across a drunk in the same category as stumbling upon a village of lepers.

"Now, Milly, what if the man's sick? Suppose he's had a heart attack?" His breathy speech suggested ill-fitting dentures, but his heart was in the right place. He knew leprosy wasn't contagious.

"Drunks don't have heart attacks, Harold. They pass out. Like this one."

"But Milly . . ."

"Don't be difficult, Harold. Let's get out of here."

Their voices faded. I opened my eyes. From only a few inches away large, luminous eyes in a round, alien face stared at me, a creature from Dante's hell. I tried to get away from it, but my arms and legs weren't working properly. All I could do was flop about like a beached seal.

Startled by the movement, the lemur leapt onto a branch and disappeared into the foliage.

My head hurt like hell. Damn it all, that goon had probably given me a concussion. I tried to get up but failed. A tangy, acidic fluid washed up from my stomach and filled my mouth. I swallowed hard, fighting nausea. Why'd he have to hit me so hard? Unless he'd been trying to kill Henderson, in which case he hadn't hit me hard enough.

At least I didn't think I was dead yet; the dead aren't supposed to feel pain.

It took me several minutes before I had the energy to push myself into an upright position. At that point more visitors came in. They didn't' see me sitting there at first. When they did, they seemed to share Milly's philosophy: best let sleeping drunks lie.

I pulled myself up on one of the viewing benches and held my head between my knees until I felt steady enough to walk. I was dizzy, but all my working parts seemed to be functional, albeit not at full capacity.

To my surprise, Henderson's gun was still right there on the floor. Either they hadn't considered him worth worrying about, or they had left in a big hurry. Maybe Milly and Harold had saved my life. I'd have to be sure and say thanks the next time we met.

As a precaution, Henderson went out the "in." On the way down the ramp he passed several people who were bursting to tell him he was going the wrong way. At the door he hesitated. There had been two of them, one to cover each entrance. The instant Henderson stepped outside, he could end up with a bullet through his heart. On the other hand, he didn't want to take up residence in the Nocturnal House. The hours were good, but he had a feeling the food was lousy.

He pulled the door open a few inches and peeked out. There were more visitors coming. He waited until they were just a few feet away then, using them for camouflage, he made an uneven dash for some trees to his right. Nothing happened. Nothing, that is, except that his head threatened to explode. He waited until the sensation passed before searching the area, asking everyone he met if they'd seen a woman and two men pass by. No one had, or else they weren't talking. Henderson got the distinct impression from their reactions that he looked pretty rugged.

He checked at the gate on his way out, but the ticket seller hadn't noticed them either. From there it was only a few minutes' walk to his car, but it seemed longer, much longer. When you're not feeling well, time has a way of expanding, like in a Bergman movie or when you're put on hold.

I was only a few feet short of the sanctuary of Henderson's car when I threw up. My aim was good enough so that I didn't get any on myself, but the squirrel that had been hoping for a handout wasn't too happy.

The only thing in the glove compartment that even slightly resembled medicine was a package of wintergreen lifesavers. I popped one in my mouth, but it didn't help. The sour taste wasn't entirely physical. Faith had taken a chance on Henderson, and he had let her down.

I drove around the park, twice, staying as close to the perimeter as possible. I didn't see them; I hadn't really expected to. But for Faith's sake, and for my own peace of mind, I had to try.

Somehow the guy in the baggy jacket hadn't looked like FBI, but you can't really tell these days. That's what I wanted to believe. He and his partner were FBI and all they wanted was to keep Faith away from Henderson until they'd finished whatever it was they were up to.

But no matter how much I tried to convince myself that Faith was safely in the hands of the FBI, I couldn't quite shake the thought that if Henderson didn't come up with some answers soon, he would never see Faith again. It was all my fault. Fate's whipping boy, that's what I'd become. And I had sucked Faith into the morass with me.

I stopped at a fast-food restaurant frequented by families looking for cheap food and a kid-friendly atmosphere. My goal was to slip into their restroom and clean up without calling attention to myself. Slipping past a mother trying to calm her excitable brood of unruly kiddies, I was pleased to find the restroom empty. Unfortunately, only the cold faucet produced any water, and they were out of paper towels. I was forced to use toilet paper to clean the blood out of my hair. The toilet paper was the thin stuff that fast-food restaurants invariably use. It disintegrated so quickly that I had to use a ton of it to get the job done. I tossed the bloody, soggy mess of TP into the garbage just as a man and his son came in. They eyed me suspiciously and suddenly decided they didn't need to use the restroom, after all.

I washed my hands and splashed some water on my face. Too late I remembered that there were no paper towels. You can't dry your face in a Jet hand dryer. And when I did a final check on my appearance in the mirror, I didn't like what I saw. If I kept getting beaten up, my head was going to be shaped like an underdeveloped potato, all lumps and indentations.

I drove from the family friendly restaurant to an adult friendly coffee shop and ordered a cup of coffee and bummed two aspirin off one of the servers. It was becoming my favorite snack.

Deciding what to do next wasn't easy. Norton and Stevick thought Henderson should proceed toward their joint goal of clearing Norton's name and figuring out who was trying to make life tough for Stevick. But Henderson wanted to concentrate on finding Faith. There was a good possibility she was in imminent danger. It seemed to him that the only right thing to do was to put aside self-interest until he was sure she was safe.

When other people had arguments with themselves, I bet they didn't have names attached to the differing points of view like I did. At times it felt like I had a multiple personality disorder. I was never certain when Henderson's instincts would take over, or if Stevick would involuntarily swoon over a good brandy, or if I really was no longer Warren Stevick but a blend of identities.

Into that mix of thoughts and arguments, I was having a hard time getting a handle on what Faith had told me about working for the FBI. That didn't make sense. The FBI had nothing to fear from Stevick; they had already used him and cast him aside. Even if for some crazy reason the FBI was hoping to somehow use me again and Faith was a part of that scenario, it still didn't make sense. Unless it had something to do with Simco and the fact that he had been working for Gillis. Gillis was my only lead. So, Gillis it was.

Norton, Stevick and I were still screaming protests as Henderson headed for First Avenue. They considered what Henderson was about to do crazy and downright stupid, possibly suicidal. But the more they protested, the more determined Henderson became.

The lower end of First Avenue was lined with shoddy stores that catered to a shoddy clientele. It was also littered with more than its share of down-and-outers and certified drunkards. I always hate walking past all that human misery. It makes me feel guilty for what I have and even more guilty—and nostalgic—for what I used to have.

Henderson could never resist digging into his pockets for a couple of bucks to give a panhandler. Norton and Stevick always protested, arguing that the person would just spend it on liquor, not food. Henderson didn't care. It was their choice. His choice was to give them money in the first place.

"Thanks, buddy. You're a prince," the man with the downtrodden demeanor and Yosemite Sam mustache said as Henderson dropped a fiver in his upturned hat. He was holding a cardboard sign with uneven penmanship that said he was hungry and homeless. Somehow his expression of gratitude for the fiver only made me feel worse.

Inside the arcade, I was barely able to see in the dim light from the bulbs dangling overhead. It was like being back in the Nocturnal House, only here the animals were armed.

There was a row of pinball machines to the right. They looked like they'd seen better days, relics of the past. If the intent was to make the place seem like a legitimate business establishment, the owners needed a better marketing consultant.

"You want to buy some time inside?" a female voice asked. I turned toward an enclosed stall and saw that she was already reaching for a roll of tickets.

"No, I'm looking for someone."

"Can't let you in to look for someone." He couldn't see her clearly, but he guessed her age at about sixty. Handing out tickets for peep shows didn't seem like an appropriate job for someone her age, but who was he to pass judgment?

"I'm not looking for a customer," he explained. "I want to talk to your boss."

Her demeanor went from bored to guarded. "You a cop?" she asked.

"No, I just want to talk to Frankie Gillis. He keeps an office here, doesn't he?"

"Sometimes."

"Sometimes? What does that mean?"

"He's here sometimes, but not now."

"So, where can I find him?"

"How should I know?"

"Doesn't he pay your salary?"

"He owns the place," she reluctantly admitted.

Henderson put both hands on the glass that shielded her from the paying customers and leaned forward until he could see the smudges of mascara under her baggy eyes. "Listen carefully," he said. "I want to get in touch with Frankie, and he isn't going to be very happy with you if you don't cooperate. Do you understand?"

She obviously didn't know what to do. He glared down at her, waiting for her to make up her mind. Finally, he took out his card and slid it through the money slot. "Call him," Henderson said. "Find out if he wants to see me."

"All right. Hold on a minute." She stood up, clutching her bulky sweater around her bulky body as if she was afraid Henderson might try to rip her clothes off. "You stay right where you are. I'll be back." She slipped out of the booth and disappeared into the dark interior.

It seemed like she was gone a long time. While she was away a decrepit man with deep lines in his face above a whiskered chin came up to Henderson and asked where the girls were. Henderson went into the booth and pulled a dozen tickets off the roll and handed them to the man. Then he located the buzzer that released the lock on the door to the back room. The man smiled as he walked through the door to paradise.

When the ticket taker returned, she didn't seem pleased. "Gillis don't want to see you so much," she announced.

"He's just saying that," Henderson quipped. "To know me is to love me."

"He ain't someone to mess with."

"Look, he isn't the godfather. I just want to talk with him for a few minutes. Is it a yes or a no?"

"He says he'll see you." She was eyeing her roll of tickets as if she sensed something wasn't quite right."

"So . . .?"

"How soon do you want to see him?"

"I'm here now, aren't I?"

"He wanted to know how tomorrow afternoon would be."

"You his social secretary? Look, I want to see him right now. Can you make that happen or not?" Way to go, Henderson, you bully. Keep it up and you'll be in the same league as the creep you're trying to contact.

"Be on the corner of First and Pine in a half hour. A couple of men will drive by and pick you up."

"He isn't here?"

"That's what I told you in the first place." She picked up the roll of tickets and looked up at him. "You didn't take any of these, did you?"

"Do I look like the type of guy who gets his jollies peeping through a hole at pictures of naked women?"

"There's more to it than that," she said defensively. "It's not all pictures. But," she added quickly, "there's no physical contact between the clients and the entertainers."

"You're saying that there are women back there who tease men by stripping for them." He wasn't sure why he was arguing with her. He didn't care what went on in the back room.

"They're artists," she said. "They act out sexual fantasies."

"Artists?"

"Entertainment is an art form."

"Would you want your daughter to work here?" I considered that argument my coup de grace, but I was wrong.

She straightened up and puffed out her sagging chest. "My daughter *does* work here."

Fifteen minutes later I was standing on the street corner wondering what in the hell Henderson thought he was doing. Now that he was about to make contact with Gillis, even Henderson was starting to have doubts. Gillis had been pretty definite about warning him off. And Gillis might be a smalltime crook, but as Al had warned, he could be dangerous.

Call Garcia, Norton and Stevick argued. Make up some story about how he'd discovered the woman who had identified Stevick wasn't the real Caron Stevick and let the police worry about finding her.

It sounded like a reasonable thing to do, and it was definitely the safe thing to do. But Henderson wasn't sure the police would follow up fast enough, could *or* would. And if it hadn't been for Henderson,

Faith might not have been kidnapped. In fact, if you wanted to get technical, it was actually all Stevick's fault. He was the one hiding out. If it hadn't been for him, Faith might not have ended up in trouble in the first place. Stevick owed her whether he wanted to face up to it or not.

Somehow, he wasn't surprised to see the little guy with the big head jump out of a dark car and hold open the door for him. It wasn't a subservient gesture, more like a spider inviting its prey into the web. *Will you walk into my parlor?* Stevick and Norton made one last plea for sanity, but Henderson ignored them. He got in on the passenger side in the front seat next to the big guy with the little head.

"You carrying a gun?" the big guy asked.

Henderson saw no sense in denying it. "Yeah."

"We'll stop when we get out of town and relieve you of its burden."

"I'd appreciate that."

"I bet you would."

They didn't talk after that. The big guy concentrated on driving, and the little guy concentrated on the back of Henderson's head. Like he couldn't wait to put a bullet in it. That made Henderson more than a little uneasy, and the rest of us were scared spitless.

"Where are we going?" Henderson asked as they pulled onto the freeway and headed north.

"You'll see when we get there."

When they were about ten miles out, the big guy took an off ramp and drove until they came to a wooded area. As soon as they reached a convenient place to pull off the road, they did. Then Henderson not only had his gun removed but they informed him that he would also have to be blindfolded and tied up.

"Hey," Henderson complained. "I *asked* to see Gillis; this isn't a kidnapping."

"Gillis said to make sure you're clean."

"I let you take my gun."

"Gillis wants to keep his privacy." The big guy motioned for the little guy to proceed. Henderson took a step back.

"You can blindfold me if he's that fussy, but there's no need to tie me up."

"Those are my orders."

Stevick and Norton were screaming, "I told you so." Henderson hesitated. He wasn't sure what to do. "What's with the 'hard to get' routine anyway? I thought Gillis was a businessman."

"Let's just say he values his privacy. Now, do you want to see him or don't you?"

Reluctantly, Henderson submitted. He saw no other way of getting to Gillis. The little guy put the blindfold over his eyes and tied it in place. It was a piece of black cloth and smelled like it had been used to wipe off engine parts. Then he jerked Henderson's hands behind his back and began, none too gently, wrapping a rope around them.

"Did Gillis order you to cripple me, for Christ's sake? You're cutting off my circulation."

"We ought to gag him," the little guy said. Henderson wanted to tell him to stuff it, but then, that was what the little guy wanted to do. Also, he remembered too clearly what it had been like the last time the two had worked him over, and he wasn't exactly in a strong bargaining position.

"Don't bother," Henderson said. "I'll keep quiet."

They shoved him back in the car and took off. He was forced to lie on the floor in the back because they didn't want anyone to see him. That made sense, but it didn't make him any more comfortable. The little guy sat in the back with him, either to make certain he stayed down or to torment him with his sharp-toed shoes.

The trip seemed to go on forever. At first Henderson tried to track which way they were going, but soon his concern for comfort blocked his other senses. Every time he tried to shift to a better position the little guy kicked him.

This time you've done it, Norton and Stevick complained. This time, Henderson, you've really done it.

When the car finally stopped, Henderson's muscles were so cramped he could barely move. That didn't deter his hosts though. They pulled him up and out of the car as if he were a sack of potatoes being delivered to an eager grocer. In the process he banged his head on the door frame and wrenched his left shoulder. It was beginning to look more and more as if this had been a truly stupid move.

"Come on. We don't have all day." They shoved him forward.

Henderson hated walking without being able to see. He had visions of being taken to the edge of a cliff and blithely stepping out into space. Where on earth were they? Why were they on a dirt path? Was Gillis hiding out in the woods somewhere? He could smell evergreens, and there were no street sounds.

They didn't warn Henderson about the steps. When he stumbled and fell to one knee, they jerked him upright and dragged him the rest of the way up the stairs and through a door.

"So, this is the man who's been asking all those questions about me." The voice was unpleasant, high-pitched and piercing.

"Do I have to stay blindfolded and tied up?"

There was a moment of silence. Then Henderson felt someone working on his bonds. At the same time another pair of hands removed the blindfold.

It took him a few seconds to focus. They were in what looked like a living room with a couch, a lounge chair and a couple of end tables. But there was also a long table along one wall with several chairs scattered around it. Gillis was standing across from Henderson. He was short and round, kind of gnome-like, a jolly looking little man.

"Sit down," Gillis ordered, motioning to a chair across from the coach.

Henderson took a seat, glancing around to see what had happened to his two escorts. They were standing near the door, conferring in whispers.

"You can wait outside," Gillis said to them. He sounded more imperious than jolly.

"You sure?"

"If I need you, I'll yell." It was clear he didn't like having his orders questioned. "He isn't armed, is he?"

"No, we took care of that."

"Good."

As soon as they were alone, he sat down in the middle of the couch, raised his eyebrows, and asked, "Well? What do you want that was so important you couldn't wait until tomorrow?"

"Information."

"Information?"

Henderson looked around. The curtains were pulled shut. "Why are you hiding out like this?" he asked.

"That isn't any of your business. At least I assume it isn't." It was part question.

"I doubt it. I was just surprised by all the melodrama. You get in trouble with some of the local scum?"

"I wouldn't be a wise-ass if I were you. Not unless you want to walk home."

"OK. You're right. What you're up to out here isn't any of my concern. All I want is any information you might have on how I can find Faith Devine."

"I'm not in the religion business."

"Funny," I said. "It's a name. Of a woman."

"Nice name."

"Simco was playing watchdog to her when he was killed."

"So, why come to me?"

"I've been told that Simco was working for you."

"Not recently."

"But you must keep a close eye on that sort of freelance stuff. Maybe you can give me an idea about who he might have been working for."

"Maybe."

"Will you?"

"Why should I?"

"I'm willing to pay."

"I don't need your money."

"Look, she may be in danger. All I want is to see that she doesn't get hurt."

"What are you, the patron saint of women?"

"No." Obviously appealing to his better nature wasn't going to work. Henderson decided to be honest, at least in part. "It's my fault she's in trouble. That's all. I feel an obligation to try and help."

"Aa man with a conscience. Quaint."

"Look, Gillis. If it isn't anything you're involved with, then it's a simple business deal. Anything wrong with that?"

"A man has to look out for his friends. And his enemies. Which are you?"

"Neither. I'm just a private dick trying to make the best of a bad situation."

Gillis snorted. "You're a fool," he said. "You'd risk your life for some piece of ass. It doesn't make sense. There are hundreds of thousands of women in the city. What makes you so hung up on this particular one?"

"I don't know hundreds of thousands of women, but I do know this one."

"Fool," Gillis said again. The word hung in the air between them like a bad smell.

"Will you help me?" He had to ask; it was what he had come for.

"I'll think about it."

"When will you let me know?"

"When I'm ready."

Henderson felt deflated. He'd known all along the plan might not work, that in fact it had been unwise to contact Gillis, but he'd also let himself hope.

"Look," Henderson said, making a last-ditch effort to change the man's mind. "Faith doesn't have any connection with what's going on, does she? I mean, the reason you're hiding out."

"I told you that's a private matter. Your troubles are your own problem." He turned toward the door. "Milton!" he shouted. The big guy immediately appeared in the doorway.

He was Milton? It was like The Rock being named Dwayne.

"Mr. Henderson is ready to leave. Will you see him out?"

"This is important," Henderson said, even though he knew it was useless to plead. "She could be in danger."

"We are all in danger, Mr. Henderson." There was a gleam in his eyes. Like he enjoyed danger, as long as someone else was experiencing it.

"I know you're a man who keeps his word." Surprisingly, the lie didn't stick in Henderson's throat. "And I know you don't act out of spite. I'm not asking this for myself; I'm asking for Faith. She doesn't deserve to pay for someone else's mistake."

"I said I'll think about it."

"Thank you." Hating himself for being so meek in front of such an asshole, Henderson let Milton lead him out of the room. In the hall the little guy was waiting with the rope and the blindfold.

"You don't need the rope," Henderson said.

"Tie him up," Milton ordered.

Again, Henderson submitted. There wasn't much choice. That was the problem with life in general. When you got right down to it, there weren't enough choices. Or else there were entirely too many.

CHAPTER 20
FAIR TRADE

He wasn't sure if he was going to survive the trip back to the city; he wasn't sure for two reasons. In the first place, Milton had been called back at the last minute by Gillis for what Henderson assumed to be new instructions. But even if Henderson had misjudged Gillis, he hadn't been wrong about the little guy. The little guy, whose name was apparently Butch—go figure—was a lowdown, cowardly creep.

"Hey, that's my ear you're kicking," Henderson said. He was aware that Butch already knew that, but he felt compelled to complain to prove he wasn't a complete cream puff.

"Is this what you mean?" Something hard and sharp jabbed him in the ear. "Maybe you'd like me to do that again?"

Henderson was reminded of the schoolyard bully Stevick had encountered his first week in one of the many grade schools he'd attended. The bully had made fun of the fact that Stevick brought his lunch in a brown paper bag instead of in a lunchbox with some cool theme like Star Wars or Ghostbusters. Outweighed by almost fifteen pounds and unsure of himself in his new environment, Stevick had run away. That had earned him the nickname of "Rabbit." The next time Stevick's mother proposed moving on, Stevick had been relieved instead of disappointed.

Dammit, Stevick might be a rabbit, but Henderson wasn't. He'd risked his neck trying to find Faith. He didn't deserve to be kicked around by some little pipsqueak who was only brave enough to pick on someone not in a position to fight back.

"You kick me one more time, little man, and when I get loose, you'd better run like hell."

"Oohh my, don't we talk big."

"Gillis didn't say to rough him up," Milton said from the front seat.

That was a relief. Although it would have been even more of a relief if Milton had added that they'd been ordered not to kill him either.

The rest of the trip passed slowly, but there was no more kicking. Whether it was because of my threat or Milton's comment wasn't clear. When they finally stopped and removed the bonds and blindfold, we were in the same wooded area where we had stopped on the way out. It was the ideal location for permanently getting rid of someone. So, when Milton reached into his jacket pocket and pulled out a gun, I wasn't surprised. But Henderson was surprised when Milton held out the gun to him, butt first. It was his own gun, the one they had taken from him on the way to Gillis' hideout.

When Henderson was invited to sit up front for the rest of the trip, it was all he could do not to scream "Halleluiah. And thank you, Lord."

"You want to be dropped off where we picked you up?"

"That's fine. I left my car near there."

"You're lucky, you know."

Henderson thought he *did* know, but he said, "Oh, how's that?"

"Gillis didn't like it none when you were nosing around before. He didn't have to be nice to you this time, you know."

"Like I said before, I'm not involved with anything that has to do with Gillis. Simco was working for someone else when I got interested in his affairs. All I want is to figure out who that someone is."

"I saw him talking to a guy once, not too long ago."

On a hunch, I said, "Tall, dark-haired fellow, baggy jacket, long face?"

"Might have been."

"Know anything about him? Like who he is or who he works for?"

"I might."

"Anything that you're willing to tell me?" Had Gillis decided to help him for free? It wasn't impossible that Gillis wanted Henderson to cause trouble for Simco's most recent employer. Then again, maybe it was Milton's way of making a few extra bucks. Although he doubted Milton would act on his own without Gillis' knowledge and approval.

"What's it worth to you?" Milton asked.

"Depends on what it is."

"What am I offered for a license number?"

Later that day, Henderson found himself waiting on a street corner for the second time. Even though I kept telling myself there was nothing to worry about, I was uneasy. I didn't trust Milton any more than I trusted Gillis. They might be planning on taking Henderson's money and giving him nothing in return. But it seemed a pretty elaborate setup if that was all they were after. And it was entirely possible they may have been keeping tabs on Simco and actually had seen the guy in the baggy jacket meeting with him.

When the car came around the corner, Henderson's hand automatically went to the gun in his pocket. He had checked to make certain it was in working order after they had dropped him off. As far as he could tell, it they hadn't tampered with it. And if they had intended to rough him up or do away with him, surely they would have done it before. Unless Milton and Butch were acting on their own to make a little cash on the side.

The car pulled over and stopped. Butch got out and motioned for Henderson to take his place in the front passenger seat. Just like before. Henderson got in and pulled the door shut.

"Got the money?" Milton asked.

"Got the number?"

Milton nodded.

Henderson took an envelope out of his inside pocket and placed it on the dash. Butch was leaning forward, carefully watching the exchange from the back seat. Neither man asked to see what was inside the envelope. He knew they didn't exactly trust him, but they were probably confident that he wouldn't pull any funny stuff with them. Not before he qualified for Medicare.

Milton took a piece of paper out of his shirt pocket and handed it to Henderson. Henderson left it folded and slipped it into his pocket.

"How can I be sure this license plate number is legitimate?" Henderson knew it was a stupid question.

"You can't."

So, bigmouth, now what do you say? "Well, I can guarantee the money is good." See, I'm holding up my end of the bargain.

"If it isn't, your life won't be worth much. Gillis doesn't like to be crossed."

"He's in on this?"

"Let's just say I don't keep any secrets from him."

"That's smart."

"OK, sport, end of the line."

My heart missed a few beats; then I realized they were waiting for Henderson to get out of the car.

"I appreciate this," Henderson said as he opened the door.

"It's not a favor."

"I still appreciate it." They drove off the instant he was out of the car, Butch still in the back seat. Like Mutt and Jeff or Jeff and Mutt. I didn't know which had been the tall one and which the shorter of the two in the comic strip. In fact, I didn't understand why the thought had even crossed my mind. I'd never read the strip, and if I hadn't, then none of my selves had.

It wasn't until they were out of sight that I took the piece of paper Milton had given me out of my pocket and looked at it. If it had said, "Ha, ha, you've been had," I wouldn't have been surprised. But it didn't. There was a license number and a description of the car written in a barely legible hand. If they could be believed, Henderson was looking for a burgundy Lincoln Town Car with an out-of-state license. Damn. How was he going to trace and out-of-state car?

The options seemed to be narrowing and were, at the same time, becoming more undesirable. To get somewhere on this matter in a hurry, Henderson would need professional help. That meant he had to go to Castaldo. And Al would have questions. Uncomfortable questions. Questions Norton and Stevick might not want to answer. But this was getting too complicated for Henderson to cope with on his own. And Faith's life might be hanging in the balance.

Al answered the telephone himself. He wasn't too happy about being disturbed at home. "We're just sitting down to dinner," he said. When Henderson asked to meet him later, Castaldo complained that it would be awkward. Henderson assured him it was important, a life and death matter, and Al finally agreed to come to a tavern a short distance from his home in an hour.

On the way there I stopped for something to eat at a café named Liz's. Unfortunately, Liz wasn't a very good cook. The food was bland. Not even a liberal sprinkling of salt and pepper could give it life. The bottom line was that Liz's "special" wasn't all that special. At least not in a positive way. Even Henderson hated it. But he cleaned his plate. He was hungry and didn't know when he'd get another chance to eat.

Dinner might have left something to be desired, but at least I had a lead. Then again, what if baggy jacket really was FBI? And what if Faith was wrong about their intentions? Maybe at this very moment instead of her life being in jeopardy she was being safeguarded by men with short haircuts and neutral-colored clothes. Maybe Henderson was going to all this trouble for nothing. But if that was the case, what was the FBI up to? Were they using Stevick as bait for something? And why would Simco be working for them as a freelance hired gun when they specialized in that sort of thing themselves?

No matter what I came up with, the pieces didn't fit together.

Henderson arrived at the tavern a few minutes early. He went in and sat at the bar and ordered a beer. Stevick had occasionally drunk some expensive imported beer when the occasion called for it, but he had never been a real beer drinker. Henderson was fast becoming one, but he didn't like it. No, that was wrong, Henderson *did* like beer. At least he pretended to. It amounted to the same thing.

When Castaldo showed up, they moved to a table away from the other customers. Al sipped his beer with relish, smacking his lips with exaggerated gusto. "Damn fine," he said.

"You drink like a thirsty man," Henderson observed.

"It's the wife. She says beer isn't good for me."

"So, you're not supposed to be drinking beer."

"Don't worry, I have a package of breath mints in my pocket."

"And you're not supposed to be here in this bar either, I suppose."

"Smart man."

"Where'd you tell her you were going?"

"The office."

"What if she calls there?"

"I'm not there yet."

"And if she calls back?"

"I'd already left."

"Doesn't sound like the basis for a trusting relationship."

Al sighed. "We've been married for almost twenty-five years. All but the last few have been great. But now, all of a sudden, she's concerned about my health. She's driving me crazy trying to keep me healthy."

"She loves you." He said it with a feeling of regret, not regret that Al had a wife who loved him, but regret for his own solitary state.

"You should get a woman, Eric. They're not all bad."

"Yeah, I'll shop around for one first chance I get."

Al picked up his beer and drank half of it down.

"Actually, Al, that's the reason I'm here. I'm looking for a woman."

"This joint isn't the best place to find one."

"I'm looking for a particular woman."

"Then I can guarantee you won't find her here."

"Very funny."

"You should see me after *two* beers."

"OK." Henderson took the hint and went over to the counter and picked up another two beers, even though he hadn't finished his first one.

"So, who are you looking for?" Al asked before taking a drink.

"A woman named Faith Devine. Ever hear of her?"

"She a stripper?"

"No."

"Then no, I haven't."

Henderson took out a copy of the license number Milton had given him. "She may have been, ah, kidnapped. But I'm not sure. At any rate, she went off in this car." He handed Al the piece of paper.

"Involuntarily?"

"I think so." He didn't know whether Gillis was being honest with him about the Lincoln Town Car. It could even be some kind of trick or joke. But he had to follow up.

Al became very serious. "This is a job for the police, Eric."

"I don't think so, Al."

"Care to tell me why not?"

"Because I think they would kill her rather than turn her over to the police."

"You can't take on a 'they' single-handed."

"All I need is a little help. Once I track her down and assess the situation, then I'll know whether I need to call in the gendarmes."

"Eric . . ." Al rolled the beer glass back and forth between his hands and watched the foam bounce around.

"Al, spare me one of your police officer lectures. I know you're a straight arrow. And I know I have no right to always come to you with my problems. I wouldn't be asking you to do this for me, but it's a question of time. If she *is* in trouble, then she's going to need help fast. The police can't go barging in somewhere without probable cause. But I can. I'm not asking you to approve of my methods, but I'm asking you to help me, for her sake."

"She your client?"

"No."

"She the daughter or wife of a client?"

"Sort of."

"That's all you can give me?"

"I've already told you too much. Look, Al, I can promise you I won't rush in if I think it will put her in danger. And if she's being held against her will and there's no easy way to get her out, I'll call in the police. Honest. But at this point, based on the information I have, I don't think the police would take any action. You know how that goes."

Al frowned. One of his gripes with the system was how the police were often prevented from moving in on a potentially explosive or unstable situation until they could get sufficient evidence for a warrant. By then, far too often the damage was done.

"All right, Eric. I don't know why, but I'll do it."

"Great. Thanks . . . oh, just one more thing."

"Oh, oh. Why do I feel like this is going to be a whopper?"

"No, nothing like that. It's just, well, after you get the name of the owner, do you think it would be possible to see if he, ah, works for the government?"

"You're not interfering with a government agency, are you?"

"I hope not. That's what I want you to find out. So I don't step in it, big time."

"Someday, Eric . . . someday." Al took a long drink.

"You'll still do it?"

"I said I would."

"Great."

"You're repeating yourself."

"OK, 'good' then."

"I suppose you want all this done yesterday."

"That's right."

"See? I told my wife the truth. I *am* going to the office. The only thing I have to lie about is the *three* beers."

"You'll make it quick?"

"I'll make it quick." Henderson waited while Al finished off his second beer. Afterwards Al went downtown and Henderson went back to his office to wait for Al's call.

CHAPTER 21

ILLEGAL LANE CHANGE

I t was 6:00 a.m. when Al finally called. I'd had a fitful night trying to get comfortable slouched down in Henderson's office chair with my feet on the desk. Every time I'd dozed off something had happened. My feet slipped off their perch. I got a cramp in my calf and had to hop around until it went away. Then there were the building noises. Distinct but unidentifiable. Twice I'd gone out in the hall to listen, but I'd never discovered the source. All in all, it was a terrible night.

"You're still there," Al observed.

"I told you I would be."

"You could have gone home. You *do* have a home, don't you?"

"More or less. But I wanted to be ready to act when the information came through."

"This woman must be important to you."

"I don't want to go all soft on you, but she is pretty special."

"Well, I hope what I got helps."

"I do too."

Al read what he had, and Henderson copied down the information. "That's K-r-a-u-s-e?"

"Yeah, Langdon Krause," Castaldo repeated. "He's the car's registered owner. From Nevada. The address is an apartment in Las Vegas. And the car hasn't been reported missing or stolen or anything."

"Langdon Krause?"

"Yeah, almost as bad as Alphonso Castaldo, isn't it? Maybe *he* had a rich uncle too."

"Not Uncle Sam by any chance?"

"Huh?"

"I mean, did you find out whether Krause is a government employee?"

"Oh, that. No, as far as I can tell he isn't."

"What does that mean?"

"That means he doesn't appear on any records I have access to. Nor does he have a criminal record. At least not under the name of Krause."

"But he still might be working for the government?"

"I doubt it, but you'll have to take it from here."

Al sounded cranky and tired. Chances were he, too, had missed out on his normal sleep. Henderson felt guilty, but then, he hadn't asked for the favor for himself.

"This really helps, Al. You went to a lot of trouble on this . . . I owe you one."

"Sure. I'll put it on your account. And by the way, there's one more thing."

"Oh?"

"He got a ticket yesterday. Illegal lane change."

"Yesterday?" Henderson could feel his heart pumping.

"Thought you might like that. It was right here in town. Sometimes you're a lucky sonofabitch."

Not a particularly lucky SOB, but maybe this time Henderson had been dealt a break. For once. *It's got to happen, happen sometime. Maybe this time I'll win—*

Henderson was really irritated when he found out the police officer who had given Krause his ticket the day before wouldn't come on duty until 8:00 a.m. He was tempted to try and get the officer's home telephone, but that would have taken some doing. Instead, he turned to another task, trying to find out where Krause was staying in the city.

Starting at the top of the alphabet, Henderson slowly worked his way through the list of hotels and motels within the city limits, calling the ones he considered most likely, then going back and starting on the second-tier possibilities. Nothing too ritzy, nothing too cheap. Middle priced, easy access. He'd given it an hour. But no one named Langdon Krause was registered at any of the places he'd called. And no one he talked to remembered a burgundy Lincoln Town Car with Nevada plates.

Henderson arrived at the station at 7:30 and hung around the entrance to the coffee room. The officer at the desk told him that Officer Richards always stopped for a cup of coffee before checking in. He was medium height and weight with brown hair and no distinguishing features. He would, however, be wearing a name badge.

It seemed to Henderson that all of the officers stopping by for coffee were nondescript, and their name badges were not intended to be read from a distance. Twice he'd resorted to asking, "Officer Richards?" when he couldn't make out the name.

Richards showed up at 7:50. Henderson stepped up close, checked his badge and introduced himself.

"Look, I haven't had my coffee yet," Richards complained.

"Could I come in with you and explain what I need?"

"Sure, why not?" Richards was more apathetic than agreeable.

They went inside. It was a large room with several coffee makers on a counter at one end and a cluster of tables in the middle. Newspapers had been left behind on a couple of the tables, the sports pages prominent. Several officers were there drinking beverages. They nodded at Richards and checked out Henderson as they passed by.

"I know you don't have much time," Henderson said. "And I wouldn't normally bother you like this, but it's important."

"It always is."

Richards seemed too young to be so listless and cynical. Henderson wondered if perhaps he kept late hours.

"A woman's life may be in danger."

Richards still didn't seem interested. He poured himself a cup of coffee and motioned to a nearby table.

"We suspect she was abducted," Henderson said as he took a chair. This time he got Richards' attention.

"You police?"

"Private"

"Private, huh? You don't look it."

Henderson was curious about the remark, but the minutes were ticking away.

"You ticketed a burgundy Lincoln Town Car registered to a Langdon Krause yesterday for an unsafe lane change." Henderson pulled out a map. "Here," he said, pointing to where the ticket had been issued in case the officer needed a memory prompt. He didn't.

"Him!"

Henderson had scored. Krause had done something memorable.

"What an idiot. He was clearly in violation of code, but he had the nerve to argue with me. Cheeky bastard."

"Was he alone?"

"Yeah."

"Is there anything you can tell me about him? Anything stand out in your mind?"

"Not a sharp dresser." Henderson already knew that.

"You didn't happen to ask where he was going or where he was coming from, anything like that?" It seemed unlikely; he didn't know why he bothered to ask.

"No, but it was obvious where he was headed."

"Oh?"

"Yeah, people getting off the bridge don't realize they have to make an immediate right to get to the waterfront. They get in the left-hand lane to pass the slow traffic then end up cutting across at the last minute to make the exit. A lot of accidents happen there." And a lot of officers make their ticket quotas there, Henderson guessed.

"So, you think he was trying to get down here." Henderson pointed to the waterfront area to the left of the bridge.

"Seems obvious to me." Richards tossed back what remained of his coffee and stood up. "I hate to eat and run, but I need to get to work."

"You've been very helpful."

"That's good." He left without saying "Goodbye" or So long," It was 8:00 on the nose.

I drove directly to the bridge where the Lincoln Town Car had made the illegal lane change, being careful to stay in the right-hand lane, even though the temptation was to pull out and pass the SUV that had slowed down to drive over a speed bump. There was a police car under the bridge, waiting for its next victim no doubt. Well, it wouldn't be me. I legally got off at the exit Richards had pointed out and immediately found myself in an industrial area. The street followed the waterfront past businesses, warehouses, and docks crammed with boats. I drove the full length of the street until it intersected the main road, then made my way back for a second look.

Surely Krause wouldn't have taken that exit unless he was headed for some destination along this street. It wasn't on the way to somewhere that couldn't be reached by an easier route. And if he hadn't had this location in mind, why would he suddenly have made an illegal lane change? Henderson was sure he was onto something. That meant I needed to make a thorough search for the car to see if my luck was holding or if Lady Luck had moved on to someone with less complicated issues.

The buildings in the area weren't like normal office buildings, all in a row with parking to one side or the other. These businesses had apparently sprung up before city planners got involved. Sometimes there were parking spaces in front, other times cars were parked off to the side or around back. Some of the buildings bordered the street, leaving no place to pass by on foot without taking your life in your hands. Most were only a couple stories tall. A few looked like repairs should have been done decades ago.

I wasn't too hopeful about finding the burgundy Lincoln Town Car. It was a longshot; I was a day late, and it was a large area where a car could easily be parked out of sight. But it was my only lead.

When I spotted what looked like a burgundy Lincoln Town Car in the distance, I wanted to believe it was the one I was looking for, but nothing is ever that easy, so I was prepared to be disappointed. Then, as I got close enough to read the license plate, a southern phrase one of Stevick's lawyer colleagues used to say when something worked out better than expected came to mind: *Well, butter my butt and call me a biscuit.* At the time, I'd found the hokey cliché irritating, but it was right on in this instance. Through some miracle, I was looking at Langdon Krause's car. Henderson, you lucky SOB.

The car was parked in a medium-sized lot between a boat moorage and a marine supply store. Just past the lot there was a narrow space next to a small grocery that didn't exactly look like legal parking, but there was no sign saying it was private either. From there I could keep an eye on the Lincoln without being right out in the open. I could also pull out in a hurry if the need arose. I put on a baseball cap I leave in the car for daytime surveillance and settled in.

After only about twenty minutes I started doubting the feasibility of sitting there in my car waiting for Krause to appear. Maybe he'd dropped off his Lincoln yesterday and took off in a boat for who knows where or how long. Or, maybe he *was* somewhere in the vicinity, but that didn't mean he would be coming out to his car any time soon. He could be holed up in one of the buildings, intending to stay out of sight for a day or two, or even a week or two. The possibilities were endless. And luck always runs out eventually; I needed to show some initiative.

My first stop was the marine store. It didn't take long to figure out that Krause wasn't there. But, on the off chance the young woman at the counter had seen him or talked to him, I asked her if she knew the owner of the burgundy Lincoln Town Car in the parking lot. To avoid having her wonder why I was asking, I explained that I had parked too close to the car and had dinged his door when I got out and wanted to make amends. I was hoping she'd find the Good Samaritan act appealing and be cooperative. Unfortunately, she didn't have any idea who the Lincoln belonged to. But she thought it was nice of me to try to find the owner.

The next stop was the moorage office of the small marina that shared the parking area with the marine store. The office was a single room at the back of an old wood building that appeared to be mostly warehouse space. The woman behind the counter looked to be almost as old as the building, evoking visions of peeling paint and years of misuse. Henderson wondered if they had built the office around her.

"There is no moorage space rented to anyone named Langdon Krause at this marina," she assured me. She didn't look or sound like someone who could be encouraged by a twenty-dollar bill slipped across the counter, so I tried a ruse instead, one I hoped would appeal to her customer service instincts.

"I'm supposed to meet him and a couple of other guys here, and I can't remember the name of the boat."

"As I said . . ." she enunciated the words slowly so I would under-stand. ". . . there are no slips leased to Langdon Krause."

"Maybe he's subletting."

"We do NOT allow sublets.".

"I see." She had me stymied. Henderson should have come up with a better cover story before approaching her. But I could hardly just walk away. "Perhaps you can tell me if you've seen the owner of that burgundy Lincoln Town Car in the parking lot. I think it belongs to one of my buddies." He pointed at the Lincoln, but she didn't bother to look out the window.

"I don't pry into the lives of our tenants or their visitors."

Still refusing to give up on his only good lead, Henderson said: "He's rather tall, dark hair, longish face."

With no hesitation, she replied: "That doesn't sound familiar."

How could it not "sound familiar"? It probably described a quarter of the male population. He felt as though he could accurately describe her own mother and she would say the same thing. Feeling desperate he said, "Look, I wouldn't trouble you if this wasn't important." He took out a card and held it out across the counter for her to take.

"You can leave it there." She nodded toward the counter.

"Look, a woman is missing, and I have reason to believe she may be on one of the boats at this marina. Probably being held against her will by the man with the Lincoln Town Car. If I go wandering around the docks, they see me and make a run for it."

"I thought you said you had a friend at the marina."

"That's my cover story. I didn't want to upset you with the true situation."

She seemed to soften a little, but not much. She did, however, reach out and pick up his card. Then she shook her head. "I'm afraid I can't help you. Sorry."

Being "sorry" was an improvement, but not very helpful. "Can you suggest any tenants who might be around that I could talk to? Maybe they've seen something suspicious."

"Well . . ." She seemed to be considering the possibility of actually parting with some useful information.

"You might be helping to save a life."

Either the thought of saving a life made a difference or she was getting tired of having Henderson hanging around. In any event, she gave him the names of several boats with liveaboards. There were apparently about a dozen at the marina—boat owners, crew, even the occasional boat sitter. People were supposed to report in at the office and pay a fee if they planned on staying aboard for any length of time, but she admitted they didn't always do so.

Living aboard a boat, that was something Henderson hadn't considered before. Very portable. Maybe in his next life.

CHAPTER 22
THE MARINA

The docks were made of thick wood planks, uneven and rutted by years of heavy use. The pilings on either side were battered and dark with streaks of environmentally unfriendly creosote. Henderson passed a sign that warned against leaving gear or garbage unattended and wondered if the person who had made the sign had seen the humor in it.

It had rained earlier that morning, leaving the dock slippery in places. The "unattended gear and garbage" littering the narrow dock was interspersed with smatterings of goose poop imprinted with tread from tennis shoes. Nice.

The woman in the moorage office had given him the names of three liveaboard boats. Until he'd talked with her, he hadn't even heard the term "liveaboard." The *Ocean Star* was first on his list, for no other reason than its proximity to the parking lot. She'd said it was a commercial boat, and one or more of the owners was there doing some work on it.

The *Ocean Star* turned out to be a big boat, perhaps a hundred feet. Equipment, floats, and crab pots were crowded against the far railing on its large foredeck, leaving the rest of the deck accessible for repairs. Overall, the boat appeared to be old but well cared for. He wondered how much time the boat had spent at sea and how much bad weather it had seen. Stevick had been out on cruisers for social events or when on vacation, but he'd never been on a working boat.

Henderson didn't see anyone around. He took one last glance back at the Lincoln before climbing aboard. He wasn't sure if he was supposed to knock or not, and if so, where. Maybe he was supposed to yell, "Ahoy, matey."

There was a door at the back of the main cabin. As he approached, he could smell coffee. Someone was definitely there. He decided to knock on the door, a gentle "rap, rap, rap."

The young man who answered couldn't have been more than twenty-five. He was dressed in an old pair of jeans and an even older shirt with a collage of patches on the arms. His hair was longish, and he sported a scruffy beard. He could have been a poster child for a Haight-Ashbury hippie from the sixties, except for his erect posture and alert eyes.

"What can I do for you?" he asked.

"I'm looking for someone. I was hoping you could tell me if he's on one of these boats out here. His name is Langdon Krause. He owns the burgundy Lincoln Town Car in the parking lot." I watched carefully for a reaction to either the name or the car, but didn't see one. Even though unlikely, I knew there was a possibility that *this* was the boat I was looking for. That Krause might be hiding somewhere, maybe with Faith locked away below. That was why I'd kept my right hand in my pocket on Henderson's gun.

"Sorry. Don't know anyone by that name. Come on in though. Jay may know." He turned and yelled up a stairway. "Jay! Come on down. There's a guy here who wants to ask you something."

Henderson moved inside, casually surveying the cramped interior, leaving his hand in his pocket, keeping the gun at ready. There was a diesel stove and a small sink to his left, a settee and table to his right. Inside, the aroma of perked coffee seemed to be everywhere. He took a deep breath.

"Want some coffee?" There was a steaming cup already on the table next to a newspaper.

"Smells great."

"We make it the old-fashioned way, in a percolator, so you can see the color in the glass bubble and know when it's just right."

Jay appeared just as the coffee was being poured into a white mug with a tiny chip on the lip. He was a duplicate of the first guy, only his beard was well-trimmed. He grabbed himself a cup of coffee and sat down across from Henderson. Neither man had asked for his name, so Henderson took out a card, introduced himself and explained who he was looking for.

"Yeah, I've seen him," Jay said. "If it's who I'm thinking of, he's on a boat on the end dock. Doesn't dress like a fisherman. Looks like he's out of his element. Can't explain what I mean by that exactly, but he just acts, oh, strange somehow."

"Do you have any idea which boat he might be on?"

The two men discussed which was the most likely boat while Henderson drank his coffee. It was good, really good. Maybe the taste experience was enhanced by being in a small space totally immersed in the rich aroma. Like making coffee over a campfire in the early morning when your senses were primed to take in the singularity of nature's freshness instead of exhaust fumes mingled with the myriad of city smells.

All of a sudden, he was remembering a camping trip he and Caron had taken one summer with the kids when they were about seven and eight. Caron had been miserable; she'd hated everything about camping. But Tammy and Warren Jr. had loved every minute. Stevick's hadn't been enamored with the experience, but he did have positive memories of the trip. Food tasted better, the air seemed cleaner, and he had reveled in time spent with his kids. Unfortunately, that had been the one and only time they'd gone camping as a family.

"It has to be either the *Falcon* or the *Zenith*," Jay was saying. "I think I saw smoke coming out of the stack on one of those two."

"Are there any other, ah, liveaboards on that dock?"

"I think there's someone staying on the *Eagle II*. Most of the others over there are company boats."

"You haven't by any chance seen a young woman around the docks, have you? Sandy hair, blue eyes, good legs."

"Wish I had," Jay said. Both men grinned.

"I take it that's a 'no.'"

They nodded in unison.

"If you do . . ." Henderson tapped his card that was on the table in front of Jay. "Give me a shout."

"It must be interesting being a private investigator," Jay said.

"I was thinking the same about what you do for a living."

They offered him a second cup of coffee which he reluctantly declined. It was time to get moving.

When he stepped off onto the dock, he checked to make sure the Lincoln was still there. It was. He was getting closer, too close in some ways. Why hadn't Henderson had the sense to wear a real disguise? More than a baseball cap. The more I thought about it, the more nervous I felt. There wasn't time to make a complete change of appearance, but the least he could do was to wear something that fit in a little better. He hurried over to the marine store and bought a green rain jacket and a wool hat. They both screamed "brand new," but it helped make him *feel* like be belonged. That, as Henderson well knew, was more than half the battle.

Emboldened by his new "look," Henderson wandered over to the dock where the two fishermen thought Krause might be staying. It was lined on both sides with boats, two and three deep. The *Falcon* was next to the dock about half way out; the *Zenith* was tied outside another boat on the end. There was no one around that he could see.

Before he could make a move, he needed to be certain which boat Krause was on and how many men he had with him. For all he knew there might be an entire gang aboard. He couldn't go barging in waving a gun and demanding Faith's release. He didn't even know for sure if she was with Krause. He just hoped like hell she was.

The thought crossed my mind that this might be the point at which Henderson should bring in the police. But what would he tell them? What could he actually prove? Al would probably follow his reasoning and accept his conclusions, but so what? They couldn't get a search warrant on trust. And if they sent an officer or two to knock on the door and ask to talk to Krause, that would just alert him to the fact that they suspected something was going on. He would obviously lie and then pull up stakes and hightail it to a new location.

And maybe get rid of Faith to cover his trail, if he hadn't already done so.

Dammit. Henderson was on his own. At least until he had a little more information. Stevick and Norton were lousy backup, but they would sink or swim with him. So, what was new?

He sauntered back down the dock and moved his car into a better position from which to view the end of the dock. There was still no activity. He felt almost like he'd been dropped onto the set of a "day after the end of the world" movie. Day one, the attack. Day two, all the people are gone or dead. At least there weren't any bodies littering the dock.

While he was waiting, he checked his burner to see if there was a message from his mysterious caller. Since he hadn't been able to take the call at the scheduled time the day before, he'd texted the number asking for another day. There was a return text: "Will call same time Friday. You better be there." Hopefully he wouldn't be tied up then, figuratively, or literally.

By mid-afternoon he was beginning to wonder if *anything* was *ever* going to happen. Then he saw a man coming down the dock in the direction of the parking lot. It wasn't Krause, and he was fairly certain it wasn't the other guy who had been with Krause at the zoo. In fact, the closer he got, the more certain Henderson was sure he was another fisherman.

He got out of his car and moved toward the man. "Say," he called. "I wonder if you can tell me which boat a friend of mine is on. He owns that Lincoln Town Car over there."

The man was in his late thirties, clean-shaven, with a full head of curly brown hair. He was wearing striped overalls covered with grease spots. There was also a grease smudge on the side of his face.

"Yeah, I know that turkey. He's a friend of yours you say?"

"Well, I'm looking for him."

"You with the IRS or something?" He sounded hopeful. Obviously, Krause had made a real positive impression.

"No, nothing like that, I'm afraid." Henderson considered making up something, but most people were willing to talk to a private investigator if they felt he was working on a good cause. Usually, the less said the better though. He took out a card and gave it to the man. "I'm looking for a young woman. Sandy hair, blue eyes, good looking."

The man shook his head.

"She may be with Krause, but I'm not sure."

"Why not go out and ask?"

"He may be holding her against her will."

"It's like that, huh?"

"Yeah."

"Somehow that doesn't surprise me."

"I take it you aren't fond of Krause."

"You've got that right. I'm on the *Eagle II* out there, the boat on the inside of the dock. And I'm working on a few things, see. Since he and his friend have been hanging around, I've had nothing but grief. They track through whatever I'm doing. They don't care what kind of mess they make. And then they had the gall to complain because they got dog crap on their shoes. They should look where they're stepping. They don't have to give my dog a bad time. That SOB even tried to kick Clyde once. What kind of a person kicks a dog that's trying to be friendly?"

"Not exactly good neighbors," Henderson summed up.

"Damned unpleasant neighbors." He suddenly looked sheepish. "Sorry, I shouldn't have run off at the mouth like that. But they act like they're big time and I'm a nobody." He smiled. "The name is Hal by the way."

They shook hands. Some of the grease on Hal's hands came off on Henderson's and he had to resist the urge to wipe it off right away.

"Do they own the *Zenith*?"

"I don't think so. The owner has been trying to sell the boat for some time now. But I don't think . . ." A gleam came into his eyes. "You don't suppose they're squatters?"

"Don't get your hopes up. I don't think they'd invite trouble with the law just now."

"Too bad."

"Look, you keep referring to 'them.' Is that 'them' as in two men or more?"

"I've only seen the two."

"And you haven't seen a woman."

"No, sorry."

Henderson was sorry too, although they would hardly make it known that they were keeping Faith there if it was against her will. "Can you tell me a little about what the inside of a boat like the *Zenith* is like?" He didn't say why he wanted to know, but he felt certain Hal could make a guess. He wished it wasn't so risky or he would have asked the man to help as a decoy. But he couldn't take a chance on involving anyone else.

"Want to look around my boat? They're similar."

"Am I keeping you from something?" he asked to be polite.

"I was just going to pick up a part I need, but it can wait."

"Let me grab my jacket," Henderson said. He went back for his new jacket and hat. It was clear from the look on Hal's face that he didn't need to tell him why he was wearing them. And being with Hal made it even less likely they would pay any attention to him.

"They haven't been out today," Hal offered as they made their way back down the dock. "At least I haven't seen them go anywhere. I'm pretty sure they are both on board."

"I'd rather they didn't see me," Henderson acknowledged.

"No problem. Unless they come on deck, they can't really see much from their boat. Just stay on my left and keep your face turned away."

The guy had possibilities. If only the bad guys weren't quite so bad.

"Look out for that cable," Hal warned as they came up to the *Eagle II*. "I've been greasing it. Makes quite a mess, but it preserves the cable."

Henderson gingerly stepped around the cable and climbed aboard in the same place Hal had. The door to the cabin was on the dock side of the boat. They went straight in without pausing to look around. Once inside, Henderson noted how different the layout was from the vessel he had been on earlier. But it had that same sense of cozy confinement.

There was a corridor that went to the forward part of the cabin. On the left was a large dining area with a pass-through counter that led to the galley. The galley looked very similar to one that might be found in a mobile home, although the stove was probably diesel and everything looked well used, not like something cranked up for a once-a-year trip.

There was a washer-dryer on the right, next to a stairway that led down into the engine room. Hal took him down below so Henderson could see what was there. It was a maze of unfamiliar machinery and equipment to him. He couldn't imagine understanding how to operate everything.

The rest of the lower cabin area was devoted to bunks and storage for living. There were three separate staterooms, with a head and shower at the far end. Henderson was amazed at how much was compacted into such a small space.

Up above was the pilot house and navigation station. As they went up the narrow stairs, their footsteps seemed to reverberate throughout the boat. In the pilot house there were a number of complicated looking instruments, some that Henderson couldn't even identify as to function. There was also a large chart table, another narrow bunk, and two very comfortable looking pilot seats.

"Look out that window and you can get an idea of how the *Zenith* compares."

Henderson obeyed, keeping to one side in case anyone on the *Zenith* was watching. He could see that the two boats were indeed similar. That probably meant Faith was being kept in one of the staterooms. *If* she was there.

"I suppose the only way in is through the main door," Henderson said.

"You can usually get in through the pilot house by climbing up an outside ladder. See, there it is on the *Zenith*." Hal pointed and Henderson's eyes found the ladder. "And there's usually a forward hatch. Yeah, there it is." He pointed again. "But if you try to get in that way, I think you might be too visible."

Henderson smiled. "That obvious, huh?"

"Uh huh. But I'm not blabbing. It's your business."

Henderson stood there looking at the *Zenith*. It was going to be one hell of a trick getting in without getting caught. He would prefer to try it when there was only one of the two men aboard. He would also prefer to try it in the dark. Of course, that had its advantages and disadvantages. If only it wasn't so damnably quiet out there.

"Want to earn a few bucks?" Henderson asked Hal.

"Doing what?"

"I'm going to hang around here today in the hope that they come out, but if they don't, I'll still have to take a look inside. And, as you've pointed out, it won't be easy."

"You want me to hold the flashlight while you pick the lock?"

"Nothing quite so glamorous. No, I was wondering if you could start your engine when I went aboard. A little sound cover would be a big help."

Hal looked almost disappointed.

"And, if something happens. I mean, if anything goes wrong . . ." He wasn't quite certain how much to say and how to phrase it. "I wouldn't want you to try to come to my rescue. Everything should be OK, but if it isn't, there's a police officer you can call." He wrote out Al's name and number on the back of one of his cards.

"A cop? You want me to call a cop?"

"You seem surprised."

"Well, it doesn't sound like what you're doing is exactly what I'd call legal."

"No, not exactly. All I want to do is find this woman and make certain everything is all right. If it is, no problem. If it isn't, and I suspect it isn't, I'm hoping to get her out of there. That could prove tricky. I might need police backup." He didn't want to say he might be shot and wanted to make sure someone, Al, knew what had happened.

"All right. I need to run the engine anyway. If it's noise cover you want, you've got it."

CHAPTER 23
THE BLUFF

We had everything planned. If one of the two men left to go somewhere, Henderson was going to move in right away. If not, Plan B was for Hal to start his engine at 9:00 p.m. There was no Plan C, but Norton, Stevick and I thought there should be.

It had been a long day. Hal agreed to go and get us something to eat. While he was gone, Henderson continued his vigil from his car. It seemed strange that Krause and his partner were staying cooped up in the boat for so long. Unless they were under orders to stay out of sight and out of trouble. If so, for how long? And by whose orders?

While Henderson was sitting there waiting, I thought of all the things he could be doing. For one thing, he could be researching the ownership of the *Zenith*. Maybe the owner was involved. He could be finding out more about Langdon Krause. Or, he could be trying to track down the gym locker owner. It would be nice to know who he was before the next time they talked. He definitely needed to get on that soon. The minute he knew Faith was safe.

My head jerked, and I realized that I had dozed off. Damn. Henderson couldn't afford to do something stupid like that. A look at his watch told him it hadn't been long. Hal should be back any minute with the food. He could use something to eat. That should perk him up.

It was at that point he noticed something that sent the blood rushing through his veins: the Lincoln Town Car was gone! Maybe it was the sound of the Lincoln's motor starting that had awakened him. Damn, damn, damn. If he had bungled it, he would never forgive himself.

There was no time to wait for Hal. He had to act now. Hopefully it wasn't already too late.

He hurried down the dock. It was starting to get dark but visibility was still good. Maybe too good. With no sound cover and in the light, he would scarcely be able to sneak up on anybody. But he was going to give it a shot anyway.

Hal's dog came bounding over to him as he climbed aboard, barking and jumping up and down on him. "Sit, ah, Clyde," he ordered softly, but Clyde wanted attention, not orders. For just a moment Henderson felt sympathy for Krause or whoever had kicked the damn dog. Why couldn't he calm down?

The door was unlocked on the *Eagle II*. He grabbed the dog by the collar, shoved him inside and closed the door. Then he stood very still and listened. Except for Clyde's whining from inside the *Eagle II* everything was quiet.

Rather than charging right over to the other boat, Henderson got hold of his emotions and decided he needed a more cautious approach, a Plan C.

He let himself into the *Eagle II,* fighting Clyde off, and went up the stairs into the pilot house. Clyde followed in his wake. "Leave me alone," Henderson warned softly. His tone must have convinced the dog he wasn't going to be petted or played with. Tail down, Clyde headed downstairs.

There was a light on in the cabin of the *Zenith,* but there didn't seem to be anybody in the pilot house. That was the way Henderson had originally intended to get in based on the theory that the two men would most likely be hanging out in the dining area, hopefully with either music playing or a television on. Now he wasn't so sure.

Clyde barked again.

There was movement on the other boat. Someone was on the back deck. He wasn't sure, but he thought it might be Krause's partner. He was smoking a cigarette.

Henderson quickly raced down the stairs. Clyde tried to squeeze out the door with him, but he forced the dog back inside. Moving as quickly and quietly as he could, he went around to the side of the cabin. He couldn't see the other man from there, but he could see the door leading into the main cabin on the *Zenith*. Should he try and take the guy out, or should he try to sneak past him and get inside?

Stevick had always prided himself on his calm, rational approach to problems. Neither he nor Norton made snap decisions. But Henderson often had to. The thing that made it so difficult this time was the realization that Faith's life might depend on which choice he made. His own life might, for that matter.

As he went over the side of the *Eagle II* and stepped onto the deck of the *Zenith*, all he could think about was that any wrong move might prove fatal for Faith or for him. It was an almost paralyzing thought.

Henderson was relieved to find the door of the cabin unlocked. He went inside and moved down the corridor toward what he assumed to be the staterooms. There was no sound of pursuit. The dog was barking again though. Hopefully not at a returning Krause.

Oh, oh. It was.

When he heard the voices, he barely had time to hide. He slipped into a dark room and closed the door. Moments later someone came inside the boat.

"We stay?" It was half question, half complaint.

"That's what I said."

"For how long? I'm going stir crazy hanging around here."

"Don't think I like it, do you?"

The voices faded. The two men must have gone into the dining area. He could still hear them talking, but he couldn't make out the words. At least he had only heard two distinct voices. When he first realized someone was coming, he had feared there might be more than the two men. But it was probably just Krause and his friend, like he'd originally thought.

Well, Henderson, aren't you smart? You sneak into the enemy camp without a plan and on an empty stomach. Now what?

He felt his way around the room and verified that he was in a space lined with bunks. At least he hadn't barged in on a room full of sleeping infantry or a meeting hall filled with mob bosses. He noted that the mattresses were bare. And when he stumbled across what appeared to be a closet, it too was bare. At least the room wasn't in use. One bit of luck. He could probably hide out there indefinitely. Maybe even catch a few winks. Sure.

On the other hand, if he'd waited, he might not even have made it his far. But in this silence, how in the hell was he ever going to search the boat with two men sitting just a short sprint away? Come on, Henderson, think!

When the engine started up next door, he felt a surge of gratitude. Good old Hal. He must have figured out what had happened. Or, if not, he was at least assuming that, for some reason, Henderson had been forced to act without waiting for him to do his part. And he was doing just what Henderson would have wanted him to do if he'd been able to ask.

The *Eagle II's* engine was surprisingly loud. Henderson knew sound traveled over water, but he hadn't realized how noisy diesel engines could be, especially when two steel hulls were rafted together. The rapid chug, chug, chug reverberated throughout the boat. If the two men stayed put, he had the perfect cover.

If he could be sure there were only two men and that they were still in the dining area, he would feel a lot more confident. But nothing in life is certain. You had to act on reasonable assumptions and hope for the best. He crossed his fingers and went out into the all with his gun in readiness.

The next door squeaked as he opened it. Cursing under his breath, he quickly went in, pulling the door shut with another squeak. The loudest squeak he had ever heard. He waited in the dark for someone to come and check what was going on. But no one did.

This time he felt around for a light. He didn't want to waste time feeling his way around the room. There was a switch right where it should have been near the door. He took a deep breath, flicked the switch, and blinked against the glare.

The room was definitely occupied, only the current occupant was fortunately not in residence. There was a double bunk, built-in dresser, and a small sink. The bed was made up, but not neatly. Henderson looked in the closet and saw a man's jacket, a couple of shirts and a pair of pants. Time to move on.

The engine on the *Eagle II* was still running, but the world's nosiest door squeak seemed to Henderson to scream for attention. He waited a few moments with the door standing open before going out into the hall. He reasoned that it would be better to be in the room than in the hall if someone came to investigate. But again, no one did.

He moved on to the next room.

He went through the same routine, only this time when he switched on the light, he saw someone was in the lower bunk, just a few feet away. His gun came up, but if the other person had been armed, he would have been too late. Wyatt Earp he wasn't.

It only took a couple of seconds to realize that the person in the bunk was Faith. She had her eyes open and was staring at him. He was so relieved to see her he almost said her name out loud. Catching himself just in time, he put a finger to his lips to indicate she should be quiet. Then he realized that she couldn't say anything even if she wanted to: she was gagged.

He left the light on and went over to her. She was tied up, both hands and feet. He put his gun down to untie her, clumsy in his attempt to get it done in a hurry. The bonds were tight and hard to undo.

When he thought he heard a noise in the hall he picked up his gun and went over to the door. Was it possible to see the light under the door from the hall? He mentally weighed the odds and switched off the light. Then he waited.

There was definitely someone moving around out there.

He flattened himself behind the door and waited.

Moments later the door opened. Then the light came on.

"How are you doing, honey?" the voice said. "Need to get up once before going nighty-night?"

Faith shook her head "no."

He moved into the room, but not very far. Henderson could have jumped him, but then he would have had the other guy down on him in seconds.

"You sure? I'm not going to offer again."

Faith shook her head and turned her face away.

"You're a real bitch, you know." He started toward her, then changed his mind. Henderson held his breath. If the man turned to the left, Henderson would be forced to act. But he didn't; he turned to the right and didn't see Henderson standing there ready to attack. He switched off the light and left.

If you're so damned brave, Henderson, then why in hell are you sweating? And why in hell are your hands shaking? And why in hell don't you hurry up and get this over with?

He waited until he was fairly certain the man had gone away. Then he made his way over to Faith in the dark. This time he removed her gag before returning to the problem of untying her bonds. He wasn't sure why he hadn't done that before. "Don't speak," he whispered. She made a small smacking sound as if she was trying to moisten her lips. He wondered how long she had been gagged like that.

Getting the ropes untied in the dark was neither easier nor more difficult than it had been with the light on. His fingers were slippery with sweat and they didn't seem to be working properly. "You can do this," he said to himself.

Her hands were cold. The ropes had most likely been cutting off her circulation. Those bastards. Henderson would get even with them for this. He didn't know how, but he would think of something. *If* he managed to get the two of them safely off the boat and away.

As soon as he'd freed her hands he moved on to her feet. That went faster.

"Can you walk?" he whispered.

"I'll manage." Her voice was raspy, and she sounded weak.

How were they going to get off the fucking boat if she could barely walk? His escape plan hadn't been much. He'd assumed they would get out the same way he'd originally intended to come in: through the pilot house. Now he had doubts about her ability to make it up the steps. And he was so rattled he was having trouble remembering where those steps were in this boat. Well, there was no turning back now.

He helped her up. She was unsteady and almost collapsed when her feet touched the floor. "Easy," he whispered. "Make sure you can move your hands and legs before we leave this room. We might have to make a run for it at some point."

"Eric." The one word said everything he needed to hear. Whatever he asked of her, she would give it everything she had.

They moved over to the door. This time if someone came, he would have no choice but to attack. He opened the door and listened. He could hear the faint sounds of a television in the distance, but he had no way of knowing whether both men were in that room. He couldn't even be sure one of them was.

He concentrated on visualizing the layout. Hal had been right, the two boats were quite similar. If it held true throughout, then the pilot house stairs were in front of the room where the television was. But the two men shouldn't be able to see the stairs from there. And if the *Eagle II* engine was loud enough, and the television show distracting enough, and the two men were actually watching TV, then maybe they could manage their escape. Too many ifs. And Faith was trembling. He didn't know whether she was cold or frightened or fatigued, or all three. But there was no time to wait; they had to make their move.

They went through the door with Henderson in the lead. He kept one hand on her arm to steady her, his gun in the other. As they drew near the dining room, he could hear the television more clearly. There would be a few lines of dialogue followed by a laugh track. For once I was glad to hear exaggerated audience laughter.

The stairway was right where I had hoped. I shoved Faith up ahead of me and started up the stairs backwards. It was impossible to see anything without a light, and the steps were narrow and steep. I heard Faith stumble, but the sound didn't seem loud against the backdrop of other noises.

Someone below was moving about though. I stopped. Faith continued moving upward.

"You're imagining things," I heard a voice yell.

"This place gives me the creeps," came the reply.

"I just checked on her a few minutes ago." They were both in the hallway now.

"You look around back; I'll see if she's all right."

I quickly moved up the rest of the stairs without feeling my feet touch the steps. Faith was waiting for me at the top. "They'll know in just a few seconds that something is wrong," I whispered. My other selves waited with Faith to hear the plan, but nothing came out. There were only two ways out, both down narrow stairs. If Krause and his friend started shooting, could I hold out until Hal called the police? One barely used gun against two experienced gunmen?

All at once the room was flooded with light. "Fuck!" What was happening? Faith's face was a frightened mask with shadows playing across it.

"They don't know about you yet," she whispered. Even if I wasn't thinking, she was.

There was no sound of movement down below. I motioned for her to hide between the chart table and the pilot seat. It wasn't much cover, but it was somewhat out of the way. I took a position midway between the two sets of stairs so I could see anyone coming from inside or outside. If each man came up a different set of stairs at the same time, I would be in big trouble.

The light suddenly got more intense. A loud voice that sounded vaguely familiar announced: "The police are on their way. If you harm the girl, I will personally see that you don't make it off that boat alive."

Good old Hal. He must have turned on the spotlights on the *Eagle II*. And he was trying to bluff the two men into surrendering. He wouldn't succeed, I was sure of that, but it might buy them some time.

He heard a voice say, "What the hell is going on?" Then everything was quiet again. Except for the sound of the *Eagle II's* engine.

Then the *Zenith's* engine started up. Oh my god, they were going to run with the boat. He and Faith would be trapped with no chance of escape.

CHAPTER 24
A SIMPLE SOLUTION

F aith was standing next to him. "I can keep a watch on the outside stairway," she whispered.

"They're going to leave with the boat," Henderson said unnecessarily. That meant one or both of the two men would be coming up the stairs to the pilot house at any minute. Either Henderson had to ambush them as they came up or he and Faith had to get out of there, fast.

"There's no one out there," Faith said.

"It could be a trap."

"Who was the voice?"

"The fisherman on the next boat over."

Clyde began barking frantically. Damn. He didn't want Hal taking any risks. He hoped he had emphasized sufficiently that these men were dangerous.

Someone was coming up the inside stairs. If he had been alone, he might have chanced it, but with Faith to consider, things were different.

He pushed Faith ahead of him out the door. Then the two of them stumbled down the metal steps, trying to look in two directions at once. He lost his balance for an instant when Faith screamed. Then everything started happening at once.

The sound of the shot was ear shattering. Someone had a rifle. The sound of shattered glass followed, and the lights went out on both boats.

They were on the deck now. I didn't know where the two men were, but to get from one boat to the next they needed to get around back. And that was risky.

"Can you swim?" he asked Faith.

"Yes, a little."

"Jump in. I'll try to head them off." Faith hesitated and started to say something, but Henderson had made up his mind. With her out of the way I could maneuver better. I would at least be able to stall them long enough for her to swim to safety. It couldn't be more than a dozen yards to the dock, and if Hal was watching, he'd be there to pull her out.

I practically shoved her over the side. In all the commotion the splash was barely audible. I waited until she surfaced before moving along the side of the cabin toward the rear of the boat.

A shot zinged past. It wasn't from a rifle.

Suddenly the rifle sounded again. It was coming from the *Eagle II*.

All at once he realized the *Zenith* was moving. He felt the boat rock as it strained against the line that was still tied to the bow of the *Eagle II*. That meant that at least one of the men was in the pilot house.

I zipped around the end of the cabin in a flash, practically running head on into my opponent. It was all over in an instant. No shots were fired. I knocked the gun out of the man's hand and hit him over the head with the butt of his own gun. It was neat work; I felt a jolt of pride. Thanks, Henderson, I murmured. But I didn't have time to stand around congratulating himself.

I ran up the steps to the pilot house taking them two at a time.

"Is that you . . .?" Krause said. I was on him before he got a chance to finish his sentence.

The fight only lasted a minute or so. When one guy is trying to steer a boat and is attacked by an unknown wild man with a gun, the odds are in favor of the attacker. Even a half investigator and half lawyer attacker.

When it was over and Krause lay moaning at my feet, I had to fight the urge to keep on beating and pounding on him. All I could think of was Faith lying on the bunk, gagged and tied up, with Krause's partner calling her a bitch. These two men deserved to suffer. But first I had to make certain Faith was safe.

It was dark in the cabin except for the instrument panel. The boat was pulling at its bowline, still trying to make its escape. I didn't know what to do, so I opened the door and shouted into the night: "Hal, how in the hell do you turn this damn thing off?"

The spotlight from the *Eagle II* came on. I waved. Hal cautiously moved out of his pilot house so he could hear better.

"I've got them," I yelled. "But I can't turn the damn engine off." The boat was straining to get away. If the line snapped, I was going to be the captain of the ship, and I didn't know fuck all about ships.

Hal appeared only minutes later and quickly silenced the engine. I gave him a gun and told him to keep an eye on the guy on the floor. "I made Faith jump overboard," I explained as I rushed off.

"You what?" Hal yelled after me.

"And watch out for the other guy. He won't stay passed out forever."

I stepped around the body on the back deck and rushed toward the dock. "Faith!" I screamed. "Faith!"

I found her clinging to a piling. She was so cold she could barely talk. My first thought was to jump in after her, but then what? "Aren't there any ladders around here?" I asked no one in particular.

There had to be a ladder. If not a ladder, then a rope. I jumped back aboard the *Eagle II* and started searching for a rope or a pole or something I could use to pull her out. Hal appeared on the back deck of the *Zenith* with Krause. "Did you find her?" he called.

"She's right here, but I can't figure out how to get her out of the water."

Hal pushed Krause to his knees and was across the side of the boat before Henderson could protest. He shoved the gun back into my hand. "I'll do that," he said. "You watch those two bastards."

I wanted to protest, but I guessed Hal knew what to do, and I obviously didn't. Reluctantly, I went back over to the other boat. Krause was just standing up and I motioned with Henderson's gun for him to get back down. Then I ordered him to put his hands behind his head. I had to prod him with the gun to make him obey.

The man on the back deck was coming around. In a few minutes it would be harder to keep things under control.

"Don't even think about trying to get away, Krause," I warned. "I have no qualms about shooting you. In fact, I might even enjoy it."

"How do you know my name?"

"I know all about you," I said. I was having difficulty concentrating. The adrenaline rush was fading, and I was worried about Faith.

When I saw the two shapes moving across the dock in the distance, I was flooded with relief. "Thank god," I murmured.

"You took a big chance for her," Krause said.

"Who's your friend?" I asked, pointing to Krause's colleague.

"Deek."

"Deek?"

"Yeah, Deek."

"And who do you and this Deek work for?"

"We ain't saying."

"You will," I warned, trying to sound menacing. As a matter of fact, I felt menacing. As soon as I was sure Faith was all right . . .

I looked over and saw Hal lifting Faith over the side of the boat and carrying her into the cabin. Neither said anything to me. I felt foolish standing there. It was my show, but I no longer felt in control.

I knew I should be doing something about the *Zenith.* The boat was basically loose, angling off the bow of the *Eagle II,* still trying halfheartedly to get away. Hal had saved the damsel in distress and Henderson was left to clean up the mess.

"OK, Krause, let's get this boat tied back up."

"What do you suggest?"

"It's your boat; you figure it out. Just remember, one wrong move and you'll be walking the plank." Where had that come from, some old Errol Flynn movie? Lack of food and a brush with death was obviously affecting my brain.

"I can't do it single-handed."

I kicked Deek. "Rise and shine, Deekie. You're going to help your friend here."

The maneuver involved having one of the two go over on the *Eagle II* to take a line. I directed Deek to do that, letting them know that I was quite capable of shooting both Deek and Krause before either had a chance to get away. That was Henderson bravado, but they seemed to believe it. Their faith in my threat was fortunate since I wasn't at all sure what I would do if both of them decided to make a run for it at the same time. Shoot Krause and hope for the best probably.

When the boat was secure, Henderson had Deek return to the *Zenith*. Then he called for Hal. When Hal didn't immediately appear, he called again, a little louder: "HAL!"

Hal's head popped out the back door of the cabin. "What?"

"I need some help," Henderson said.

"I thought you told me to stay out of this."

"I've changed my mind, OK? How's Faith doing?"

"She's half frozen and completely exhausted, but other than that she's fine. I put her in my bunk. Once she warms up properly, she should be all right."

"Well, right now the problem is what to do with these two. I can't tie them up and keep an eye on them at the same time. How about lending me a hand."

"Just a minute."

Hal disappeared inside the *Eagle II*. When he came back, he was carrying some rope. "This ought to do it," he said.

They took the two men back inside the *Zenith* and into one of the staterooms. Henderson kept them covered while Hal tied up Krause, then Deek.

"They might be able to get loose," Hal observed. "What if I also tie them to these posts?" There were sturdy looking posts at the outer ends of the bunks connecting the bottom one to the top one.

"You have the mind of a criminal," I said.

"I thought we were the good guys."

"By the way, I haven't thanked you yet. Your moves were brilliant."

"How'd you like the voice of God touch?"

"It was perfect."

"I thought you'd want to know that the cavalry was on its way."

"You called the police?"

"No, I meant 'me.'"

"I see." I ran my hand across my forehead. I felt almost faint. And it was getting harder and harder to think.

"Now what?" Hal asked.

"I need to talk to them," I said.

"You don't need me for that."

"I want to see Faith first."

"They should be OK here for a while."

"I'll be back shortly," I warned Deek and Krause. "You might want to think about giving up the name of your boss. It will make things go faster. And it will be a lot easier on you."

Faith lay covered with a pile of blankets. I'd noticed her wet clothes on the counter on my way in. Hal was certainly a fast mover. Another thing I'd noticed for the first time was that Hal's hair was wet.

"Did you have to go in the water to get her out?"

"Yeah. I swam her around to a ladder on the other side of the dock. She couldn't have climbed up on her own."

"I thought there must be a ladder."

Faith's eyes opened, and she smiled up at them. No, that wasn't accurate, she was smiling at Hal. And Hal was smiling back.

"Faith," I said softly. "I'm glad you're all right."

She turned her eyes to me. "Eric."

"You remember my name." It was a foolish thing to say. And I knew it sounded more like a jealous boyfriend than a disinterested investigator, but then all along I'd been aware that I was helping her in part because Henderson was attracted to her.

"Thank you, Eric."

"She needs to rest," Hal said.

"I need some answers first."

"Can't they wait?"

"No. If you would leave us alone for a few minutes."

"It's OK, Hal," Faith said.

Reluctantly, Hal backed out of the room. "I'll make you some hot chocolate," he said as he left.

"I could use some," I called after him. "And something to eat if you have it."

"I meant for Faith," Hal corrected. "But sure, I have some food."

As soon as he was gone, I asked, "Do you know who those two are working for?"

"No, I'm sorry."

"Do you still think the FBI is responsible? Are they FBI?"

"Not them. They couldn't be."

"Why not?"

"I'm not sure exactly. Except—" Her eyes filled with tears.

"What is it?"

"They were going to kill me. I heard them talking. They were waiting until their boss gave them the go-ahead. Oh, Eric." She started to cry. I wanted to comfort her, but I hesitated, and Hal picked that moment to reappear.

"For Christ's sake, what are you doing to her?" He pushed past me and gathered Faith in his arms, rocking her back and forth, murmuring what sounded to me like a series of "there there's." She clung to him the same way she had clung to the piling, as if her life depended on it.

Feeling like a third wheel, I picked up the plate of food Hal had set down on the dresser and went out into the galley. It was at least five minutes before Hal returned. By then I had finished my food and was feeling physically better.

"She's been through hell," Hal said.

"I know."

"She needs rest."

"I know that too. But I had to ask about what she knew. It isn't over yet. Not until I get to the guy who gave the order to kill her."

"They were going to kill her?" Hal sounded genuinely shocked.

"It wasn't going to be a Love Boat cruise."

"I didn't realize."

"Those were real bullets flying around out there, in case you hadn't noticed. In fact, I remember you taking a few shots at one point."

"You needed some cover."

"Thanks. I did thank you, didn't I?"

"Yeah, you did."

I poured myself a cup of coffee from a pot on the stove. "I'm afraid I have still another favor to ask of you."

"What?"

"There are two problems remaining: those two on the *Zenith* and Faith. Both have to be kept under wraps until I have a chance to figure out who's giving the orders."

"You're not going to turn them over to the police?"

"Not yet. They would just lawyer up. Then Faith would still be in danger."

"Well, Faith can stay here with me."

I had figured as much.

"As for those two . . ." Hal thought for a moment. "I don't especially want them on this boat. The police frown on keeping people tied up like that."

"I know. But if I leave them on the *Zenith,* it will be too easy for whoever is calling the shots to find them."

"Not if the boat isn't there." Hall was grinning.

"What do you mean?"

"We'll move the boat."

It was all so simple, why hadn't I thought of that?

CHAPTER 25

72 HOURS

I t took almost two hours to complete the operation. The first thing they did was improvise an outside lock for the stateroom door where we were "detaining" the two men. The carpentry was primitive, not something the owner would consider an improvement, but it served the purpose. Even if Deek or Krause managed to get untied, there was no way they would get out of that room on their own.

The next problem was to move the boat. They got away from the *Eagle II* without incident, but after that things didn't go as smoothly. Henderson just wasn't a boat person, Stevick had been out on boats from time to time but only as a guest, and Norton was a total novice. Our combined presence wasn't much help to Hal.

Hal steered the *Zenith* down the waterfront about a quarter mile and alongside the hulk they intended to tie to. He got in quite close, but I waited too long to leap across the abyss between the two boats, and he had to make the approach a second time. Then I couldn't figure out what I should tie to. It was too dark to see well. I stumbled around, groping for something solid while the two boats slowly drifted apart. By the time Hal made the third approach, tempers on both sides were short.

It was a company dock with a warehouse blocking the view from the main road. The *Zenith* was the fifth boat out, overshadowed by the inside boats. Hal was fairly certain that nothing was going on there at present, so with luck, the *Zenith* could remain unnoticed for quite some time. Even if someone did get curious, it would probably take a while to get things sorted out. By then Henderson hoped to have the case resolved.

As soon as the boat was securely moored, Hal and I untied the two men, one at a time, and gave them bathroom and food breaks. Deek didn't talk much, just did what he was told, wolfing down his food like he was starving. But Krause ran at the mouth, trying to convince us we were making a mistake. He pleaded his innocence in the situation, and when that didn't work, he warned us, at the top of his lungs, that his mysterious boss would make us pay for what we were doing. We encouraged him to keep on shouting—there was no one around to hear him, except us. And we didn't give a rat's ass what he had to say, unless he gave up his boss.

I was feeling guilty about involving Hal as much as I had, so I sent him outside while I made one more attempt to browbeat the men into telling me something worthwhile. At that point Krause fell silent. Obviously both men were unnerved by the fact that the boat had been moved, and that we were unconcerned about how much noise they made. So, when Henderson told them how he had always wanted to pull out someone's fingernails, they didn't know whether to believe him or not.

"I swear," Krause said. "We were only supposed to keep her out of circulation for a while."

"Until when?"

"Until we were told to let her go."

"Just like that, you were going to let her go. She'd seen your faces, hadn't she? And she probably knows your names."

"We weren't going to hang around for her to sic the cops on us."

"And she'd seen your car, hadn't she? It's registered in your name, Krause. How do you think *I* found you?"

"I swear it on my mother's grave."

"What does that mean?"

"It means that I'm telling the truth."

"Let's try again." Henderson sighed. It's not easy making a "sigh" sound threatening. "Who owns the *Zenith*?"

"Some guy. We paid him to let us use it as a base. Deek thought it would be a good place to hang out. He's always liked boats." He glared at Deek.

"Not anymore," Deek offered. "Too cramped."

"How'd you find it in the first place?"

"It's up for sale."

A dead end.

"OK, I've about had it with you two. You can claim you don't know the name of the person at the top. But you have a contact or a number or something. You have to. You're getting orders from someone. And . . . you're getting on my nerves." I took out Henderson's gun and tapped the barrel in the palm of my other hand as if contemplating which man to shoot first.

"I'm telling you the truth. They gave me a phone, and they call me on it when they want to deliver a message. It's always from a different phone. You know what that's like these days. No one has a regular number anymore."

"That the best you can do, Krause?"

"I can't tell you something I don't know." He looked and sounded scared.

"I gotta take a leak," Deek said.

"Too bad."

"Seriously, man, I gotta take a leak."

"We just gave you a break."

"But I drank that bottled water."

"Next time, don't." I felt absolutely no sympathy. "I'm giving you the same consideration you gave Faith." He paused a moment, then looked from Krause to Deek and back. "And if I find out you're lying to me . . ." Henderson sounded so mean he almost frightened *me*.

"If I had a name, I'd give it to you," Krause said.

I was starting to believe him, but I didn't intend to make it easy. "If I find out either one of you is a lying SOB, neither of you will get off this boat alive. Do you understand?"

Both men looked terrified. That gave me some small satisfaction. They had let Faith lay on that bunk for days wondering when they were going to kill her. Now it was their turn to wonder whether they were going to get out of *this* room alive.

They had ferried a car over before moving the boat, so in no time at all they were back at the *Eagle II*. Faith was waiting for them in the galley. She was wearing one of Hal's work shirts and some long underwear bottoms that sagged below her crotch. Even in that ridiculous outfit, she was appealing.

"How'd it go?" she asked.

"Not so good," I admitted. "I didn't get anything out of them, I'm afraid."

"I didn't think you would. They seem like pretty low-level muscle."

She poured them all some coffee, and they crowded around the small table, Henderson across from Hal and Faith. They already seemed like a couple.

"What next?" Faith asked.

"You stay here with Hal while I go out and see what I can dig up. Just don't show your face outside until you hear from me, understand?"

She didn't look at all displeased by the plan.

"How are you feeling?" Henderson asked.

"By comparison, just great. Before Hal pulled me out of the water, I thought for sure I was going to die." She gave Hal a quick smile of gratitude. "I'm still a bit stiff, and my wrists and ankles are sore, but it feels so incredibly good to be sitting here drinking coffee."

I hated to put a damper on her good spirits, but there was one more thing that had to be said. "Hal, Faith, I'm going to leave now. If I don't come back or call within 72 hours, you're to go to the police, you understand? Blame everything on me. Tell them I took the *Zenith* and you don't know where it is. They'll eventually find it. Krause and Deek will lawyer up, so you don't have to worry about what they will say. And if they accuse either of you of anything, just deny it."

If Henderson had expected sympathy or a plea not to go, he was disappointed. I finished my coffee and left them there, huddled against each other in the warmth of the small cabin.

• • •

Bright and early the next morning, Henderson headed back to the gym. The young woman behind the counter was wearing a tight tank top and floral pants that could have been a second skin. She seemed all bouncy and bright, either from being so physically fit, or she was on steroids.

"I have a problem," I explained. "Somehow I ended up with someone's cell phone by accident when I was here the other day." I held up the phone as evidence. "I'm pretty sure it belongs to the guy with locker 328. Any chance you can give me his name so I can give this back to him?"

She held out her hand. "I can do that for you."

"No, I want to apologize to him." I smiled. "And I want *my* phone back. I was here as a guest, and my phone's locked, so he can't track me."

"I'm sorry, but I can't give out a member's name." I didn't think it would be that easy, but I'd thought it was worth a try. "Well, why don't you give him a call and tell him that I have his cell and would like to meet and exchange phones. Could you do that? I'm sure your member would appreciate getting his phone back."

She considered the proposition a moment, then said, "Yes, I don't see why not." She turned to the computer on the desk behind the counter and typed in something. I waited until I was fairly certain she was on the right screen before waving in the guy I'd hired from a long line of young men standing in front of a home improvement warehouse store. Like about a dozen others standing there, he'd been hoping to get day work. He'd seemed intelligent and not too fussy about what he had to do to earn a few bucks. To him it must have seemed like easy money.

He came bursting into the tiny lobby. "Hey, lady," he said to the young woman at the computer, waving his hand in front of her face. "I need some help. Can you take a look?" He doubled over as if in pain.

"I'm not a nurse," she said.

He straightened up. "I know that. I was exercising and hurt myself. I need help."

It wasn't a very convincing approach, but it was definitely a distraction.

"This is *not* a clinic," she said, determined to get rid of him with a frown and a few discouraging words.

"Lady, I need help. Get me some help." He was starting to sound frantic. Perhaps a bit of overacting, but it worked.

"Wait here," she said, disappearing into the other room.

I quickly went around the end of the counter to the computer and noted the name of the owner of locker number 328, scribbled down the telephone and address listed, and managed to get out from behind the counter before the woman came back with a muscular man who looked like he could take care of a whole mob of unruly people on his own.

"Hey, it's OK," I said. "This young man has calmed down. I'm going to take him to a clinic down the street. Everything's just fine."

"Thanks, man, appreciate." He leaned on me as I guided him to the door. We stayed together until we were out of sight of the gym. When I let go of his arm, he gave me a big smile and asked, "Was I good, or what?"

"You were great," I said, and I meant it. I gave him double what we'd agreed upon as payment and dropped him off where I'd picked him up earlier. Although I'd asked him to keep our little drama under wraps, I knew he'd probably tell his fellow day laborers. But I doubted any of them would care about someone taking a peek at a computer screen in a gym. Although they probably wondered what all the fuss was about. It would give them something to talk about while waiting around for someone to hire them for honest work.

CHAPTER 26

THE MURDER WEAPON

I was in shock. I'd barely managed to hold it together long enough to get in my car and drive until I found a parking spot where I could pull over and think. My thoughts were tumbling over each other as Henderson tried to put the pieces together. And I felt as though the big guy with the small head had delivered another gut punch.

None of it made any sense. When I'd look at the name of the owner of locker 328 on the gym's list of members, my first thought was that I had somehow messed up and had the wrong number. How I'd managed not to tear my hair and run screaming from the room when I saw that familiar name, I'll never know. Maybe all the dots would connect themselves once I heard what he had to say. But at this point, I didn't have a clue what Norton should do.

Just to be sure I hadn't made a mistake, I got Coral, my answering service message taker, to call the local FBI office and ask for special agent Calvin Edwards' extension "so her boss at the field office could call him directly." The combination of her sweet, innocent voice and the fact that she called over the lunch hour when the regular person who answered the phones was out did the trick. Calvin Edwards, the FBI agent who had arranged for Stevick's testimony in exchange for a new life as Nick Norton, was currently on assignment at the local FBI office.

. . .

I answered on the first ring.

"What happened to you the other day?" Edwards demanded. I recognized his voice now, or thought I did, even though he continued to disguise it.

"I got hung up."

"You're running out of time, Norton. Make up your mind. Which is it?"

"The exchange."

"Good."

"But first I want to make absolutely certain you can come across with the goods."

"You've got my word."

"Not good enough."

Edwards obviously knew Norton would require proof; he had an answer ready. "How about if I send you a bullet fired from the murder weapon?"

"Sounds good. But let's say the bullet *is* from the murder weapon. How will I know there are any prints on the gun?"

"You can check it out, but I'm not going to hand the gun over until I get something in return. As a bonus, I'll give you the name that goes with the prints. The exchange either happens or it doesn't. It's up to you."

It wasn't perfect, but Norton thought it was good enough. Henderson and I went along because we wanted to see how things played out. "All right," I said.

"Just name the place and I'll send the bullet along."

One thing I wasn't about to reveal was Norton's link to Henderson. "OK," I said. "Send it to Dean Whitman. He's a lawyer. You can look him up."

"Dean Whitman it is. I should have it to him first thing tomorrow morning."

"Good. Want to set a time to talk, or can I call you back?"

"How about I call you at noon tomorrow?"

Lunchtime. After work. Never during the work day. If it was a legitimate FBI operation Edwards wouldn't have to go to the gym and use a burner phone each time he called. "I'll be waiting with bated breath." Whatever that meant.

Edwards left his office at 6:00 p.m. Since he had no reason to think he might be followed, it was an easy tail. He never looked back once. He was alone. And no one appeared to be following him, other than Henderson, that is. He walked to a parking lot a block away, got in what looked like a rental, and drove directly to an extended stay hotel south of downtown. It was in an industrial area, a boxy building that had seen better days, but not for a long time. A place Edwards wouldn't be living in if he intended to hang around indefinitely.

I didn't have long to wait. Edwards came back out just minutes later carrying a small box, got back in his car, and headed north again. The next stop was a 24-hour courier service. When he got out of the car, he was wearing a baseball cap. He, too, apparently assumed that most people remembered the cap and not the face beneath it.

It was looking more and more like this was something Edwards was doing on his own. The question was whether it was with or without the blessing of the FBI.

On his way back to the hotel Edwards went through a drive-thru at a fast-food burger place. The entire block smelled like fried chicken and French fries. Henderson's stomach started to protest its lack of fuel, but there wasn't time to get anything to eat. He would have to live on fumes for a while.

Once back at his hotel, Edwards jumped out of his car and hurried to the front door with his bag of food. Probably wanted to eat it before it got cold. My stomach gurgled in protest again.

Under normal circumstances Henderson would have followed the person he was tailing into his hotel, but in this instance, he didn't know whether Edwards would recognize him with his "new" face under *his* baseball cap. No, it was better to wait.

While watching to see if Edwards reappeared or was in for the evening, Norton gave Dean Whitman a call. Whitman had been one of Norton's regular civil opponents, a dour, serious man who always seemed to need a shave. He and Norton hadn't exactly been buddies, but Norton considered him honest. And that was what we needed, a go-between we could trust.

Before Whitman would agree to do as Norton asked, he gave Norton a strong lecture on why he should turn himself in to the police. "I know you didn't do it," he concluded. "So, what do you have to hide?"

"Until this is cleared up," Norton explained, "turning myself in would pose some, ah, complications for a client." That seemed the kind of thing an idealistic criminal lawyer like Norton might be expected to say.

"Your lawyer-client privilege should cover any complications," Whitman argued.

"I know, but it's *really* complicated." Really, really complicated. "All I'm asking is that you pass along a package that someone is sending to you to Captain Al Castaldo at police headquarters. And if anyone asks what you did with it, don't tell them, okay? Not that anyone will necessarily ask. But just in case they do, I don't want them to know the package went to the police. If you'll do that for me, I'll be that much closer to solving this, ah, little problem."

"Well . . ."

"I'm doing the right thing, believe me."

"If you were asking for anything else . . ."

"But I'm not. At least you can't be accused of keeping anything *from* the police. After all, you'll be sending something *to* them."

'I'll do it. But I want to go on record as advising you to turn yourself in."

"The record shows you so advised."

Norton hung up and Henderson put in a call to Al. When he explained what Al would be receiving, Al was irate. He didn't seem to appreciate that if things worked out, the police would be in possession of vital evidence in a murder investigation.

"Where did you get hold of this bullet?" Al demanded.

"Didn't I just tell you that I couldn't say? At least not at this time."

"You're asking me to run a check on a bullet from a potential murder weapon and you won't tell me where you got the bullet?"

"That's right. And I don't want you to mention our deal to anyone else for at least 24 hours."

"Deal? What kind of deal is this? I put my butt on the line and you say you'll tell me everything *eventually*. Eventually isn't good enough."

"Sorry, that's the way it has to be, Al. Thanks."

He stayed in his car and watched for another hour before calling it quits. He knew where Edwards worked, and he also knew nothing was going to happen until the following day. He might as well get something to eat. But first he had one more call to make.

Fred took his time getting to the telephone, apparently Henderson had interrupted a game of pool. When he finally had him on the line and explained what he needed, Fred asked, "How soon?"

"Tonight."

"That'll cost you."

"The question is, can you get it? It doesn't have to be clean, just in good condition."

"I think so. Call back in half an hour."

That gave me just enough time to go back to the drive-thru and order a hamburger and a cup of coffee. I ate in my car and used the coffee to wash down two aspirin. The aspirin were becoming an addiction. At least Henderson didn't have time to smoke anymore. Stress or tar in your lungs, either one could kill you.

When it was time, I called Buffy's again. Fred answered on the second ring. "Yeah. I can get it for you," he said. "Rush jobs cost though."

"How much?"

"Since it doesn't have to be clean, let's say eight Jolly Green Giants."

"That's robbery."

"Tell it to the po-lice," Fred said, laughing.

Normally Henderson would have bargained with Fred, but since Fred knew he was in a bind, it seemed pointless. "OK, when can I pick it up?"

"Two hours."

"I'll be there."

I went back to the apartment to get the cash. My head still ached, so I took another couple of aspirin, this time with a double scotch on the rocks. That was apparently the right combination. My headache started to subside almost immediately.

The only thing left to do was to get Edwards' room number. After giving it some thought, I decided on the direct approach. I called the hotel and told them I wanted to send something to Calvin Edwards and needed his room number. As simple as that.

Two hours later I was at Buffy's. Fred looked up from his game, eyes bright in anticipation of easy money, Henderson's easy money. He didn't rush over though. That wasn't his style. He finished the game, took his time collecting his winnings, and motioned Henderson toward the back room.

The exchange only took a few minutes. Fred's lips moved as he fanned the eight one-hundred-dollar bills. Counting to eight wasn't that big a deal, but Fred liked to put on a show. Then he handed Henderson a large bubble mailer envelope and a pair of rubber gloves. "It's been wiped," He said, "Go on, check it out."

Henderson put on the gloves and pulled the gun out of the envelope. It looked fine. The game was afoot. A very high-stakes game.

I was waiting at Edwards' extended stay hotel the next morning. I didn't have long to wait before he came out, got in his car, and drove off. Just to be sure he wasn't coming back right away, I waited for another twenty minutes before getting out of Henderson's car and heading for the hotel entrance. I was wearing a generic workman's overalls and cap, a pair of cloth gloves over a pair of latex gloves, and was carrying a red metal toolkit. The toolkit was covered in eye catching stickers and decals. I wasn't sure what the routine was for cleaning rooms or how much hall traffic I would encounter, so I wanted to be somewhat disguised and have a focal point that wasn't my face. Check out this snazzy tool kit.

Finding his room was easy. All of the rooms were clearly numbered, and each hall had a sign telling you which numbers were down which hallway. His was the last one at the end of a nondescript hall that looked like all of the other nondescript halls in the building. Without the numbers, it would have been easy to lose your way in the blur of beige rugs and beige walls. It was like being in a sandstorm.

The fact that his room was at the end was both good and bad. It wasn't in a high traffic location, but it would be hard to get away if someone caught me in the act of breaking in. Fortunately, the room had a standard hotel lock, and I was able to get inside before anyone saw me in the hall. Henderson enjoyed showing off his skills, but Norton, Stevick and I were about to have a joint nervous breakdown. We all hated this sort of thing. And I was having more and more difficulty figuring out who "I" was at any given moment.

Once inside, I took off my outer gloves and began my search. Everything depended on finding the murder weapon. I was fairly certain he wouldn't have it at the office, and it wasn't in his locker at the gym, so this seemed the most likely alternative.

A quick look around told me there weren't many hiding places. The most obvious was the hotel safe. So that's where I started. It took Henderson a surprising amount of time to break into the cheap safe with its standard locking mechanism. By the time the door swung open, there was sweat streaming down my forehead and into my eyes. I wiped my face with the sleeve of my uniform and peered inside.

There was a stack of cash next to a cardboard box. Nothing else. I took a deep breath and removed the box. Inside was a gun wired to a thick piece of cardboard. I breathed a sigh of relief as I got the bubble wrap envelope out of my tool kit and exchanged guns. Everything was going as planned.

There was a woman with two small children waiting for the elevator when I left Edwards' apartment. But she was focused on her kids and didn't even look up until I reached the door to the stairs. I had already turned away by then. And I didn't see another person as I left the hotel. Not even in the parking lot. It was either a miracle or the hotel wasn't doing so great.

As I got in my car, I couldn't help but smile. Henderson had done it again. Although in the process he had taken at least five years off my life. More if we were caught.

CHAPTER 27

THE PACT

The call with Edwards went smoothly. They agreed Norton needed some time to verify that the bullet had come from the murder weapon. Edwards didn't ask how he was going to do that, and Norton didn't offer any information. They scheduled the exchange for Sunday evening. Edwards would call Norton for the location.

Next, Henderson called Hal to tell him he might need more than the 72 hours he'd originally thought to resolve things. Hal seemed glad to hear it was going to take a little longer and volunteered that Faith was doing fine. She was helping him around the boat. And, as requested, they had been feeding Krause and Deek and giving them bathroom breaks on a regular basis. The two men weren't going to be pleased to hear about having to remain locked up longer than promised, but they didn't get a vote.

Sunday morning Henderson called Al at home and asked if they could meet somewhere. The television was blaring in the background, a cartoon show. Al yelled for the kids to turn it down, then came back on the phone and said, "In about an hour." There had been no perceptible change in the volume of the program as far as Henderson could tell. "At the House of Pancakes, the one down the road from my place."

They had met there before. They made good omelets and Al liked their pancakes.

I waited about forty minutes before tucking the envelope in an inside jacket pocket and heading for the House of Pancakes.

It was raining. Hard. I made a dash for the car, slowing down when my head started to pound. Getting wet was better that getting another headache.

The next time I started over, if I ended up in a rainy climate, I would definitely build my personality around an umbrella. A black one, the kind that popped open when you pressed a button. Maybe I could be a suave John Steed type, the umbrella-carrying agent from the old Avenger series. Of course, my recollection was that his "brolly" was also a weapon. In my next life, I hoped I didn't need to always have a weapon at hand, especially an umbrella with a sword inside the handle.

The House of Pancakes was busy, as it always was. Al wasn't there yet. Henderson waited until a booth opened up. Then he sat down and ordered coffee. It was unusual for Al to be late. Henderson ordered an omelet with a side of pancakes. Al came in just as the waitress brought his breakfast.

"Where's mine?" Al asked as he slid into the seat across from Henderson. He had on a wool jacket, no hat. People who'd lived in the Pacific Northwest all their lives seemed oblivious to the rain. But they went crazy when it snowed. Henderson didn't get it.

"Sorry, I figured you'd already eaten."

"I did," he said grimly. "Vitamin fortified grain cereal and orange juice. Skim milk on the cereal." He made a face. "You have to suffer to stay healthy."

"Want something?"

"Nah. I'll just eat your pancakes. Promised the kids I'd take them to the Science Center. It's environmental awareness day."

"Sounds like fun."

"You should work on your sarcasm." He pulled Henderson's pancakes over and asked him to pass the syrup.

Henderson let him take a couple of bites before he pulled the envelope out and put it on the table. "I have a favor."

"I didn't think you asked me here for breakfast."

"This is an easy one."

"Just like the last one was."

Henderson took a bite of omelet. "When will you have the results by the way?"

"I have them now."

Henderson stopped with his fork half way to his mouth. "Well?"

"You already know the answer, don't you?"

"My guess is that the bullet came from the gun that killed Stevick. Am I right?"

"You're right." Al added a glob of butter to what remained of Henderson's pancakes and washed them with syrup. "Just don't forget what I said about not being able to sit on this for very long."

"By tomorrow I should have the answers I need to clear my client."

"Good. Now what's in the envelope?" Al reached for it and shook it like he was checking out a Christmas present. Henderson was glad he'd wrapped the original envelope in newspaper and put it in a larger envelope. It was bulky, but not obviously a gun.

"If I'm right, all the answers I need to clear my client are in that envelope. As soon as I know for sure . . ."

"The envelope is sealed," Al observed.

"And I want you to promise you won't open it until I call you." Henderson paused. "Or if I don't get in touch within the next 48 hours."

Al put his fork down. "Is this something you're sure you can handle on your own?"

"No, that's why I'm giving you this envelope for safekeeping."

"If you tell me what's going on, maybe I can do more than hold onto an envelope for you while you're out playing hero."

"I wish I could, Al, but I can't. It's like we've discussed before. Being a policeman gives you some advantages over us poor, degenerate private eye types. But you also operate under some disadvantages. I don't want to put you in an awkward position. So, as soon as I've resolved a couple of issues, I'll give you the whole enchilada. I promise. Meanwhile, you're holding onto an envelope for a colleague."

Al stared at what was left of the pancakes. They were saturated with syrup, dark islands of sugary brown goo. Avoiding eye contact, Al said, "Eric, we've known each other for some time now. We've had . . . some good conversations. You've asked for a lot of favors, but you've done a lot for me too. That's why I've never refused to do anything you've asked for." He looked up. "But I'm afraid you're in over your head on this one. I wish like hell you could see your way clear. . ."

Henderson cut him off. "Sorry, Al. It isn't that I don't trust you. I'd trust you with my life. But I won't put you in a situation that will go against the grain of that policeman heart of yours. Just give me time to pull a few loose ends together, and I'll hand you everything on a platter. It's better this way, believe me."

Al seemed to remain unconvinced, but he didn't argue further.

"Just forty-eight hours," Henderson said as they stood up to leave. "Maybe less."

"All right, Eric. If that's the way you want it."

"Thanks, Al. I appreciate being able to depend on you."

Al looked like he was about to say something more, then apparently changed his mind.

It was still raining. Henderson ducked his head and ran to his car while Al strolled over to his wearing a wool jacket, no umbrella. A wool jacket in the rain; it didn't make any sense.

CHAPTER 28
ANOTHER DEATH

I left the apartment well ahead of schedule with Norton's disguise in a small overnight bag. I didn't like carrying the stuff with me like that, but as long as there was some hope for Henderson's survival, I wanted to disassociate him from Norton as much as possible. At a minimum, I didn't want Norton to be seen coming in and out of Henderson's apartment building.

Good old Henderson, there was no reason why he couldn't acquire a taste for Polish food and start carrying an umbrella. With time, he might even become a comfortable companion. But first, he would have to dispose of the little matter of a potential murder charge against Norton. And make life safe for Faith.

Reviewing events as a one-man operation put a lot of things into perspective. It even explained why Garcia had acted so inconsistently, first hounding Henderson, later encouraging him. From the beginning, one of the things that had bothered me was why the police hadn't discovered that the body belonged to Hicks, not Stevick. The answer was that they *had*. Edwards had no doubt used his position with the FBI to put pressure on Garcia to keep quiet about that minor detail. Garcia may have agreed to go along, but he had stirred the pot a little by getting Henderson all worked up and then pointing him in the right direction with a few hints disguised as off-the-cuff comments. I wondered what story they had given Caron. If she was trying to collect insurance, the FBI must be keeping her in the dark.

Enter the criminal element with their well-muscled truth seekers. Accused of a crime they might have liked to commit but had nothing to do with, they must have been curious. In retrospect it seemed fairly obvious that Smith and Jones—big guy and little guy--hadn't known any more about what was going on at the time than had Henderson.

Everything made sense when you assumed Edwards' main goal was to force Stevick to disclose the names and evidence he had withheld from the government two years before. With that information, Edwards would be in a position to blackmail some of the richest men in the country. All he'd had to do was wait for the right moment to make his move, long enough after the fact for the Stevick case to be considered old news, but before the information became dated. Caron must have made it necessary for Edwards to act when he did. By hiring Foster to look for her ex, Edwards was forced to make his move before Foster's search drove Stevick further underground.

It had probably been easy to set up Hicks. Edwards could have lured him to Norton's office in any number of ways. Like Faith, Hicks would have assumed the FBI didn't kill people, not without a damn good reason, at least. He couldn't have known that Edwards was a completely unprincipled agent working only for himself.

Switching the ID on Hicks was a nice touch. It let Norton know Stevick's cover was blown and that once the body was properly identified, Stevick would be the prime suspect. It would look as though the murder was Stevick's futile attempt to make the world think he had died. With both the police and organized crime figures after him, and with my FBI cover destroyed, I would be forced to make a deal with Edwards.

If it hadn't been for Henderson, Norton would have been caught that morning at his office, standing over the dead Hicks. Edwards must have called in a tip, not realizing Norton would vary his routine and show up early. Fortunately, Norton-as-Henderson was a good deal more resourceful than Norton-as-Stevick.

Edwards' biggest mistake was letting Norton escape before he could threaten him with exposure. The letter to Norton had been a long shot; Edwards couldn't have known for sure that Norton would return to his office. Nor could he have been sure the police wouldn't intercept the letter. By that time, however, he'd had too much invested in the operation not to take more risks. Like putting pressure on Garcia to stall making the true identity of the body public. Edwards probably claimed he was trying to protect an informant in an ongoing operation, but even so, it had been a dangerous ploy. Of course, once he had what he wanted from me, I had no doubt that he planned to either let the mafia do his mop-up or make it look as though they had. He couldn't afford to leave anyone alive who could point the finger at him.

Even if I managed to turn the tables on Edwards, Norton would have to go. But it was still possible Henderson was safe. Simco's orders to do away with Henderson had probably been real enough, but the fact that later on Krause and Deek had abducted Faith and left me alive suggested Henderson wasn't considered terribly important in the scheme of things. Someone to get rid of only if it wasn't too much bother.

With all that figured out, and if I was right, then tonight's exchange could even the score.

On weekends there was very little activity in the area near Henderson's office. There were no restaurants or bars in the vicinity, only block after block of office buildings, interspersed here and there with an occasional warehouse or run-down apartment complex. Unlike the high-rise quarter of the city where companies lit up their buildings like Christmas displays, most of the windows in this area remained dark after hours. It was a question of economics.

Of course, there were always a few janitors or cleaning people around. Or an occasional security guard. But they tended to be an incurious lot, even the guards. Their approach to work was in keeping with the wages they received by taking care of buildings in a low rent district.

A little further south, Norton's office building was similarly isolated and even more deserted because there was no cleaning service on weekends. There was no alarm system, and the security guard worked the entire block. At most, he came by Norton's building once or twice an evening. And oftentimes he spent the greater part of the evening in a lounge chair in the lobby of the building next door, with his feet propped up, sometimes taking a nap. Norton had seen him doing that on numerous occasions and hadn't reported him. Tonight I was glad he hadn't.

I made the switch from Henderson to Norton at Henderson's office. It was a safe place to leave Henderson's ID and it was close to Norton's office building. The less time spent on the street as Norton, the better.

Edwards called just as I was attending to the final touches. If he was surprised that I wanted to meet him in Norton's office building, he didn't let on. Nor did he make any objections. Why should he? He still thought he held all the cards. He had no way of knowing the game had taken a new twist.

Once outside I felt almost lighthearted. No one seemed to be following me. And, if things went as planned, by this time tomorrow, Norton would be in the clear. He could put in a brief appearance for the sake of clearing his name, get his car out of the parking garage, and create the impression that he had left town. Faith could resume her life as Faith Devine, perhaps with Hal, and Henderson could return to his meager and uncultured existence. It was better than starting completely over.

There was a registry at the information desk in the lobby of Norton's building. Tenants were supposed to sign in after hours with their name, date, and the time. If the guard came around earlier than I expected, it might take him some time to figure out that the signature I was signing in with was a phony. Most likely he wouldn't bother to look. But just in case, I wanted him to think a tenant was in the building so he wouldn't be suspicious if he heard noise.

It took me almost forty-five minutes to get everything set up the way I wanted. In addition to making some adaptations on one of the main elevators, I had done some work on a service elevator so I could operate it without a key.

Norton had cautioned Edwards to come alone and to get in the elevator at the far end of the lobby. He'd emphasized that he would have to engage the mechanism by pushing the brass handle forward. "Don't bother trying to shut the grilled gate," Norton had told him. "There are glass doors on all the floors. Keep going up until you see me. Then stop the car and we'll have our exchange."

Waiting in the dark silence of the tenth floor, the creaks and clicks of the aging building began to get on my nerves. The building was like some giant living creature mumbling to itself in an alien language. Then, all of a sudden, gears and cables whirred and buzzed as the elevator came to life, grinding its way upward, slipping past each silent floor.

The instant Edwards came into view, Norton signaled for him to stop the elevator. Edwards had his hand on the handle, but his reflexes were slow. The elevator came to a halt about a foot above floor level. I had jammed the glass doors in the open position, and Edwards had left the grilled gate open as instructed, so all I had to do was to step up and inside. Taking the controls from Edwards, we started up again. Then I locked the handle in place with a mechanism I had fashioned out of a piece of wire so Norton could give his full attention to Edwards.

Edwards had been grinning when Norton first came into view, probably in anticipation of the fine joke he was about to spring. *Surprise, but you didn't expect to see Edwards, your friendly FBI man, did you?* When I didn't react, lines scrunched his forehead as he reassessed the situation.

"Hello, Cal," I said. "Does the Bureau know about this one?"

"Stevick?"

"Let's say I represent Stevick. And Norton."

It didn't take Edwards long to realize the face behind the Norton disguise wasn't the Stevick he remembered. The realization came into his eyes with an "aha" flash. "Did you . . .," he began. Then he started as he saw the gun pointed at his now paunchy stomach. "What's this? What are you trying to pull?"

Edwards was one of those guys who didn't like it when the joke was on him. "Don't bullshit me, Edwards. I know about Simco and Faith." Stevick paused for emphasis. "I know about your gym locker and the hotel where you've been staying while on special assignment with the local office."

Henderson saw the shock and anger on Edwards' face quickly turn to fear. Instead of springing the trap, he was caught in one.

"Take your gun out nice and slow," Stevick ordered. When Edwards didn't respond, Stevick tensed his trigger finger. "Norton is already wanted for one murder. Yours would give me great pleasure. Now move. And no tricks."

For a moment Stevick thought Edwards was going to try and pull something. Edwards did too, but in the end, he took his gun out of his shoulder holster and dropped it on the floor as instructed.

The elevator creaked upward, the tiled floors disappearing downward one after the other. They were on the thirty-third floor now. Five more to the top.

With the toe of his shoe, Stevick pushed the gun over to the space between the elevator and the shaft. He gave it one final nudge and it went clanging downward, bouncing off cement walls, until it reached the bottom of the shaft. It was like those seconds waiting for the ball to stop in a game of roulette.

"That was unnecessary," Edwards said finally, his voice husky.

"Possibly."

"If you kill me the Bureau will know it was you."

"Can it. I know you're on your own on this one."

"Without the murder weapon . . .," Edwards began, then stopped. Stevick could see in Edwards' eyes that he was slowly coming to grasp the situation.

"Don't worry," Stevick said. "You *do* have something I'm willing to bargain for. And the murder weapon, or its facsimile that you either have on you or in your car or back at the hotel, well, that isn't it."

"Facsimile?"

"Those hotel safes aren't all that secure."

"You have the gun?"

Stevick nodded.

"So, what do you want?"

"Security."

"I don't understand."

"It's simple. I don't trust you. I want to make certain you can't ruin things for me or for Faith."

They were at the top floor. Stevick stopped the elevator and reversed direction. They began their descent. Now the floors seemed to be leaping up at them as they moved downward.

Stevick reached into his pocket for the piece of paper. "I want you to sign this."

"What is it?"

"Insurance."

Edwards took the paper and read what was typed on it. "You've got to be kidding. Why should I sign this?"

"Because if you don't, I'll kill you. That's my other option."

"It's obvious I didn't compose this."

"That doesn't matter. It will be enough to convince the big guy in Chicago to send someone after you. And it won't be to talk things over."

"You don't have the name of the person this is going to be sent to filled in."

"Of course not. I can easily add that, and he won't know you haven't seen his name. He will think that Stevick told you about his identity and business, and he will guess why you wanted it. He won't stand for that."

Edwards was really beginning to look rattled.

"If anything happens to either me or to Faith, this letter will be sent. In addition, I have a few other pieces of information that might be of interest to the police. Those, too, will be kept available, in case you get any foolish ideas."

"It won't do you any good."

"Why not?"

"Well, for one thing, Faith is already dead."

Even though he knew it wasn't true, Stevick's stomach muscles knotted. The bastard.

"Sign it!" He thrust a pen at Edwards and raised his gun level with Edward's head. "Now."

Edwards signed the paper and gave it back to Stevick. "You're making a mistake. If you give me the names I want, I can make us both rich. You don't have to be involved. I'll handle the nego-tiations."

Stevick moved the handle to stop the elevator. They were on the fifteenth floor. Stevick was going to let Edwards off and make his getaway. He had what he wanted. Edwards couldn't make a move without putting his own life in jeopardy.

He was about to motion for Edwards to get out when he heard footsteps somewhere down the hall to their left. Then another set coming from the other direction. "Damn you." He shoved Edwards aside and pushed the elevator handle forward. "I told you to come alone." Stevick was dangerously close to shooting Edwards, and Edwards knew it.

"I *did* come alone." Edwards sounded sincere, but there was no way Henderson believed him. Even if the footsteps didn't belong to FBI agents, Edwards could have brought hired muscle along as back-up.

Stevick reached over and grabbed the front of Edwards' jacket with one hand and rammed the gun into his ribs with the other. "The truth, goddammit, I want the truth."

"I came alone." Edwards fear was a palpable thing, as alive and real as Stevick's rage.

"And Faith, what about Faith?" Stevick was screaming now, his voice echoing up and down the shaft as the cables groaned and squeaked. "Did you order them to kill her?"

"I'll split the profits with you fifty-fifty." Edwards sounded desper-ate. "You can buy a hundred women like her."

Stevick hit him then. Hard. As he turned to avoid Stevick's fist, Edwards made a grab for the gun and missed. The floors were gliding by, empty hallways, like the cells of a sleeping brain. In the distance Stevick could imagine Edwards' men racing up the stairs, trying to beat the elevator's ascent.

Stevick pushed Edwards away. This time Edwards stumbled and fell back through the open elevator gate. He smashed into the glass door at the twentieth floor and collapsed. Then, slowly, with all the force the machine powered cables could bring to bear, Edwards' head hit the overhead cement opening.

He didn't even have time to cry out. One second he was splayed against the glass door, the next he lay at Stevick's feet with most of his head missing, blood flowing darkly across the blue carpet.

I knew he couldn't possibly be alive. Still, I knelt down and said his name. One eyeball was dangling from a thin strand of muscle, obscenely looking first this way and that. I wanted to push it back in its socket, but there was nothing left of Edwards' face except a pulpy mass of flesh and blood.

For several seconds, I was too stunned to act. I had hated the man, but I hadn't intended to kill him. And I wouldn't have wished that kind of death on anyone.

Finally, I stood up. *My* life was over too. It had ended when Edwards' head hit the opening. Once the elevator stopped, his men would catch up with us. If they were FBI, they would take me into custody. If they were hired muscle, they might kill me or turn me in. No one would ever believe it had been an accident.

My three selves began wrestling for control. Stevick wanted to give up, confess what had happened and take whatever punishment the judicial system dished out. He was tired of running, tired of struggling to make ends meet, and tired of life in general. Norton wanted to run, but he didn't have a plan. It was up to Henderson--two to one in favor of running.

The first thing I did was to switch off the interior light. Only the faint glow from the panel showing the floor numbers remained. I reversed direction again and started down. It would all be a matter of timing.

On the way down I removed Edwards' ID and dropped it down the shaft. Then I took out my wallet with Norton's ID and stuffed it in Edwards' pocket. The switch wouldn't fool anyone for long, but it was a nice touch, considering. Then I readied myself for what might be my last hurrah.

We were back on the twentieth floor. I was thankful the lights were out so I couldn't see the blood. I didn't like to think about it. There had been entirely too much blood of late. All I wanted was to escape.

Nineteen, eighteen, seventeen, sixteen—

As the elevator descended, I summoned every ounce of courage

Henderson possessed. "Now!" I said to myself when the fifth-floor button lit up. "Now."

I leaped out into the void.

When I landed on the cool, tiled floor, tears of relief filled my eyes. I could have ended up like Edwards, not quite human in death. Instead, I was alive, alive and still fighting for survival.

The elevator continued downward. I could hear footsteps running down the interior stairwell in pursuit, as I had hoped. But I didn't hang around to celebrate. I was still a long way from home.

The service elevator I had locked into position on the fifth floor in case of an emergency was right where I'd left it. All I had to do was turn Henderson's makeshift key in the lock and I was on my way.

The noise made by starting the elevator seemed as loud as a jet taking off. If Edwards' men were on their toes, the odds were good that I would have a reception committee waiting for me at the bottom. But there was the possibility that their own noisy chase down the stairs and the sound of the main elevator would mask the clanking of the service elevator. And even if they heard it, they might waste time trying to stop it part way, not realizing that it was headed non-stop for the basement.

The cards had been dealt, and the bets were in. All that remained was to play the hand.

When the elevator reached the basement level, the door opened slowly, ever so slowly. As soon as I could slip past, I stepped out into the darkness.

There was no reception committee.

I made my way down the hall to the service entrance. The alley too was dark, but there was a faint light at the end where it joined the main street. I went outside and walked as calmly as I could manage toward the light. Running people always call attention to themselves.

Without stopping, I ripped off Norton's beard, removing what felt like at least an inch of skin in the process. I discarded the beard and the padding in a handy garbage bin. By the time I reached the street I was almost Henderson again.

There were two men covering the front entrance. They stood up a little straighter as I came out of the alley, and I deliberately moved toward them, passing directly under the street lamp. I was gambling that my relaxed and open approach would fool them into thinking I was some innocent passerby. It all depended on how much they knew about what had happened inside the building.

When they didn't try to stop me, I cut across the street and headed uptown. It no longer seemed wise to circle around to pick up the car. The two men at the entrance to Norton's office building had changed everything. They weren't Edwards' men after all. Neither FBI nor private muscle. They had been wearing police uniforms.

CHAPTER 29
BETRAYAL

There was no use going back to Henderson's office now. The apartment probably wasn't safe either. Norton had been followed. It might have been Garcia's men. Perhaps there had been tails all along, good ones that Henderson hadn't been able to spot. There was, however, one other possibility, one that made sense and meant that Henderson was definitely compromised.

Well, the police didn't have anyone in custody yet. And tomorrow the banks would be open. A virgin set of ID was waiting. The only other choice was to give myself up. Only this time the murder evidence wasn't circumstantial. This time they'd have no trouble making it stick.

One more night on the run followed by a lifetime on the run. Was it worth it? Stevick, then Norton, then Henderson . . . and now? An exciting new lease on life, some would say. What a laugh. An exhausting existence requiring constant vigilance, lies, and self-deceit. On the other hand, the choice was prison or begin again. Which would it be?

At least Faith would be safe now. That much had been accomplished. Hal and Faith, together on a fishing boat. It was another world, and not a bad one at that.

What the hell. When you got right down to it, everyone was playing a part. He could start again as an accountant in California, an engineer in New Mexico, maybe even a fisherman. Stevick had never had time to go fishing.

As soon as he knew if he was right about who had betrayed him, he would call Faith and Hal and let them know it was over. Then he could call the police and tell them where to find Krause and Deek. He doubted the two men would want to reveal the truth about how they'd ended up in that situation. I would then skip town and keep going until I found a sunny place where no one carried umbrellas. But first I had to know.

He answered immediately, as though he'd been expecting the call.

"It's me, Eric."

He didn't respond right away. "Eric," he said finally, a shade too hearty. "What's up?"

"It was you, Al, wasn't it?"

Again, there was a brief silence. When he finally spoke, his voice sounded old and tired. "I had to, Eric. I couldn't risk anything going wrong. Please try and understand."

It was strange, but Henderson *did* understand. Most people wanted desperately to be someone they could feel about. Their self-esteem was measured by their position in society, by how they were perceived by others. When someone was stripped of whatever identity they had spent a lifetime building, there was little left. And Al was first and foremost a police officer.

"You know all about me, don't you?"

"Yes," Al admitted. "I've known for some time. At first it was just a game, trying to figure out who you really were. Then, once I knew, I couldn't ignore it completely."

"What made you suspect me in the first place?"

"Little things. Mannerisms, inconsistencies. For instance, you always pretended to be indifferent to the quality of your liquor and your food, but I could tell you weren't." He was warming to his explanation, proud of his police officer's insight. "Then one day I came up behind Norton in the federal courthouse. I started to call out to you, but you turned around. After that, well, it didn't take long to figure out that Norton and Henderson were the same person."

That made sense. It would have been easier to trace the connection from Henderson to Norton to Stevick than the other way around. Henderson and Norton both appeared about the same time in the same city. About the same time that Stevick disappeared.

"You opened the envelope, didn't you?"

"Yes." Reluctantly.

"Then you know or soon will know that Norton didn't kill Hicks."

"I never thought he did."

Thanks for the vote of confidence, Al. There was nothing more to say, yet he didn't want to hang up.

"Eric, you still there?"

"Yeah."

"How'd it go down tonight?"

"I think you know."

"What happened?"

"An accident. When I heard your men, I thought Edwards had tricked me. We fought . . . and he fell." I'd let his men explain the details.

"Where are you now?"

"You don't really expect me to tell you, do you?"

"In spite of what has happened, Eric, I'm your friend. I want to help you."

"Like you helped me tonight?" Betrayal was betrayal, no matter how powerful the reasons. Still, he knew deep down that Al meant what he said. But it was too late.

"No one knows about Henderson," Al said. "Except me."

"But they followed Henderson to his apartment, didn't they?"

Al hesitated. The full consequences of his actions were coming home. "If you went from the House of Pancakes to your apartment this morning, then yes. But that doesn't mean . . ."

Norton had come out of Henderson's office and had driven Henderson's car to Norton's office building. They had probably been on the lookout for Norton anyway. Some police officer was bound to put it all together. Al couldn't gloss over it, not now that Edwards was dead.

"Goodbye, Al. We've had some good times." Henderson would not have done that to you though. He wouldn't have done the same to you.

"Goodbye, Eric. I'm . . ." Al didn't finish his sentence; both men knew it was too late for apologies. But he added, "By the way, the nameplate came on Friday. Thanks. It was exactly what I wanted."

The next day, a virgin set of ID was used to begin again.

NOTE FROM THE AUTHOR & ACKNOWLEDGEMENTS

I am fascinated with how ingrained our habits become and often fantasize on what it would be like to completely re-imagine who you are. Personally, I've changed careers a number of times, including going from academia to blue-collar work, trying my hand at entrepreneurship, and then turning to higher-paying corporate positions. Each change required lifestyle adjustments as well as some fundamental shifts in how I interacted with peers. But I didn't have to give up *everything* and totally re-create myself. That's why I love being an author—the only limitation is your imagination. Thus, Warren Stevick and his alternative "selves" were born.

I don't usually list people who have helped and encouraged me as an author. They know who they are. For example, my husband and I share a passion for writing as well as an office, so we have a symbiotic working relationship for both writing and emotional support. Especially when writing books together. Perhaps I owe a special shout-out to friends and relatives who not only read my books but listen to me talk about the highs and lows of publishing, sometimes a bit too much. And I'll be forever grateful to my now-retired agent Donna Eastman and the many editors and publishers I've worked with since I published my first book in 2019.

More recently, I've enjoyed working with Sue Trowbridge who does the interiors for my books, puts up with far too many last-minute edits, and has had to deal with the challenge posed by inserting the correct diacritical marks for the Tlingit language in my Jonah St. Clair Mysteries. Finally, it's been a joy to get to know (via email) writer and cover designer, Chris Holmes. She can do cozy, haunting or bizarre. No matter what strange design requests I have, she emails me and says, "That sounds like fun."

Finally, I want to thank my readers. Writers don't write simply for their own pleasure; they write to share their stories with others. Thank you!

ABOUT THE AUTHOR

Award-winning author Charlotte Stuart PhD writes mysteries that fall into a number of different sub genres: cozy tales of murder and mayhem, character-driven stories featuring a female PI, a laugh out loud comedic series, as well as more traditional mysteries. And now this foray into soft-boiled noir. She also co-authored a legal thriller with Don Stuart. In general, she favors twisty plots with a dollop of adventure and strives to find a balance between humor, suspense, and social themes.

Before she started writing full time, she left a tenured faculty position to go commercial salmon fishing in Alaska, spent a year sailing in the Washington and Canadian San Juans, became a partner in a management consulting group and later a VP of HR and training. After living on boats for over a decade, boating and forays into wilderness areas often find their way into her stories.

Charlotte lives on Vashon Island in the Pacific Northwest, enjoys walks in the woods, licorice, and the companionship of her imaginary cat Macavity.

Other books by Charlotte Stuart include:

The Discount Detective Mysteries

The John Smith Mysteries

Macavity & Me Mysteries

Bogged Down (A Vashon Island Mystery)

Raven's Grave (A Jonah St. Clair Mystery)

Raven's Legacy (A Jonah St. Clair Mystery)

Forget or Forgive? NEVER! (Suspense, Dark Secrets, and Revenge with a Twist)

Midnight for Justice, a legal thriller by Charlotte Stuart and Don Stuart

———

You can visit her website or contact her on social media:

Website: www.charlottestuart.com

Twitter: https://twitter.com/quirkymysteries

Facebook: https://www.facebook.com/charlotte.stuart.mysterywriter

Goodreads: https://www.goodreads.com/author/show/19305587.
Charlotte_Stuart

Instagram: https://www.instagram.com/cstuartauthor/

BookBub: https://www.bookbub.com/authors/charlotte-stuart

Amazon author page: https://www.amazon.com/stores/Charlotte-Stuart/
author/B00GMQNV5C

www.ingramcontent.com/pod-product-compliance
Lightning Source LLC
Chambersburg PA
CBHW050306110726
47899CB00007B/2135